A SCANDALOUS WEDDING

Pretty Samantha Northrup knew her duty was to marry, but this orphaned vicar's daughter wanted to be swept off her feet by someone whose kisses made her toes curl. She never dreamed her orderly life would be turned upside down when a mysterious stranger came knocking on her door one stormy night. And when they were found in a compromising position, she found herself marrying a man she barely knew...but couldn't resist.

A NOT SO

CONVENIENT MARRIAGE

What Samantha doesn't know is that her unknown bridegroom is Yale Carderock, the disinherited son of a duke, banished by his father years before. Now the prodigal has returned—rich, but only somewhat reformed. Yale is bewitched by his bride's innocent fire, and he knows he's powerless to resist her awakening sensuality. But is this outcast from society worthy of her tender love?

Avon Books by
Cathy Maxwell

CATHY MAXWELL

Because of You

An Avon Romantic Treasure

AVON BOOKS
An Imprint of HarperCollinsPublishers

This is a work of fiction. Names, characters, places, and incidents are products of the author's imagination or are used fictitiously and are not to be construed as real. Any resemblance to actual events, locales, organizations, or persons, living or dead, is entirely coincidental.

AVON BOOKS
An Imprint of HarperCollins*Publishers*
10 East 53rd Street
New York, New York 10022-5299

Copyright © 1999 by Catherine Maxwell
Inside cover author photo by Glamour Shots
Library of Congress Catalog Card Number: 98-93459
ISBN: 0-380-79710-0
www.avonromance.com

First Avon Books printing: February 1999

Avon Trademark Reg. U.S. Pat. Off. and in Other Countries, Marca Registrada, Hecho en U.S.A.
HarperCollins® is a trademark of HarperCollins Publishers Inc.

Printed in the U.S.A.

10 9 8 7 6

For Terri Wollen Wilke
and
Tammi Wollen Watkins,
with love

Chapter 1

The Village of Sproule
Northumberland, England
1806

The persistent banging woke Samantha Northrup from a sound sleep.

She lay in bed, hoping it was only another of the vicarage's many loose shutters being buffeted against the side of the house by the north wind. A visitor in the middle of the night meant bad news.

"Wake up in there!" a man's voice shouted. "I need help!"

The man's words, and years of serving the parish's needs, roused Samantha. She threw a heavy wool shawl over her flannel nightdress, slipped her feet into a pair of old boots, and shuffled out of the bedroom into the kitchen.

The small house was attached to St. Gabriel's Church, a stone Norman building that had weathered many a Northumberland winter, although this one promised to be colder than most. Samantha shivered as a draft skittered up beneath her nightdress.

Her visitor pounded on the door again, the force of the blows making the heavy cedar door shake.

"I'm coming, I'm coming," she said crossly, her words coming out in little puffs of frigid air. No fire burned in her hearth. Not at night, when she could conserve fuel by sleeping under a mountain of blankets.

She lit a candle and glanced at the clock on the sideboard. It was shortly past midnight.

Samantha could usually tell who was outside by peeking out the window to the side of the door. However, the night was too dark for her to make out anything but the man's tall shape. He could be any of a number of the villagers.

He was just starting to knock again when she threw back the bar, opened the door—and found herself staring into the eyes of a tall, dark stranger.

She immediately attempted to close the door.

The man had anticipated her move and put his foot in the door so she couldn't shut it. He was tall, broad shouldered, with a headful of dark hair and glittering, angry eyes. She didn't know how she could have thought he looked like any of her friends or neighbors.

He didn't force the door open but held his ground.

"What is it you want?" she asked through the crack in the door.

"I want the keys to the Ayleborough vault."

Samantha almost laughed in his face. "Are you daft? Those keys are for the family only. Besides, it is the middle of the night."

The stranger's voice hardened with determination. "I want the keys." He spoke in the clear, concise English of an educated man. But she bristled at his high-handed attitude and was all too conscious of the slight lilting burr of the northlands in her voice.

"You cannot have them without the permission of the duke of Ayleborough," Samantha answered, with an authority gained from years of making grown men cringe in guilt and recalcitrant schoolboys swallow cod oil. She attempted to close the door but he pushed it with his shoulder, throwing it open and shoving her aside.

He was so tall, he had to stoop or hit his head on the low ceiling. His presence filled the room. "I want the keys."

Another woman might have quaked from fear—and the truth be known, Samantha's knees were shaking—but she was six-and-twenty, a woman in charge of her life. The Vicarage of St. Gabriel's had been responsible for the Ayleborough family vault for almost two centuries. It was a sacred trust between the vicar and the noble family that paid St. Gabriel's benefice, and she would not betray that trust.

She moved around the table, wanting to put

something between herself and this intruder. The candle's wan light cast ghoulish shadows behind him. "You can't have them."

The stranger's eyes narrowed. "I must not have heard you correctly," he said in a low, silky voice. His gloved fingers opened and closed menacingly.

Samantha's throat went dry, but if need be, she'd die to protect those keys. Since her father's death a year ago, the villagers had been hinting broadly that the time had come for her to move out of the vicarage. Now was her opportunity to prove her worth. "You can't have them," she repeated stubbornly.

His eyes took on an almost unholy light of anger. He was obviously unaccustomed to being defied. Well, so was she.

She just wished she wasn't so aware of how big and brutally strong he was.

Then, to her relief, he took a step away. He pushed his thick, heavy hair back from his face with his hand. His was a strong face with a straight nose and a lean, square jaw. When he attempted a smile, the expression seemed almost uncomfortable for him.

"I'm sorry," he apologized, his tone brisk. He looked around the small kitchen. "I imagine my behavior appears rude to you, barging in as I have in the middle of the night." He didn't sound apologetic at all.

"Who are you?" she dared to ask.

He ignored her question. His dark gaze flicked

over her half-dressed appearance with disinterest. "Where is the vicar? I must speak to him."

"He's not available," she announced curtly, and prayed the man wouldn't realize she was alone. She should never have opened the door to him. How often had the villagers warned her to be more careful?

She crossed her arms against her breasts, suddenly aware of her vulnerability as a woman.

"But I must see him," the stranger insisted.

"You can't."

"And who are you?"

Samantha drew a deep breath. "I'm his daughter. I am responsible for the Ayleborough vault."

"Well, Miss—?" He paused.

"Northrup," she said, for the first time a little self-conscious of her unmarried state.

"Well, Miss Northrup, I have traveled a long way. I want the keys to the Ayleborough vault."

Samantha almost groaned her frustration. This man was stubborn. "What right do you have to them?"

The line of his jaw tensed. "That is my affair and mine alone."

"Then we are at an impasse, sir," she said firmly. "You are wasting your time and my precious sleep. I'm responsible for those keys, and I will not let you have them without authority from the duke himself. Whoever told you to come here in the middle of the night has sent you on a fool's errand. Your time would be better spent in petitioning Ayleborough directly."

He reached into his overcoat pocket to pull out a leather purse heavy with coin. "How much do you want for those keys?" He didn't wait for her answer but threw the bag down on the table. "Here, there's five gold pieces. Take it and let me have the keys."

For a second, Samantha was tempted. Even before her father's death, there hadn't been much money in the house. She'd never seen a gold piece before.

Then she remembered the stories her father used to tell of angels, disguised as strangers, who were sent out into the night to test the mettle of good Christians. As a child, Samantha had always hoped that God would choose her to be tested and send one of the angel beggars to her door.

But this man was a far cry from her image of an angel. Or a beggar. And he looked ready to throttle her, not save her soul.

"The keys are not for sale," she said, her voice proud. "You cannot have them without the permission of the duke of Ayleborough."

The man glared at her as if he couldn't believe she would refuse his money. In the candlelight, she could see he had brown eyes, dark almost to the point of being black. Dangerous eyes.

And he had not liked her answer.

Conscious that she wore little more than her nightclothes, Samantha sent a hesitant glance back toward her bedroom, which had a good, solid door but no lock.

That moment of hesitation cost her. The stranger whirled suddenly and lunged for the hook next to the hearth. A set of keys hung there, the keys to the church and the Ayleborough vault.

He was out the door before Samantha could shout for him to stop. She charged into the night after him.

There was no moon, but she knew the way across the churchyard into the cemetery. Apparently, so did the stranger, although she heard him grunt as he stumbled over a half-buried headstone.

Samantha cried out, "Help me! Please, someone, help me!" But she knew her shouts would go unheard. On a winter's night like this, all the villagers would be huddled deep under the covers, their cottage shutters closed, their heavy doors latched.

The white marble of the Ayleborough vault glowed a shadowy gray in the night. For an instant, the man's form was silhouetted against it as he reached the vault gates.

Above the whisper of the wind, Samantha heard the gates creak open. Her father had always meant to oil that hinge but had never found the time. Now the creaking sounded ominous in the night. In another moment the stranger would be inside the vault.

She heard him swear as he tried first one key to the vault's heavy iron door and then another. She reached the gates just as he opened the door, its hinges whining in protest. He slammed it shut behind him.

"Stop! Please stop!" she begged him, knowing he would not listen.

The vault had been built over two hundred years ago. Styled as a miniature Greek temple, it contained two rooms, the tiny antechamber, and the burial crypt itself.

Samantha wrenched open the iron door open and was surprised to see a candle flame in the burial crypt. The stranger had known, even in the dark, where the hidden alcove with the tinder box and candles were. She slowed her step.

Who was this man?

She backed outside, suddenly uncertain. Then the flickering flame disappeared and she realized with a sense of horror that he had entered the burial crypt. The heel of her foot bumped into a good stout log and she almost stumbled. Instead, she picked up log, hefting its weight in her hand. Armed, she reentered the vault, ready to do battle.

Yale Carderock stood surrounded by his ancestors. He held up the candle and in the soft light immediately found what he'd been searching for. He walked over to the marker carved in the marble:

LELAND CARDEROCK
4TH DUKE OF AYLEBOROUGH
1743–1805

His father. Beside him lay Yale's mother.

Almost with disbelief, he traced the outline of the letters.

He'd recently arrived in London and had gone to the tailor's to be fitted for a wardrobe worthy of a prince when the tailor had informed Yale that the fourth duke of Ayleborough was dead . . . and had been for almost two years. Yale had immediately left the man's shop and hired a horse. He'd ridden hell bent for terror all the way to Sproule and the sacred ground of St. Gabriel's because he didn't believe it could be possible. His father couldn't be dead.

He still didn't want to believe it, even as he rested his hand upon his father's grave. The man's presence seemed to radiate from the stone.

Yale closed his hand into a fist. The angry words he and his father had spoken the last time they'd met rang as clearly in his mind as if they had been spoken only that afternoon. The anger, the contempt, the final edict.

For eleven long years, Yale had sweated blood, scraping and working and planning for the day he would return to England and prove his father wrong.

And now, here he was . . . and his father had, once again, had the last word, but not in the way Yale had anticipated.

He was so stunned, he couldn't move.

All those years, wasted.

Then, Yale Carderock, the disinherited second

son of the fourth duke of Ayleborough, did the only thing he could do. He tilted back his head and laughed. The sound was bitter and full of anger, but he couldn't stop. It was either that, or howl at the moon like a lunatic.

The sound of his laughter echoed off the crypt walls . . . and he feared he might be going mad, especially when he felt the sting of tears.

He stumbled back from the grave a lost man.

"Don't touch anything or I shall be forced to bash your head in."

The crisp order with the soft northern burr reminded Yale that he was not alone. Miss Northrup stood in the entrance only feet from him. She brandished a half-rotted log in his direction.

Her presence was exactly what he needed to regain his equilibrium. He scratched at an incriminating tear at the edge of his eye as if it were nothing more than an irritating itch. Opening his arms in a conciliatory gesture, one hand holding the candle, he said, "See? I've done no harm."

She eyed him suspiciously. The deep auburn and gold highlights of her brown hair caught the candlelight in these close quarters. She was younger than she had first appeared to him . . . and more attractive.

Of course, dressed in a high-necked nightdress and unlaced boots, her sleep-loosened braid swinging with anger, she didn't seem threatening. At some point in the chase across the graveyard, she'd lost her shawl, not that she was in any danger of being compromised. Her over-large nightdress was as concealing as a nun's habit.

However, the martial light from her brandy-colored eyes was anything but pious. Her indignation had also brought color to her cheeks. He had no doubt she would clobber him until her weapon disintegrated in her hands if she got the opportunity.

He didn't remember her, but it had been some twenty years since he'd lived in Sproule. His mother had preferred life in London, and considering how much he and his father had argued, he'd had little incentive to visit him at the family's ancestral home, Braehall, a good three miles from this village.

Even if he had visited, he wouldn't have stepped inside a church.

"I didn't mean to frighten you," he began, and then stopped as the candlelight fell on another marker that had not been here years ago when Yale had last entered this vault, at his mother's funeral. This marker was not as new as his father's.

"I want you out of here now, sir," she demanded boldly, but Yale dismissed her with a wave of his hand.

He squatted, the better to read the lettering on the marker:

YALE AETHELRED CARDEROCK
1776–1799?

His family thought him dead? The air in the crypt turned suddenly colder. Or was the chill inside him?

"I want you to leave," Miss Northrup was saying, a touch of desperation in her voice. "Now!"

Yale looked up at her. It took him a moment to find his voice. "How did he die?" *Why did they believe him dead?* "How did both the duke and his son die?"

She didn't answer him. "Please leave." Her voice now shook slightly.

He came to his feet. "That rotting log is probably full of crawling ants. I'd drop it if I were you."

Her eyes widened and she glanced at her hands, but she did not drop the log. Miss Northrup was obviously made of sterner stuff than most of the English women of his acquaintance.

"I want you to leave, and hand me the keys before you go," she insisted.

Yale pulled them from where he'd tucked them in his waistband and held them out to her. "You can have them and I'll go, but first I want you to answer my question."

A frown line worried her forehead. She pressed her lips together.

"You don't trust me," he said, "and I don't blame you, considering the way I've barged into your life in the middle of the night."

"And trespassed on private property," she added.

Yale hid his smile, agreeing readily, "And trespassed."

"Who are you?" she demanded.

Yale hesitated. He glanced at the grave bearing his name. Would his family rejoice to discover him alive . . . or had they all been relieved that the black sheep was no longer able to upset their orderly lives?

"Marvin," he said calmly. "Marvin Browne." It was the name of the tutor he'd had when he was a child, and the first name that came to mind. "Browne with an 'e,' " he added, mimicking his tutor.

Miss Northrup relaxed her stance a bit, lowering her arms, apparently deciding a man named Marvin couldn't be all that dangerous. "Mr. Browne, you must be aware that you are on very private and sacred ground. Why did you force your way into this vault?"

"I was once close to the family," he answered truthfully. "I was startled to learn the old duke was dead. I couldn't believe it until I saw it with my own eyes."

"Now that you've seen it, I will ask you to be respectful and leave. I'm certain any questions you have can be better answered on the morrow."

Yale hid his smile. He'd never met such a persistent woman. "I will leave, *after* you've answered my questions, Miss Northrup."

"What questions do you have?"

"I want to know about these men's deaths." A

thought struck him, one that filled him with remorse. "Did the duke suffer when he . . . died?" He should have been by his father's deathbed. He should have begged forgiveness.

The set of her mouth tightened and he thought she would order him to leave again. Instead, she said, "His was a wasting illness. He'd been ill for several years. The doctors thought it was consumption, but I disagreed."

"*You* disagreed?"

She lifted her chin proudly. "There are few doctors this far north. Only Dr. Rees from Morpeth. The duke's children didn't like him, so since the duke insisted on being at Braehall, they brought up London doctors. I was often asked to care for His Grace after the physicians returned to Town."

"Do you know of medicine?"

"I have an understanding," she said in her soft, almost lyrical voice, lighter than a Scots accent and pleasant to the ear. "My own mother was ill for years. I served as her nurse until her death last year."

"I'm sorry for your loss," Yale said, more because of his own father than out of real empathy.

But it was the right thing to say. Her expression softened. "It was actually a blessing when she passed on. Just as it was for the old duke. Mother and His Grace both had time to say their good-byes and make sense of their lives. My father died suddenly only two weeks after her death. It was the influenza that took both my parents, but my father slipped away so quickly, and there was no time to say anything."

Her words went straight to something he'd thought he'd lost long ago, his heart.

"But then your father didn't suffer much," Yale said. "At least, that is one blessing."

"I don't know that His Grace suffered that much, either. The Carderocks are a large and loving family and they worked hard to make his last days comfortable. He was surrounded almost daily by his children and grandchildren."

"Grandchildren?" *Grandchildren!* But then, it had been eleven years . . .

"Yes, the current duke has three sons," Miss Northrup volunteered. "His sister is also married and a mother herself, although I'm not certain how many children she has. Of course, the Carderocks rarely come to Sproule anymore. The new duke doesn't enjoy country life the way his father did."

Yale had been so focused on his father, he hadn't given much thought to his brother and sister, both of whom were several years older. Before Yale had left England, his brother Wayland had seemed firmly ensconced in the country and destined to remain there. He'd rarely seen his sister Twyla, even though she'd lived in London with her husband. Brother and sister had never gotten along, and matters had only grown worse when Yale had shown up drunk at her wedding breakfast. He'd spent the previous night out carousing gaming dens and other pleasures with some of his cronies. Twyla had not been amused.

He rubbed his temples, feeling the beginning of a headache. While he had pursued his goal of impressing his father, he'd never stopped even to wonder about his brother and sister.

"Please, Mr. Browne, the hour is very late and it's cold here in the crypt. I ask you once again to leave."

Yale ignored her request. "What about him?" He nodded to the marker bearing his own name.

Miss Northrup gave a weary sigh. "You're not going to let me return to my bed, are you?"

Yale grinned, liking her lack of missish airs.

She set the log down, dusted off her hands, and crossed her arms to keep warm. "Yale Carderock isn't buried there."

That was an understatement!

She continued, "It is believed he died at sea. I know very little about his story, other than it has a bad end."

"Then tell me what you know."

She shook her head. "I know only rumor and gossip, sir. I've never met the man since he spent most of his life in London with his lady mother."

"What is said of him?" Yale asked, curious.

"Oh, he was a rake of the worst sort," she assured him. "His extravagances and peccadilloes—"

"Peccadilloes?" Yale repeated, wondering what the blazes that meant. Remembering himself at a younger age, it could mean almost anything. He'd not been a saint.

"He was disinherited by his father," she said, with a frown for his interruption. "The villagers who worked up at Braehall say his father used to rant and rave for days over the scrapes and nonsense the younger Carderock tumbled into. But the lad had only himself to blame. He had an inheritance from his mother that he squandered. They say he gambled it away."

"They" weren't wrong, Yale thought dryly. How many times over the past eleven years had he wished he'd been wiser, and a better steward of his inheritance?

"When he'd spent that money," Miss Northrup said, "he asked his father for his inheritance, which the old duke refused to give him. The boy then behaved in such a wild and ill-advised manner, he shamed the whole family. Oh, Yale Carderock was a bad one. From the stories I've heard, he was the very opposite of his brother, Wayland. You could go far and wide and never find a better man than the new duke."

Yale felt a stab of the old jealousy he'd always felt when hearing Wayland praised. Funny, that it could hurt him after all these years. Regrettably, the picture Miss Northrup painted of him in his youth was only too true. "So Yale got himself disinherited, and then what?" he asked.

Miss Northrup shrugged. "And then nothing. Almost immediately he disappeared. His father worried incessantly. My father counseled him on a regular basis. Yale had kept bad company, and his family feared he'd been murdered and tossed into the Thames."

Yale had never once wondered if his father worried over his whereabouts. He'd assumed his father had been glad to wash his hands of him.

Miss Northrup continued. "The old duke told Father it was almost a blessing when word reached the family that Yale had died in a storm at sea almost two years after the disinheritance. Of course, they didn't hear this until almost four years after his death. Apparently, Yale had signed on with a merchantman. I think the duke gained comfort in the idea that his son had passed on attempting worthwhile employment versus the more nefarious ways he could have gone."

Yale knew what storm she referred to. It had blown up on them around the Cape of Good Hope. The ship had been destroyed. A good number of the crew had been lost, although Yale had not been one of them.

He frowned at Miss Northrup. "Was he really that much of a blackguard?"

"His story is a lesson for the sinner," she assured him without hesitation. "My father commented more than once that the story of young Carderock paralleled that of the prodigal son, except it lacked the happy ending of a reunion with his family. He often used him for his sermons—without mentioning the family name, of course. Still, everyone in Sproule knew who it was Father used as an example." She frowned at Yale's headstone. "His was a sad and wasted life. They say he was a handsome boy but died a victim of his own good locks and folly."

Yale didn't know how he felt about being a morality tale.

And yet he didn't correct the impression he was dead.

"Did anyone mourn for him?"

"The younger Carderock?" she asked. "The old duke mourned, although he was too ill to attend the funeral. Unfortunately, the elder son had obligations in London that prevented him from coming, and the daughter, I believe, was expecting her fourth child. My father officiated at the funeral to an empty church, save for myself. Since there was no body and no duke, the villagers weren't interested in attending." She sighed. "We had a hard time coming up with good things to say about the man. Few decent, reputable people knew him." She shook her head before changing the subject. "Now that I've answered your questions, will you please leave?"

Yale nodded dumbly, too stunned to do anything else. No one had attended his funeral? That was worse than being thought dead.

His feet heavy, he walked past the vicar's daughter, that guardian of his ancestor's remains. She watched in silence, unaware of the turmoil, rage, and pain roiling inside him. He'd been such a bloody fool.

His father had waited for him. His father had been the one person in all the world who had cared.

Why had Yale waited so long to come home? He could have returned at any time over the past five years. He'd had the money. *But it hadn't been enough money.* He'd wanted a fleet of ships and his company and warehouses and a huge home as grand as Braehall. And he had had them, too, back in Ceylon.

But now it didn't matter. Now it was too late.

He lingered outside the vault. The cold night air felt good against his hot skin.

He handed the vicar's daughter the keys and she locked up. She then waited for him to be on his way.

Gallantly he picked up her shawl from the ground and offered to her. She protectively threw it around her shoulders, the color high on her cheeks.

He smiled at her obvious embarrassment. Only in England did a woman worry about such silly things. He'd seen more naked women than he cared to remember. Miss Northrup's nightdress was not going to throw him into a frenzy.

"Thank you," he said.

"I hope you found what you were looking for."

Her words surprised him. "I don't know," he admitted sadly.

She looked as if she were going to say something but then changed her mind. "Good night, Mr. Browne."

"Good night, Miss Northrup."

She stood waiting, and he knew she expected him to leave. He walked to the edge of the cemetery toward the road leading into the small village of Sproule. He'd already taken the liberty of stabling his horse with the village blacksmith.

But instead of making his way toward the only inn in Sproule, the Bear and Bull, he slipped into the shadows of a huge hemlock tree.

Miss Northrup waited until she was convinced he was gone before returning to her house attached to the stone church. He watched as she blew out the candle in the kitchen and the windows went dark.

Yale hunkered down, his back against the trunk of the hemlock, and stared off in the direction of the decorated iron doors guarding his family's vault. The damp cold seeped up through his boots, but he ignored the discomfort.

He didn't know what to do or where to go, other than he needed to stay here and keep a silent vigil. It was a sign of respect for the man who had been his father.

It was the only thing he could do.

Miss Northrup didn't go to bed immediately, but spied on him from the dark window. So she knew he hadn't left. He could feel her presence, disapproving but curious.

What would she say if she knew his true name? What a twist that fact would give her biblical lesson. The prodigal son returns, but instead of the welcoming arms of his father, he finds an empty life.

At last she determined that he meant no harm and returned to her bed. Yale concentrated on the vault. He was not a praying man . . . but that night he learned to pray.

In the wake of a bleak dawn, Yale rose. His joints were stiff and aching from the cold. His years in the tropics had thinned his blood. He walked the length of Sproule to the Bear and Bull.

As a boy, he and his father had visited the inn a time or two—but no one recognized him now. They all thought he was dead.

Yale registered under the name Marvin Browne, ordered a bottle of brandy to warm his blood, demanded privacy, then did something he hadn't done since he'd awakened aboard that ship eleven years ago. He got good and properly drunk.

When he finished that, he ordered another, pausing only long enough to compare his life to the empty bottle. As twilight of his first day home approached, the lonely coldness of the night before seemed to have settled in his bones and made them heavy. He closed his eyes and passed out into blessed unconsciousness.

And that was when the fever started.

*　　*　　*

John Sadler, the innkeeper, didn't know what to do. Mr. Browne had come down ill. At first, Sadler had suspected the man was little more than passed out drunk.

However, in the early hours of the morning, the sound of his retching woke both John and his wife.

"He's only getting what he deserves," his wife said. "A man shouldn't drink like that."

John wasn't so certain it was only the drink.

When Mr. Browne didn't make an appearance at breakfast, John decided to wake him. "It will serve him right for keeping us up half the night," he told his wife, and she agreed.

He pounded on Marvin Browne's door, but there was no response.

He beat his fist against the door again, harder. Nothing.

He turned the handle. There were no locks on the doors at the Bear and Bull. The inn was too small and out of the way for such an expense.

John walked inside and quickly backed out.

"The man's bloody sick," he told his wife.

"How sick?"

"I don't know, but he looks close to dead."

"Then let us send for Miss Northrup," his wife said. "She'll know what to do."

"Aye, she will." He dispatched his eldest son to go and fetch the vicar's daughter.

Chapter 2

Samantha scraped the bottom of the tea drawer and managed to collect only the most pathetic pile of leaves in the bottom of her cup. The water in the kettle was already boiling hot and she dearly needed a good strong cup of tea.

It was so cold today, she'd been forced to use some of her precious fuel and build a fire in the kitchen hearth. She even wore both her dresses, a trick she'd learned from exercising the strictest economies over the past year. One was the black mourning dress she'd just set aside, and the second was a serviceable brown dress. She wore it on top because she was heartily sick of black.

She felt bleary-eyed and cranky. After her adventure the other night with Marvin Browne, she'd spent a good portion of yesterday running errands and nursing the Chandlers' youngest daughter, who had come down with the fever. She should have slept soundly last night. In-

24

stead, she'd tossed and turned, her mind full of worries.

It had all started when the ladies of the village, led by Squire Biggers's wife, had paid her a morning call. Apparently, a village meeting had been held at the Bear and Bull on Monday night. Samantha had not been invited to the meeting because it was about her.

After drinking the lion's share of her meager supply of tea, the village women had announced that a vote had been taken and it had been decided the time had come for Samantha to leave the vicarage. Her mourning was over and the new vicar, who'd recently married, wished to move in.

Remembering their ultimatums, Samantha caught her hands shaking as she carefully poured the cup half full of boiling water and let it steep.

Of course, she had been expecting such a decision. By rights, she should have moved from the vicarage after her father had died—but she had nowhere to go. Her mother had been an orphan, and her father's family had all passed on before him.

She'd hoped perhaps the village would offer her a cottage. After all, it would only be right, since her father, who had always worried over their penury, had spent the majority of his living to help feed and clothe the poor.

But upon his death, the villagers seemed to

have forgotten all Vicar Northrup had done for them ... or else they considered letting Samantha live in her home during her time of mourning to be repayment enough for his lifetime of service. Her own charity and nursing skills they took for granted.

For a moment, her thoughts strayed to Marvin Browne and their strange meeting in the graveyard. A bit superstitious, she realized his appearance had been the first warning that her life was about to change.

She moved restlessly around the small kitchen. There had to be *more* to life. She just didn't know what "more" was ... but she was reasonably certain letting the villagers scuttle her off to live with the two spinster Doyle sisters wouldn't help her find it.

A part of her yearned for what other women had: a husband, children, a home of her own. But at her advanced age, Samantha knew that would never be.

She lifted her teacup, silently toasted her impending future, and was about to take a sip when someone knocked on the kitchen door.

She was tempted to ignore it. Then a young voice called, "Miss Northrup! Please, Miss Northrup, we need you!"

She recognized the voice. It was Tommy Sadler, the innkeeper's oldest son. The innkeeper would not send for her unless there was sickness.

Setting her teacup back on the table, she rose

and hurried to the door. A blast of frigid air greeted her as she opened it. "Whatever is the matter, Tommy?" she asked, waving him inside.

The redheaded boy pulled his hat off. "One of the guests has taken ill, Miss Northrup. Pa needs you to come and see the man. He's been very sick, miss. We fear he's dying."

Samantha did not hesitate. "Let me gather my basket and my cape." Her basket was filled with different medicines, herbs, salves, and, of course, the book from Dr. Rees, the physician in Morpeth, whom she often consulted. She also had her own journal of different remedies she'd found could help.

Tying the ribbons of her black bonnet beneath her chin, she shot a regretful look at her tea. Well, there was naught to be done. The habit of tending the sick ran deep inside her. She would not turn her back, even on a stranger.

Outside, heavy gray clouds threatened more bad weather. Samantha huddled deeper into her cape. The cold seeped up from the hard ground and through the thin soles of her boots.

No one wise would venture out on such a cold day. However, she and Tommy were halfway through the village when a loud "Yoooohooo!" called out to them.

Samantha turned to see Hattie and Mabel Doyle hurry out of their cottage toward her. Both sisters had to be well over fifty years old and looked enough alike to be twins, although most people guessed Miss Mabel was the older by a year or two. Their shoulders were humped over by age and their huge black capes swept the ground as they scurried toward Samantha, reminding her of nothing less than two fat, happy beetles.

She slowed her step and hid her impatience, unwilling to give the appearance of a snub. Both women were notoriously sensitive—and she might shortly be living with them if she could not think of a way out of the situation. "Hello, Miss Hattie, Miss Mabel," she said respectfully.

"Good morning! Good morning," they chimed in unison.

Miss Mabel spoke first. "Where are you off to—?"

"Where are you going?" Miss Hattie added.

"One of the guests at the inn is ill. Now, if you will excuse us—"

"One of the guests?" Miss Mabel said.

"Must be that dark-haired man," Miss Hattie answered.

"Dark-haired?" Samantha questioned. The memory of Mr. Browne's thick dark hair flashed in her mind.

"Yes, the one who came to the village yesterday morning," Miss Mabel said. "Mrs. Sadler said he was waiting on the front step before they'd even risen for the day."

"Said he drinks," Miss Hattie offered helpfully, drawing out the syllables as was her custom. "Drinks terribly."

A hint of foreboding tickled Samantha's neck.

"This guest at the inn, does he have a name, Tommy?"

"Aye, miss. His name is Marvin Browne. Browne with an 'e,' " the boy said dutifully.

So Marvin Browne had not left the area. She wondered what had kept him here. It was rare to find a mystery in Sproule.

"Do you know him?" Miss Hattie asked, her eyebrows coming up in interest.

"No," Samantha said quickly, and then felt foolish. But gossip spread fast in Sproule, and it was usually one of the Doyle sisters who spread it.

She took a hesitant step back toward home.

"Why, Miss Northrup, whatever is the matter?" Miss Mabel asked. "You've gone all pale. Are you feeling sickly yourself?"

Samantha shook her head while turning away from their too knowing eyes. "I'm fine, thank you." She was being a goose. *What was it to her if Marvin Browne had not left Sproule as she'd imagined? Or if he needed her help?*

She started walking toward the inn. Tommy and the Doyle sisters followed.

"Silly name, Marvin, isn't it?" Miss Mabel said, her concern for Samantha vanishing.

"I knew a Marvin Browne, Browne with an 'e,' once," Miss Hattie said.

"You did?" Miss Mabel asked.

"Aye. You did too," her sister said. "He was tutor for the duke of Ayleborough. Don't you remember now? Years ago, when the boys were young."

"Ohhhhhh, years ago," Miss Mabel said. "Yes, I think I do remember. Arrogant man, wasn't he? From London, and kept raving on about how we all talked like Scots and should mind the King's English. Silly man."

The arrogant discription fit Mr. Browne, but Samantha couldn't see the man she'd met the other night as a child's tutor. Why, that man had almost appeared to be younger than the present duke.

Samantha shook her head and tried to shut out their prattle. They talked like that all day long. The thought struck her that she would be mad in no time if she accepted her fate and moved into their cottage.

As if reading her mind, Miss Mabel said, "Have you given any more thought about coming to live with us?"

"Yes," Miss Hattie interjected. "We are excited. I have this pain in my left knee—"

"My back gives me terrible fits," Miss Mabel interrupted.

"Oh, yes, your back is bad," Miss Hattie agreed. "But my knee makes it hard for me to walk." She suddenly started limping for good measure. "It will be so nice when you come to live with us. We'll never worry about our aches and pains again. Will we, sister?"

"Well, I haven't quite made up my mind," Samantha stated tactfully.

"The village has already made it up for you," Miss Mabel said.

"Aye," Miss Hattie echoed. "We're looking forward to your joining us. Three spinster ladies at peace with the world."

The world suddenly seemed a very small place to Samantha. In a flash of insight, she realized her deepest fear—that she would live and die alone . . . and she would be very much alone with the Doyle sisters. Everyone avoided them if they could.

This past year had not been easy, but her future loomed even darker.

Fortunately, she was saved from making a comment because they'd come to the inn. She quickly ducked inside the narrow tavern door.

Everything considered, the Bear and Bull did a fair business. Other than the church, it was the social center of Sproule and the surrounding countryside. John Sadler and his family had a reputation for hospitality and a love of gossip, a winning combination for the success of any public house.

Of course, between the Bear and Bull and the Doyle sisters, nothing was a secret in Sproule.

Samantha nodded to John Sadler, who met her at the door, his expression anxious.

"I understand you have a sick man here."

"I do, I do," he said, leading her through the open public room with its huge hearth and whitewashed walls. Trestle tables and long benches were the only furnishings. "Miss Mabel and Miss Hattie, why don't you take a seat here and Tommy will fetch you a hot cup of cider?"

"Oh, that's nice," Miss Mabel said. "But we'd rather see this Marvin Browne."

"Yes, we want to see him," her sister seconded, and they followed Samantha and the innkeeper toward the stairs leading to the bedrooms.

Mr. Sadler shrugged. The Doyle sisters were almost impossible to waylay once they'd made up their minds.

His wife's voice called out, "Has Miss Northrup arrived?"

"Aye, Mrs. Sadler, she's here," her husband responded. Birdie Sadler walked into the public room from the back kitchen. "Glad we are you've come, Miss Northrup. We've been afeared this man's contagious."

"How long has he been ill?" Samantha asked, as they led her up the narrow staircase, the Doyle sisters trailing behind. Tommy hovered close to his mother.

"We heard him—" Mr. Sadler made an expressive gesture with his hand. "—Long about the wee hours of the morning. Lost every drop of brandy in him and then some, by the sound of it. Of course, he'd looked like a regular drunk when he came down to buy his second bottle of brandy. Unsteady on his feet and red-eyed."

"Drink, see?" Miss Mabel said, nudging Samantha from behind.

"Tisk, tisk," her sister said.

"Had he eaten anything?" Samantha asked, attempting to ignore the comments of her two shadows. They'd reached the short upstairs hall and Mr. Sadler had paused in front of one of the three rooms.

"Nothing at all," Mrs. Sadler answered.

Samantha frowned. "Why are you so certain his present malady doesn't stem from the overindulgence of strong spirits?"

"Mr. Sadler and I have seen more than our fair share of drunks, Miss Northrup," Mrs. Sadler answered. "This man is sick. When Mr. Sadler went into his room and tried to rouse him, the man didn't even so much as twitch."

"His skin is hot to the touch, not like any drunk I've ever seen," Mr. Sadler added. He put his hand on the door. "I'll warn you now, this isn't a pretty sight, Miss Northrup."

"I don't imagine it is," Samantha assured him.

"We are prepared for the worst!" Miss Mabel declared almost cheerily.

The innkeeper didn't bother to knock, but opened the door. Mrs. Sadler stepped aside, but the Doyle sisters pressed forward, craning their necks to see. They quickly covered their noses and stepped back.

Accustomed to sick rooms, Samantha had been prepared for a strong smell. Poor Mr. Browne. Every slop bucket in the room was full. The stench mingled with those of stale liquor and unwashed male.

And yes, it was him. She recognized him even with two days' growth of beard.

He lay flat on his back, his large frame filling the small bed. The murky light through the shuttered windows did him no good. He was still fully dressed, even down to his mud-caked boots, although his stained clothes were rumpled, as if he'd restlessly tried to remove them and failed. He appeared to be sleeping peacefully, until one noticed the ruddy flush to his complexion or the shallowness of his breathing. A sheen of sweat covered his skin.

Alarmed, Samantha moved closer and placed the backs of her fingers against his cheeks. She could feel the fever radiate from him even before she'd touched his skin.

"Mr. Sadler, please remove these slop buckets," she ordered briskly. "And don't just toss the contents out the window, but have Tommy bury them."

Mr. Sadler snapped his fingers for Tommy to do her bidding. The lad reluctantly moved forward, holding his nose.

"What is it, Miss Northrup?" Mrs. Sadler asked anxiously. "Do you know what he has?"

Samantha set her basket down. She didn't have to consult her journal to recognize his illness. "Influenza."

The word seemed to suck the very air out of the room. Influenza had already hit the village hard this winter and the one before.

Even the healthy and young in Sproule feared

the influenza after seeing how quickly the Vicar Northrup had succumbed. And last month it had claimed the life of the Rymans' baby.

Mrs. Sadler reached for her son and pulled him back. "Go downstairs and mind your brothers and sisters. Do not let them upstairs."

"I'll go with him," Miss Mabel volunteered. Miss Hattie was already moving down the stairs.

"We must get this man out of my inn," Mr. Sadler announced. "There won't be a soul who will come here if they know I've a man sick of the influenza under my roof."

"Our first duty is to offer him aid and comfort," Samantha corrected. "This man is very sick. I'm not certain it would be wise to move him." She pressed her fingers against the pulse at Mr. Browne's neck. She could feel his heart beat. It was weak but steady. As if her touch irritated him, he shifted restlessly and pushed her hand away.

"Mr. Browne?" Samantha said. She leaned over him. "Mr. Browne, can you hear me?" she asked again, louder.

Mr. Browne turned his head away, his brow furrowed. "Go away," he muttered, his rough voice weak. He was a far cry from the intimidating man she had met only a day and a half ago.

"Mr. Browne, please, open your eyes. Talk to us."

For a second, Samantha didn't think he would

respond . . . and then his eyes opened. She was startled to realize that his eyes weren't black as coal, as she'd remembered but a warm shade of brown. And there was a touch of red in his black beard.

He stared at her dazed and uncomprehending.

"Mr. Browne, do you remember me? Miss Northrup?"

He didn't answer. Then, just when she was beginning to believe he wasn't going to respond, he said in a low voice, "The grave's mistress."

Mrs. Sadler gave a small gasp at his words. Even Samantha felt a shiver run through her, especially when he added in his deep, raspy voice, "Have you come to claim me at last?"

"I don't know what you mean," she said hesitantly.

"I'm dying, Miss Northrup," he whispered. His thin lips twisted into an ironic smile. "Dying."

She took his hand. It was roughly callused, and in spite of the fever, cold and stiff. She rubbed his fingers between her own to stir the circulation of blood. He had long, tapered fingers like those of a gentleman. But there was strength in them, too. "You are not going to die, Mr. Browne. I will not let you."

He shook his head slightly, his eyes closing. "Damn hot." His voice sounded weaker. He tugged at his neckcloth, the knot tight from previous struggles.

Understanding it was important for a patient

to feel comfortable, Samantha hooked a finger into the knot and undid it. She was about to pull the strip of material from around his neck when his hand came up and grasped hers. His grip was surprisingly strong.

His eyes were wide open again, and this time he was seeing her clearly. "Get out. Get away from me."

This was the man she remembered from the other night. The dangerous man.

She met his gaze with a steady one of her own. "I will not leave you like this."

"You can go to the devil with your charity." His voice was so soft, she almost hadn't heard his words. "I don't need you or anyone."

She pulled back and he released her hand. But instead of alienating her, his words had the opposite effect. A fierce protectiveness welled up inside her. *Everyone needed someone.* She believed that all the way to the deepest reaches of her soul.

"I won't leave you be, Mr. Browne, because I won't let the influenza claim another soul. *Not one more.* Do you hear me? Whether you wish it or not, you are going to live."

His gaze narrowed and then dulled as his energy ebbed. She watched his eyes slowly close.

"Have it as you will." He slipped from consciousness.

Samantha didn't know if his words were a curse or a benediction.

"Do you know this man?" Mrs. Sadler asked.

Her blunt question reminded Samantha that she wasn't alone.

Samantha picked up her basket of medicinals sitting on the floor by her feet, and sitting on the edge of the bed, started rooting through it. If she was going to keep her promise, she needed to start immediately. "We met the other night. He wanted into the Ayleborough vault."

"He *what*?" Mrs. Sadler said in surprise.

Finding the small muslin bag she was looking for, Samantha glanced up. "He wanted into the Ayleborough vault," she repeated patiently. "Here, Mrs. Sadler, this is feverfew. Please make a tea of it, the more, the better."

But Mrs. Sadler did not take the packet from her hands. She turned with distress to her husband. "She met him lurking around the graveyard. What kind of man does that? And did you hear him wish her to the devil? The man's on his deathbed!"

"Mrs. Sadler, he is not himself," Samantha said. "He can't be held to account for what he is saying."

Her husband stepped forward, the set of his face stubborn. "The man's not staying here. Not in my inn. I want him out of here." Taking his wife's arm, he turned on his heel and started for the door.

Samantha followed. "This man needs our care. You can't turn your back on him."

"And what am I to do if he dies in that bed?" Mr. Sadler threw over his shoulder, his heavy shoes clumping down the wooden stairs. "People are very superstitious, Miss Northrup. There isn't a soul who will sleep in the room, let alone the same bed, if he meets his Maker in it. Times are tough. The new duke doesn't come up here as often as his father and all the nobs and gentry around these parts would rather toast their toes in London than brave the Northumberland winter. This man could ruin me." He marched into the empty taproom.

Samantha followed, her skirts swinging around her ankles as she hurried to catch up with him. After Mrs. Sadler had veered off toward the kitchen, Samantha said, "Mr. Sadler, I will stay here and nurse him. You won't have to lift a finger. Do you hear me?" she demanded in exasperation as the man went to the keg and poured himself a healthy draught.

"Aye, I hear you, missy, and my answer is no!" He lifted the tankard to his lips and downed the contents in one gulp.

The man's lack of compassion angered Samantha. "If my father was alive—"

"But he isn't, because he had the influenza," Mr. Sadler snapped back. "And I don't want to end up like the good vicar, God rest his soul."

Mrs. Sadler came out of the kitchen, her eyes brimming with tears. "The Doyle sisters left. Tommy said they feared for their lives. They'll spread the news of this all over the village in less than an hour."

Mr. Sadler shook his head. "Don't worry,

Birdie. I'll have him carted to the Post Road and put on the first stage going south."

"You can't do that!" Samantha said. "A mail coach ride in this weather will kill him. We have a Christian duty—"

"Bah to Christian duty!" Mr. Sadler said. "I take care of my own."

At that moment, they were interrupted by Alys Porter, the blacksmith's wife. She hovered by the front door. "Birdie, I've heard some alarming news from the Doyle sisters. Is it true you've got the influenza here?"

Mrs. Sadler groaned and fell back down on the bench by one of the trestle tables, covering her mouth with her hand.

Mr. Sadler answered for her. "Aye, it's true, but he won't be here long. I'm going to round up a couple of the lads and we'll send him on his way." He started for the door.

Samantha practically ran to step in his path. "That man will die without proper care and his death will be on your conscience."

"Better him than one of my children." Mr. Sadler walked around her and left. Samantha heard him shouting outside for Roddy, the hired hand, to hitch a wagon.

Tears of frustration filled her eyes. She whirled on Mrs. Sadler. "You cannot just throw the man out! The Lord asks us to care for one another, even if we are strangers."

Mrs. Sadler stood, her expression as grim as her husband's. "Then mayhap you should put the man under your roof, Miss Northrup. That way you may care for him all you like."

"Why, Birdie," Mrs. Porter said. "That is a good idea!"

"What is?" Samantha asked.

Mrs. Porter stepped into the room. "The idea of sending Mr. Browne over to the vicarage. You can tend him there, Miss Northrup."

"Aye," Mrs. Sadler agreed, her face brightening. "It is the best solution."

"Wait," Samantha said. "You know I can't."

"Why not?" Mrs. Sadler asked.

"Because I'm a single woman. It wouldn't be proper."

"Nonsense," Mrs. Sadler said with blunt northern common sense. "You are not some young girl, Miss Northrup, you are past your prime. Nor do these missish airs become you. Why, you've tended many a male patient. And some with little or no clothing on."

Samantha felt a rush of heat to her cheeks. "But that was different, Mrs. Sadler. I always had a member of the patient's family with me. I would be alone with this man."

Mrs. Sadler sniffed. "Seems to me, Miss Northrup, that you trot out the Lord's rules on us but don't apply them to yourself."

At that moment, Mr. Sadler walked back in. Roddy and the blacksmith, Dan Porter, followed him. They walked with deliberate purpose.

Samantha stamped her foot. "You can't do this."

The men walked right past her. She listened as the stairs creaked under their heavy boots. She heard them open the door to Mr. Browne's room. There was the sound of footsteps as they prepared to move his body.

A few moments later, the men clumped down the stairs and came in to the tap room. They carried the unconscious Mr. Browne by his arms and legs. The men were far from gentle.

Samantha watched helplessly as they marched out the front door. She couldn't let them do this. Her feet began moving toward the door.

Roddy had already hitched a wagon and it waited out front. Large, damp flakes of snow had started to fall. They settled on Mr. Browne and melted into his coat as he was unceremoniously dumped in the back of the wagon.

They couldn't be doing this, Samantha told herself. It was cruel! Uncharitable!

Roddy walked toward the seat of the wagon.

Samantha turned to plead one more time with Mr. Sadler. "This is wrong. I beg you not to do it."

"I already have, Miss Northrup," came his cold reply.

Roddy jumped up in the driver's seat and lifted the reins—and Samantha knew she could not let them leave Mr. Browne to die.

She ran to the head of the horses, her hair coming lose from its neat bun, and put herself in their path. "Stop."

Roddy reined the horses in before they ran over her.

"I'll take him," she said. "Drive him to the vicarage."

Chapter 3

Dead silence met Samantha's announcement.

Then Mr. Porter, a short, barrel-chested man, moved forward. "I don't think you should, Miss Northrup. Sadler is right. It's best we send him away."

Slowly Samantha turned on him, uncertain whether she believed her ears. Mr. Porter was a man known for his fatherly good humor, yet even *he* would turn his back on Mr. Browne.

"I don't agree, Mr. Porter. In fact, I almost fear a terrible retribution if we don't do our Christian duty. Do you not see? God tests us, and we are being tested right here and now."

Mr. Porter shifted uncomfortably. He glanced at his wife, who met his gaze and looked away.

He said to Samantha, "Have it as you will. I do not care as long as this man is no longer a threat to the rest of us."

"He will not be," Samantha promised. She faced Mrs. Sadler and Mrs. Porter. "I do value my reputation. It might be wise if one of the village women came and stayed with me."

Both women took a step closer to their husbands.

"I am certain your reputation will remain beyond remark," Mrs. Sadler assured her.

"But you will check with Mrs. Biggers?" Samantha insisted. The squire's wife was the parish authority on what was right and what wasn't. "Explain it to her?"

"Aye, I will go and do it now," Mrs. Sadler promised.

Samantha's next request was harder. She shivered, but not completely from the cold. It was one thing to offer charity, another to ask for it.

She couldn't meet their eyes as she said, "Also, if I am to care for him, I will need food, wood, and coal, too, if any of you can spare some."

Mrs. Porter made a soft sound of dismay, but Mrs. Sadler stoutly agreed. "We can. You'll have everything you need in an hour."

Samantha released her breath slowly. "Let me gather my cape and my medicinal basket and I'll be ready to go."

Mrs. Sadler ran into the inn herself to fetch Samantha's things. When she returned, Mr. Sadler helped Samantha place the heavy wool cape on her shoulders and gave her a hand up into the wagon seat beside Roddy.

Roddy snapped the reins and they were off.

It felt strange to be riding the quarter mile through the village. The Doyle sisters had done their work well and almost everyone had heard of the sick man. They came out of their cottages to watch Samantha drive by.

Mabel Doyle stood by her hedgerow fence, whispering to Mr. Chandler. Mrs. Ryman stood frowning, her arms crossed against her chest. No doubt she was thinking of her poor lost child. No one said anything . . . and Samantha felt a little like one of the lepers spoken of in the Bible.

At the vicarage, the burly Roddy hoisted Mr. Browne up on his shoulder like a sack of grain and carried him inside. Samantha was going to direct him to her parents' room and then thought better of it. The new vicar might not appreciate it.

"Please put him in my bedroom, Roddy."

The stablehand did as he was told, unceremoniously dumping Mr. Browne into Samantha's bed and then, with a polite pull of his forelock, hurried from the house. He too was afraid of the contagious disease.

Samantha hung her cape on its peg and stood in the center of her kitchen. No sound came from the bedroom, but she could already sense Mr. Browne's presence filling every corner and nook, just as he had the first night they'd met.

Tucking a few stray strands of hair back into her neat bun, she pushed open the door to her room.

Mr. Browne looked out of place lying on top of her light blue and yellow quilt cover. He still wore his mud-caked boots.

He also still smelled.

A horrifying thought struck her: if she did not get to work, he could very well die, right where he lay in *her* bed.

She moved into action.

Samantha picked up the bucket and hurried outside to pump water. The wood and metal pump handle felt icy cold to her hands. Snow swirled down around her, the flakes big and beautiful, but she didn't have time to stop and contemplate their beauty.

The water came out in a gush. She filled the bucket to the brim and carried it the few steps to her kitchen door, the weight of it straining her back.

Adding several logs to the dying fire, she brought it back to a blaze and then set a black iron kettle of water over it to boil.

A knock sounded at the door. It was Mrs. Sadler, Tommy, and Roddy. They carried cloth sacks of food.

"Please put those on the kitchen table," Samantha said.

"Roddy will be back with wood, and if you can use it, a load of coal," Mrs. Sadler said.

"I can," Samantha said, thankful. "I have a brazier that we used for my mother that will warm his room just fine with coal."

"Good," Mrs. Sadler said, with satisfaction. "Well, then, we'll be off."

She was almost out the door when Samantha remembered to ask, "What of Mrs. Biggers?

Have you explained everything to her yet?"

"I haven't had a chance, but I will speak to her when I see her. Don't worry."

She started to leave again, but Samantha asked, "And what of his overcoat?"

"His overcoat?"

"Aye. He had good wool overcoat, but you did not bring it with him."

Mrs. Sadler pinched her lips together. "He owes us for our trouble."

Samantha thought of the purse full of money he'd offered her. He had put it back into the pocket of his overcoat. "Did he pay for his room?"

"For one night."

"And one night is all he stayed. As for *trouble*, you can settle that with Mr. Browne once he is well."

"What if he doesn't ever get well?"

Samantha itched to wipe the smug look off her face. "He *will* get well," she practically growled. "I won't let him die."

Mrs. Sadler blinked at her tone of voice, and then backed down. "I will send his coat over later when Roddy brings the coal."

"Thank you."

With a nod, the innkeeper's wife left with her son, but Roddy lingered behind.

"Begging your pardon, Miss Northrup, but I've been close to that man. Do ye think I'll come down with what he has?" There was fear in his usually complacent brown eyes.

"I don't know, Roddy. He's very sick," she answered truthfully. She took his hand. "But you shouldn't be afraid. God rewards us when we do something right."

He drew his hand away from her. "That poor little baby died and it had never done anything to nobody. And look at your father. I'm the only one to take care of me ma. I can't get the influenza." He slipped out the door, almost slamming it behind him.

So. She was alone to fight this.

She found a hambone in a food bag and set it in a pot of water to boil. She then poured cold water into a basin, grabbed several soft cloths from her medicinal basket, and marched into the bedroom. Behind her in the kitchen, she could hear the kettle starting to boil. Good. Something was finally starting to go her way.

Little light came through the closed shutters. In spite of the fever, Mr. Browne's face was pale, with a thin sheen of sweat.

She dipped a thick rag in the water and laid it on his brow before leaving to brew the fever-few tea.

A few minutes later, she reentered the bedroom, a cup of tea and a spoon in her hand. He'd flung the rag away from him. She set the cup down on the bedside table and picked the rag off the floor. Rewetting it, she replaced it on his forehead with practiced patience. She knew she would do this a hundred times before the night was over.

She sat on the bed beside him. "Now, listen to me, Mr. Browne. I must have you drink this tea. It will be good for you."

No response.

She took that for his acceptance. Propping his head against her bosom, she tilted his head and dribbled the tea down his throat with the help of the spoon. It was slow business. "But then, I have no reason to expect you to be agreeable, do I?"

He didn't answer.

She usually wore an apron to protect her dress whenever she administered medicine this way, but the fair amount of tea that stained her dress didn't bother her. The battle lines were drawn between her and the influenza.

The medicine in him, she prepared to strip him naked and bathe him in cold water. It was the quickest means for getting the fever down.

Outside, the snow came down harder. She heard it hit the shutters—tiny crystal stabs. She'd always liked the sound of snow, but this time it made her feel isolated.

She moved to the foot of the bed. His mud-caked boots had streaked dirt down her quilt.

"All right, then, the boots come off first."

But saying and doing were two different things. Mr. Browne's boots had been made for him. Even worn at the heels, they fit his feet like a glove. By the time she got them off, she was breathing heavily.

She pushed a stray strand of her hair back

from her face. "Now for the rest of you."

She had few qualms about seeing Mr. Browne naked. Mrs. Sadler was right, she'd nursed many men besides her father. The secrets of male anatomy held no surprises. Both she and Dr. Rees had agreed that humans were the most pathetic-looking creatures without the shield of clothing . . . and Samantha secretly thought men looked the silliest of the two sexes.

Removing the coat from a solidly built man while he lay like dead weight was not easy, but Samantha was a strong woman in spite of her petite size. Furthermore, she was determined, and after a bit of a struggle to bend his long arms, she'd removed his coat.

His shirt was easier. She climbed up on the bed, rested his head in her lap, and reaching down, yanked his shirt up and off. She dropped it on the floor beside the coat.

As she'd pulled, the back of her hand had brushed his rough, whiskered jaw. There was strength in the lines of this man's face. Character.

"Who are you, Mr. Browne with an 'e'?" she asked quietly. "Is there someone waiting for you? Someone wondering where you are?" She paused a moment. "You're lucky if there is."

She slid out from beneath him and got up from the bed. "Now for your breeches, sir."

She efficiently began unbuttoning them. All of his clothes had been made of good material, although they were well worn.

As her fingers reached the last button, and the

more sensitive region of his anatomy, he moved restlessly and swatted at her hand. This was good. Any sign of life was good.

Slipping her fingers under his waistband, she pulled his breeches down—and then froze.

"Oh. My." Mr. Browne was not built like other men. "Impressive" was the first word that came into her mind.

The room became suddenly close.

Samantha gulped for air. She shouldn't stare.

"Oh, dear Lord," she whispered, lifting her eyes to the ceiling. With a swift tug, she pulled his breeches the rest of the way down and over his feet. She tried not to peek, but it was hard because she had a powerful curiosity about all things.

She also couldn't help noticing Mr. Browne's legs were *very* well favored. She even liked his long, strong feet.

Dipping more rags into the basin of cold water, she laid them on Mr. Browne, starting with his private parts. He reacted when the wet cloth hit his hot skin, but didn't push it off. Working quickly, she covered all of him.

She then headed outside to the pump to fetch more water. The snowy air felt good on her hot cheeks.

Mr. Porter appeared at the edge of the cemetery. "How are you doing, Miss Northrup?" he called.

Samantha felt her heart lurch in her chest. Did

her face betray her? Was it still flushed from the heat of embarrassment?

"I'm fine. Everything's fine," she managed to say.

"Good then." He waved and walked on.

She pumped the handle for fresh water. She should fill a second bucket, too, and dash its contents over her head for being such a ninny. She'd never blushed over naked flesh before.

Back inside, the hambone was starting to bubble. She poured dried peas into the water, gave it a stir, and then got up and carried the bucket into the bedroom.

Methodically she began removing the cloth rags and rewetting them with fresh cold water . . . over and over and over again. The fever had a terrible hold on Mr. Browne. But then, just when she wondered if she'd ever break it, the chills started.

His body shook almost to the point of shaking the bed.

Samantha quickly removed the cloths and reached to pull the quilt over him—except that he lay on it and she was too tired to struggle with him now. She raced to her parents' bedroom on the other side of the kitchen for more blankets and the coal brazier. Coming through the kitchen, she heard him mumbling, the words incoherent.

In her bedroom, she unceremoniously dumped the quilts on top of him before setting up the brazier with coal and lighting it. By the time she'd finished, his mumbling had turned to ranting. He was shouting orders: "Kill the bloody bastards! Strike hard!" His arms and hands began flailing in the air and he kicked the covers to the floor.

Samantha picked them up and dumped them back on him.

"Billy!" Mr. Browne shouted, his teeth chattering. "Watch your back, Billy!" He started up from the bed, his eyes open but unseeing.

Samantha bodily pushed him back onto the bed, no longer flustered by his nakedness. She lay on top of him to keep the covers around him. "Mr. Browne, you stay in this bed. Do you hear me?"

He didn't hear her. He kept warning Billy to watch his back. "The damn pirates are crawling the ship like maggots!"

Pirates?

He looked more like the sort of man who could *be* a pirate, than one to fight them.

The wild thrashing slowly ceased. His teeth still chattered even as the room heated up from the brazier. His wild words turned to incoherent mumbling, and it took her a moment to realize he was speaking in another language, one she didn't recognize.

And so went her day into night. Each time, the chills followed the fever and the fever grew progressively worse. He alternated between the deathly stillness or battling demons only he could see. At one point the room was so hot, she removed the brown dress.

The snow stopped sometime well past midnight. Samantha was exhausted. Her eyes ached from lack of sleep. She could not seem to break the deadly cycle that could claim his life. She had dragged a chair into the bedroom and sat by his side watching his fitful sleep.

Suddenly Mr. Browne went stiff. He half rose in bed, his eyes still closed. He cried out one word, "Father!" It was filled with all the pain in the world.

Samantha was no stranger to death. She had sat by its side far too often not to recognize the signs. Mr. Browne was dying.

Tears rolled down her cheeks. She slid off the chair to kneel on the floor, her folded hands on the edge of the bed. "You cannot take him, Lord," she begged. "I am so weary of death. I'm tired and I don't know if I can go on. Please, don't take him."

Her prayer was met with silence.

Burying her head in her arms, Samantha leaned against the bed and sobbed.

But her tears weren't just for him; she also cried for herself. Her life was about to change, and she had no one to turn to, no one she trusted. Her girlhood dreams of being a wife and a mother would never be fulfilled. She felt as if her spirit was dying.

A hand came down and rested on her head.

Samantha looked up through burning eyes.

Mr. Browne stared at her, his dark, fever-bright gaze filled with concern.

"Don't cry," he said, his voice hoarse.

Samantha could only gape at him. The despair that had overwhelmed her slipped away.

His hand fell from her head to land on the soft mattress. His eyes closed.

Samantha reached up and felt his forehead. The fever still raged inside him, but now she had hope.

She got up from the bed, consulted her medical journal, and brewed another cup of feverfew tea, renewing her battle for the life of Marvin Browne.

By mid-afternoon the next day, the intensity of Mr. Browne's fever had lessened. He suffered chills, but they no longer racked his body. Stubbornly, Samantha continued her treatment.

She now knew that her patient spoke many different languages. Occasionally she could pick out a word of French or Italian, but those were the only two she recognized. He fought pirates and storms and talked of ships and cargoes. Often he called for Billy . . . Billy, who never came.

He didn't call for his father again.

Samantha never left his side for more than a few minutes. He seemed comforted by her presence, and it felt good to be needed.

By late evening, she knew she had won. Sitting back in the chair, she couldn't help but grin foolishly at her victory. She had beaten the fever. He would live. His breathing was now even and natural, the color of his complexion still pale, but he was not clammy with fever or chills.

"Thank you, Lord," she said, and again felt the sting of tears, but these were of relief and thanksgiving.

She'd not slept since he'd been carried through her door, and she was tired— so very, very tired. What was left of the pea soup was cold in its pot. The fire in the kitchen hearth had died out. However, the bedroom was toasty warm from the few coals still burning in the brazier.

She had to lie down. Just for one moment.

She stretched out on the edge of bed beside Mr. Browne. It felt good to close her eyes. The bed beneath her was damp, but his body heat felt good.

The candle on the bedside table sputtered and then died as the last of the wick was used. Save for the sound of the wind, the world was so silent she could hear his strong, steady heartbeat.

She smiled. She had won. She drifted off to sleep.

The pounding on the door woke her. Samantha awoke abruptly. Disoriented, she was surprised to find herself in bed and still in her clothes.

Her black dress was wrinkled almost beyond repair.

What had happened? Had her mother had a bad spell during the night—?

Her thoughts broke off. Her mother was dead.

Samantha turned her head, and caught looking at the back of another person's head. A man . . . and she realized where she was!

She half-stumbled, half-jumped out of bed. Mr. Browne slept soundly. The bedcovers were up to his neck . . . although she was all too aware that he was naked.

How could she—?

The pounding on the door came again. "Miss Northrup! Miss Northrup, are you all right?"

Birdie Sadler! What was *she* doing here?

Samantha hurried out to the kitchen. She rubbed the sleep out of her eyes. The fire had died out and the house was freezing.

But Mr. Browne would live. Suddenly the day seemed perfect.

She glanced at herself in the mirror. Combing her hair with her fingers, she rebraided it while calling out, "Yes, Mrs. Sadler, I'm fine. What can I do for you?"

"We've come to call, but we want to know if it was safe."

We?

Samantha peeked out the window and drew a sharp breath. There, by the edge of the cemetery, the imposing figure of the squire's wife, Mrs. Biggers, sat in a horse-drawn sleigh. Beside her sat Mrs. Porter and the Doyle sisters. Mrs. Biggers raised a basket to show they came on a charitable mission. It was the custom in Sproule that neighbors brought food whenever there was death or sickness.

But Mr. Browne was not dead.

After tying off her braid with a piece of ribbon, Samantha opened the door. "Yes, Mrs. Sadler, it is safe. I beat the fever. Mr. Browne is going to live."

Mrs. Sadler's eyes opened wide in surprise. "I feared the worst."

"But it did not happen," Samantha added. "Praise the Lord."

"Yes, praise the Lord," Mrs. Sadler echoed. She turned to Mrs. Biggers. "It is all right to come in. The stranger lives."

"And he's no longer sick," Samantha called out, triumphant.

"Oh, that's good," Mrs. Biggers said, carefully climbing down from the sleigh. She made her way gingerly through the snow.

Samantha stepped back to invite Mrs. Sadler inside before hurrying over to the hearth and starting the fire.

"Miss Northrup," Mrs. Biggers exclaimed cheerily, the pheasant feathers of her velvet cap bobbing. She came into the kitchen and handed Mrs. Sadler her basket before taking off her riding cape and stamping the snow from her boots. "We have been so worried about you, my dear. Then, when you didn't answer the door immediately—well, we didn't know what to think."

Samantha doubted there had ever been a time in her life when Mrs. Biggers didn't have an opinion of one sort or another. She squashed the uncharitable thought.

The women were busy taking off their capes and bonnets. The kitchen smelled of wet clothes, snow, and Mrs. Biggers's famous veal pie.

"There's also cheese and sausage in the basket," Mrs. Biggers said briskly.

Samantha smiled. "Thank you. Will you please sit down?" There weren't enough chairs without the one in the bedroom. After the kindling caught fire, she hurried to fetch it. Mr. Browne slept soundly. She closed the door firmly behind her. The village women were making themselves comfortable.

Samantha forced a pleasant smile. "Here, Miss Hattie. Here is a chair for you."

"Can I help you?" Alys Porter asked.

"You can start the kettle," Samantha said. "There is a good supply of tea in the sack over there." She nodded to one of the bags Mrs. Sadler had used to deliver food.

Miss Hattie made herself comfortable. "Miss Northrup looks a bit peaked, doesn't she?"

She'd directed her comments to Mrs. Sadler, who agreed. "I told them we should not come," she said to Samantha. "But Mrs. Biggers insisted."

"Of course I did," Mrs. Biggers said. "Poor Miss Northrup has been here with Sproule's charity case throughout the snowstorm. My dear, you look terrible. Has nursing this poor unfortunate worn you to the bone?"

"I am fine," Samantha assured her. The kitchen started to warm from the fire and the company.

Still Mrs. Biggers shivered. "I do believe the parish should modernize the vicarage before my nephew moves in," she said tactlessly. "Then we would be able to use the parlor instead of the kitchen during the winter."

Samantha's father had asked repeatedly for the same thing over the years. She had no doubt that it would happen, now that the precious nephew was coming here to live.

"Is that tea ready?" Mrs. Biggers asked crossly.

"Takes a long time for water to boil," Miss Mabel said, and earned a glance of irritation from the squire's wife.

"It's about done," Mrs. Porter said.

Samantha went to the sideboard and took down a pot and the delicate teacups and saucers that had been a wedding gift from her father to her mother. Her fingers lingered over the fine English china. Whenever she touched them, she remembered her parents.

"I had to come today," Mrs. Biggers said. "You know how the squire feels about strangers. He wants to know everyone who comes into the shire. He'll ask me for a report. Comes from his days in the military," she confided to Mrs. Porter.

"And wise he is, too," Mrs. Porter said dutifully.

"Yes," Mrs. Biggers said. She took a sip of tea. "But Miss Northrup, where is the patient? I thought you said he was well."

"He is, but he's sleeping right now. It takes a great deal of strength to fight off illness." She was standing. There was no chair for her, and she felt slightly ridiculous, like some sort of servant. She wished they would all leave so that she could go back to sleep.

"I know what kind of strength it takes," Mrs. Biggers said. "Remember when I suffered from that cold last month?" She rolled her eyes dramatically, the pheasant feathers on her hat sweeping the air over her head. "I didn't want to see or talk to anyone."

"I remember," Miss Mabel said. "Oh, we all prayed for you. Pour me more tea, Miss Northrup."

Samantha was surprised by the hint of command in Miss Mabel's voice. She glanced around the room. No one else seemed to have noticed. They were all listening to Mrs. Biggers expound upon her sufferings.

She poured the tea thoughtfully, her worst suspicions confirmed. Life with Miss Mabel and Miss Hattie might be more that of an unpaid companion, nursemaid, and servant.

And she was the only one who objected. The others seemed to feel that was her role in life.

Samantha frowned, rejecting the image . . . but where else could she go?

Mrs. Biggers babbled on, ". . . I took to my bed

and told the squire he could—" Her voice broke off suddenly. She focused on a point past Samantha. Her mouth dropped open, and for the first time in Samantha's memory, she appeared speechless.

Nor was she the only one. Every one of the women went still as if frozen in time, their eyebrows raised to their hairlines in shocked expressions.

And then Samantha sensed him. He was here, in this room. Marvin Browne.

Slowly she turned to face him—and then her own jaw dropped. He stood leaning against the door frame as naked as the day he was born.

He was a riveting sight. A cowlick stood up in his sleep-ruffled dark hair, and there were several days' growth of beard on his jaw. He stared at them, his expression hard. Then, in a low, dangerous voice, he growled, "Where the bloody hell am I?"

Chapter 4

G roggy and disoriented, Yale stared at the five ladies, all comfortable and cozy around a kitchen table, who all stared back at him in wide-eyed shock.

What an odd dream this was!

Miss Northrup, the vicar's prickly daughter, was there. She stood off to one side, dressed in mourning black and holding a tea pot.

She appeared particularly horror-struck by his appearance.

Of course, this wasn't the first time he had dreamed of being naked in a crowd. He just couldn't understand what it all signified.

He also didn't remember his dreams being so colorful. Or so real.

One of the ladies, made a low sound of distress and dropped her tea cup.

The sound of the breaking cup sent the silent tableau of women into pandemonium.

The woman who had broken the teacup threw her arms up as if to shield her eyes from the sight of him. Another squealed, the ribbons on her lace cap bobbing as she attempted to duck under the kitchen table. Their actions tipped over more teacups. The innkeeper's wife attempted to save the cups and ended up pushing two of them over the edge of the table. Funny that she should be in his dream—

Miss Northrup grabbed him by the arm, and with surprising strength, propelled him back into the bedroom.

Her touch made Yale realize he had not been dreaming!

The heat of embarrassment blazed through him. Damn, but he was naked. In front of the innkeeper's wife—and the vicar's daughter!

Inside the bedroom, Miss Northrup slammed the door behind them, then said with great forbearance. "Mr. Browne, what do you mean walking out of this room in your—" She paused. "In your *natural state?*"

Yale reached for the sheet off the bed and wrapped it around his waist. "Where are my bloody clothes? And who is Mr.—" He caught himself before he blundered.

The night in the vault came back to him. He was posing as Marvin Browne.

"Who is who?" she said, her tone as clipped and inquisitional as a tutor's.

He changed the subject, going on the counterattack. "How did I end up here? I'm in the vicarage, correct? *And where are my clothes?*" he repeated with exasperation. "I feel like a damn fool for walking in on that hen party naked."

His words almost surprised a smile out of her. She'd hidden it, but he'd seen her mouth twitch and it gave him a bit of satisfaction.

He'd wager she was a fetching little thing, if she'd ever smile.

"Mr. Browne, let me explain everything. In fact, it might be better if you sat down. I can't imagine you're feeling completely the thing yet. You've been very ill."

Memory came back. He'd been at the inn. "Are you talking about the brandy?" He remembered throwing it up. Funny, he'd never been one to lose his liquor. He might have gotten so drunk he couldn't remember his own actions, but before, he'd always kept it all in.

"You had the influenza, sir. It's true you'd had a good deal to drink, but that's not what made you so ill. When the innkeeper realized how sick you were, he sent for me."

A thought tickled the haziness of his memory. "I remember, you nursed my father—" Again he realized he'd made an error. Masquerading as someone else was not easy.

Worse, Miss Northrup was far too quick to let anything slip by her. "Your father? I don't know your father."

Yale drew back from revealing his true identity. His feelings toward his father were too raw, too vulnerable, too unmanly. "I'm confused. The fever . . ." he explained lamely, and then realized it was true.

He was tired. The fever still rested in his bones, but he had to get away from Sproule. What would Wayland and Twyla say if they heard he'd been lurking about? Or worse, that he'd introduced himself to the village woman *en déshabillé?*

No, Yale didn't want to run into any member of his family. He'd already disgraced them enough. In fact, the best thing he could do for all would be to continue to let them believe he was dead. He would get dressed, get on that sway-backed nag he'd ridden from London and return to his ship. Before another week passed, he'd be on his way back to Ceylon.

He spied his money purse lying on the bedside table and picked it up, offering it to her. "Here, this is for the trouble you've gone to on my account. You've saved my life, Miss Northrup, and I am thankful."

"I will not take your money, Mr. Browne. I did not nurse you for money."

"It is not charity I offer, Miss Northrup, but a fair wage for a job well done." Besides, he added silently, she looked as if she could use the money. She was too thin and her clothes well worn.

While at the Bear and Bull, he'd overheard the innkeeper grumbling to his wife about the "difficult Miss Northrup." Curious, he'd eavesdropped and knew the whole village was attempting to move her out of the vicarage and in with two old women.

Seemed a pity. There was too much intelligence in her eyes for her to be branded the village spinster and placed on a shelf.

"I do not want your money," she said firmly. "If you feel you must pay, then give it away to the poor."

Yale amended his opinion. The innkeeper *had* been right: she was difficult and proudly stubborn. He understood why she wasn't married.

He tossed the money bag on the bed. He would leave it anyway. "Now, if you will be good enough to bring me my clothes, I will be dressed and on my way," he said.

She opened her mouth to argue about the money, but no words came out.

"Miss Northrup, you've gone speechless," he said crisply. "I *am* surprised."

"Oh, dear," she answered on a worried sigh.

"Oh dear?"

"I burned them."

"Burned what?"

"Your clothes."

Yale thought he would choke.

"I burned them because I feared they carried the disease," she hurried to explain. "And now I must go see to my guests." She opened the door and was through it before he could blink.

"Burned them?" he repeated. Comprehension was slow to come, but when it did—

"*She burned them!*" He faced the half-open door. "Miss Northrup, I have nothing else to wear. I brought no other clothes with me!"

Everything he owned was back on his ship in the London harbor or being readied at the tailor's. He'd been so shocked by the news of his father's death that he'd taken off without being well prepared for the trip.

And what of his overcoat? "You didn't burn my overcoat, did you? Miss Northrup? Miss Northrup!"

No answer.

"That woman is exasperating." Holding the sheet up with one hand, he marched over to the door and threw it open, ready to do battle with her and her high-handed ways. But the words died in his throat.

She stood in the middle of the kitchen, her expression puzzled. The door was open and the cold wind ran across the floor and up under his sheet.

Their gazes met.

"They left," she said simply.

"Who left?"

"Mrs. Biggers. Mrs. Sadler. The others." She took an uncertain step. "Mrs. Biggers even took her shepherd's pie. Why would they leave without saying good-bye?"

Yale walked over to the kitchen door and shut it. "Don't you think it had something to do with my walking out stripped naked?"

Miss Northrup appeared startled by the thought. "Yes, yes . . . that must be it. You were a bit much for any woman's delicate sensibilities."

"Was I?" he said, rather flattered by the thought.

She realized the double entendre of his words and her cheeks turned a very becoming shade of pink. "I didn't mean it that way."

"What way *did* you mean it?" Yale pressed, enjoying her discomfort.

She frowned before making a great show of ignoring him by attempting to make order out of the broken teacups.

Yale pulled up a chair and sat. He was not accustomed to being ignored—at least, not by women. It was a novel experience.

He noticed her hands shook as she gathered up the bits and pieces of green and white porcelain. "Is something the matter?"

She didn't answer but turned and carried the shards over to the bin and dumped them.

"Seems a waste," he said. "This must have been a nice set at one time." It was a ludicrous thing to say. He'd never paid attention to teacups and such. Wouldn't know Staffordshire from Sèvres. Still . . . it bothered him that she appeared so upset.

Miss Northrup took a cloth from the sideboard and folding it over, started to wipe the spilled tea off the table. Yale reached over and picked up one of the only two cups whole and intact.

It was an ordinary teacup to him, milky white porcelain with green leaves drawn all over it.

Miss Northrup snatched it from his hand. She set it on the sideboard with the other cup alongside the matching teapot and then immediately seemed to regret her rudeness. She turned to him. "They belonged to my mother. They are all I have of her."

Yale had received gut punches that hurt less than her words. He remembered how he'd felt when he'd lost his mother . . . and then, of course, he was still sorting out his feelings about his father's death.

He stood. "I'm sorry. I didn't know."

"You couldn't." She went back to wiping the table, her head bowed, the long braid swinging free over one shoulder in time to her movements.

Concerned, he watched her a second. He didn't see that the table needed more cleaning. Something was not quite right about her behavior. He'd never really wasted a great deal of time considering the vagaries of women. They had an obvious purpose in his life, one he enjoyed very much, but he didn't give them much thought.

But something about her quiet behavior bothered him. A small drop of water landed on the table. And then another.

Panic rose inside him. *Oh, God, she was crying*!

He wished he'd never stepped out of the bedroom. He bloody well should never have left Ceylon. This whole trip was nothing but a disaster—and for what purpose? His pride?

His pride wasn't worth dealing with a crying woman.

"No, Miss Northrup, don't cry. Just don't. Everything will be all right. You can use the money I gave you to buy more teacups."

They were the wrong words. She began crying harder.

Yale placed his hands on her shoulders. "Here, sit. Sit!" He had to tell her a third time before she finally did as he ordered.

He knelt beside her. "Come, don't be a goose. Broken teacups aren't worth tears."

"You are right," she said, struggling to bring herself under control.

Tears and red eyes did not become Miss Northrup, yet she looked endearing all the same. He pulled her braid over her shoulder and gave it a pat. Its silky texture surprised him. He liked the feel of it.

"Then what is the problem?" he asked.

"When I married, I was going to take that tea set with me . . . and it does not really matter because I am never going to marry—" She broke off with a sob and broke down into tears.

Yale didn't know what to do.

"Miss Northrup, please. Don't carry on this way." He started to put his arm around her and then pulled back when he realized it wouldn't look right if anyone walked in and saw him half-naked and comforting her.

She swiped at her eyes with the back of her hand. "I'm all right. I'm just tired and my life hasn't been going very well lately."

"Tell me about it," Yale said, grasping for anything to make her stop crying.

"Come along. Dry your tears." He offered her the trailing edge of his sheet.

He was being silly but it worked. She stared at the sheet in his hand, and then laughed. He placed the sheet in her hand, and she did use it.

"Now, what is the problem?" he asked quietly.

"Sproule. My life. Everything."

"Ahhhhh," he said sagely. "And what is wrong with your life?"

She glanced at the door and then said in a low voice, as if she were afraid the villagers would hear her, "Sometimes I wish I could fit in, but I don't. I try, but I don't have a husband, and I am rather set in my ways, and I like books and ideas . . . I can't imagine myself spending the rest of life living with Miss Mabel and Miss Hattie. I think I'd almost rather be dead."

He covered her small hand with his own, staring into her eyes. "Don't ever say that. Don't even think it. No matter how bad life is, it is always preferable to death."

She studied their hands resting on her leg. "That's easy for you to say. You're a man and can go anywhere or do anything you wish. I have no choices. I'm too old to marry. There had been thoughts that the squire's nephew, Vicar Newell, might offer, but he's recently married a younger woman with a nice dowry. I don't blame him, but now they want to move into the vicarage. Whether I like it or not, I have nowhere to go but Miss Mabel and Miss Hattie's."

Yale had never stopped to think about the role of women in society. He'd assumed they all wanted to be married—or at least, the respectable ones did. In the Orient, he'd known some bold and dashing Englishwomen who lived by their own rules. They were either extremely wealthy or married to men who let them go their own way.

"Why didn't your father find a husband for you?" he asked.

She frowned at him. "It's not that easy. Look at me."

"I am looking at you. I see nothing wrong with you." He'd actually spoken the truth. Miss Northrup was no sultry beauty, but she was an attractive woman with a fresh wholesomeness. She also had nice breasts—but he was not going to mention that to her!

"Why do you smile when you say that?" she asked, misinterpreting the reason behind his smile. "Come, Mr. Browne, I'm rather plain."

"Absolutely not!"

"Yes. But also, I didn't have time to marry when I was younger. My father needed me. Mother was sick, and he needed someone to care for her and help him with his duties. I understand why a man would wish for a prettier girl than myself. Especially one with fewer commitments."

"Then he isn't a man worth having."

He held her attention now. He drew her hand into his, giving her fingers a reassuring squeeze.

"Miss Northrup, sometimes it is possible to have all the things you've wished and still be alone. You can even have a family and not feel included."

She raised her eyes to meet his. "Have you ever been lonely, Mr. Browne?"

Her directness caught him off guard. He answered truthfully. "Aye."

She nodded as if his response was what she had expected. Actually, she was a very attractive woman, with a pert nose and determined chin. Kissable lips . . . Of course, a gentleman would never seduce a vicar's daughter.

But she was the one who broke contact first.

She pulled her hand from his. "Well, I need to find clothes for you."

He rose to his feet, a bit embarrassed by the direction of his thoughts. He liked Miss Northrup. She'd cried, but she hadn't clung or expected him to solve her problems. She was a brave woman and he hoped everything worked out for her.

"Perhaps your father had something I could wear?"

Coming to her feet, she shook her head. "You are a good six inches taller than my father. Besides, anything worthwhile I gave to the poor." She took her cape off a peg on the wall and threw it over her shoulders. She then reached for what had to be the ugliest bonnet he'd ever seen. The black silk material covering it had been faded by the weather. When she set it on her head, she looked like she was wearing a crow.

"Where are you going?" Yale asked.

"I'm going to call on Mr. Sadler and see if he has any cast-offs for you."

"Cast-offs? You want me to wear the cast-offs of an innkeeper?"

"You sound as offended as a duke. Beggars can't be choosers, Mr. Browne. Sproule is a small village. If you wish to purchase new clothing, you can do that in Morpeth. But for now, I'll have to scavenge for breeches and you'll have to settle for whatever I can find, especially since you are such a tall and brawny man."

Yale couldn't help but preen a bit. He liked the way the soft Northern burr in her voice rolled over the words "tall and brawny man."

"Did you just pay me a compliment, Miss Northrup?"

To his surprise, she smiled.

He'd been right. She was a fetching lass when she smiled. The smile lit her whole face.

"If calling a man too big to make it easy to find breeches for him is a compliment, sir, then that I did." On those words, she opened the door and left.

Charmed, Yale went to the window to watch her trudge through the inch or two of crusty snow on the ground. He scratched the growth of beard on his jaw. He hadn't shaved since he'd left London.

He opened the door, stuck out his head, and shouted, "Don't forget to bring a razor!"

She waved that she'd heard him.

He shut the door.

Silver gray clouds covered the sky. They were too high to herald more snow. He still felt weak, but was also eager to return to his life in London.

The truth was, he shouldn't have come back.

Or he should have come back years earlier—while his father was still alive. He could have returned to England three years ago, but he hadn't felt he had enough money or enough power to properly impress the great duke of Ayleborough . . . or so he thought.

He looked down at himself. He was a rich man, the owner of his own shipping company, and yet here he stood in a vicarage kitchen in the tiny village of Sproule dressed in nothing more than a sheet.

What a fool he was!

Of course, he could stop in London and see his brother Wayland and his sister Twyla.

He immediately rejected the idea. He could not face them. Not now that their father was dead.

His failure to be at his father's side in his last hours would be only one more way in which Yale had disappointed his family. Besides, because of the age difference and their separate mothers, they had never been close as family. Wayland and Twyla had always done what had been expected of them. Yale had rebelled.

How many schools had he been sent down from for miscreant behavior? He'd forgotten.

He'd also been extremely selfish. The truth was, his father had ignored him, favoring the children from his first marriage over Yale.

And it had hurt. At some point he'd learned that if he acted badly, his father had no choice but to pay attention.

Yale winced at the memories of some of the pranks he'd pulled.

Then there was episode that had gotten him disinherited. He'd been kicked out of school, this time permanently, but instead of returning home to Northumberland, he'd hired a coach and driver.

Even now he smiled at the memory of his younger self, full of self-importance and no small amount of gall, setting himself up as a man on the Town. He'd been all of eighteen. Not one merchant or a matchmaking mama had questioned him.

He'd rented rooms, purchased a horse, had a new wardrobe made, and lived the high life with plenty of women eager for his attentions and a new set of friends to take him around London. In less than six weeks he'd gambled away a small fortune—including the inheritance from his mother.

He stared out the kitchen window. Snow blanketed the graves and headstones. From this angle, he could just see the Ayleborough vault.

His breath made a fog on the window. He touched the cold glass with his finger, remembering that day when his father had come to Yale's rooms in London and found him passed out drunk, a naked opera dancer at his side.

The duke had been furious. The school had notified him that they had sent Yale home. He'd been worried about Yale's whereabouts until word had reached him through friends in London.

When his father had confronted him, Yale, hung over and full of pride, had demanded his portion of his inheritance right then and there so he could live his life the way he wished.

That had stopped his father's lecture.

But to Yale's surprise, he had agreed.

"It will make a man of you," he'd said. He'd pulled from his pockets all of Yale's debts. He'd bought them up and now held the chits in front of Yale.

"Here is your inheritance," he'd said. "Twenty-seven thousand pounds. Wasted."

And then he had disinherited his younger son on the spot.

Yale turned from the window. He now knew how hard it was to earn that sum with one's sweat. He also understood more of the world now.

Back then, he'd been hurt when his new friends had deserted him. Doors that had been open to him had slammed shut the minute notice of his disinheritance had been posted in the *Gazette*.

He'd gone off to a dockside tavern to get good and drunk. He'd succeeded. He'd also signed on as a crew member of a merchantman.

When he'd come to his senses, the ship was well out to sea. Foolishly, he'd demanded to be released from the contract he'd signed and had been soundly beaten for his rebellion.

It had been the making of him.

He'd stayed with the ship because he'd had no choice—and because he'd rather cut off his own arm than beg his father for forgiveness. When the ship put into port in Naples, a more sober, and somewhat wiser, Yale had found a small church, and there he had made an oath. He vowed he would prove his father wrong. He would not crawl home a broken man like the prodigal son but as a rich man.

In the ensuing years, there had been times he wondered if he would succeed. Life's lessons were hard.

He'd thought himself a swordsman until he'd found himself battling for his life against Mediterranean pirates. He quickly learned tricks not taught by any London fencing master. And no boxing school could teach him how to brawl the way he'd learned on the mean streets of Algiers and Calcutta.

In time, he'd learned how the world truly measured the worth of a man. His rebelliousness was replaced by a very sincere desire just to stay alive. He'd learned to live in a world where a

man's word was his bond—breaking it could be
a death warrant.

The first gold coin he'd earned by his own labor, he'd put in a leather bag that he wore
around his neck, lest one of his comrades should
steal it. It had taken him almost another full year
to earn another. He'd decided there had to be a
better way to build his fortune. He'd purchased
a few shares in a sailing ship. In a few years,
he'd owned the ship.

The keen intelligence that had lain dormant
through all his history and Latin lessons now became a powerful weapon, especially in the hands
of a man who had to educate himself. He'd
asked questions and listened hard.

He'd also learned he had a talent for making
money.

But now, it all seemed hollow—the money, the
vow, the desire to show his family he was a man.

He sat down in the chair in Miss Northrup's
small kitchen. The brick floor made his toes cold.
He curled them up under the sheet and crossed
his arms, waiting.

He must have dozed in the warmth by the
hearth because when next he knew, a rush of
cold air jerked him to consciousness.

It took him a moment to gather his bearings
and when he did, he found himself surrounded
by a group of angry men. He immediately recognized the innkeeper and the blacksmith with
whom he had left his horse upon arriving in
Sproule. The blacksmith was carrying the heavy

hammer he used to pound metal into horse-shoes. The innkeeper held a club. The other men didn't look any friendlier. The women he'd met earlier poured in the door behind the men. By the set expressions on everyone's faces, this was obviously not a social call.

"Marvin Browne?" questioned an officious man in drab brown and green hunting clothes and a great wool scarf. He cradled an aged blunderbuss in his arms.

Yale stared at him, refusing to answer.

"Aye, Squire Biggers, that is Marvin Browne," Mrs. Sadler answered for him. "See? He's wearing nothing but the bed linens."

Yale slowly rose from his chair, feeling at a disadvantage with the men looming over him. As he had expected, when he came to his full height, they took a step back—everyone, that is, except Squire Biggers.

"Where is Miss Northrup?" Yale asked.

At that moment, she pushed her way forward from the back of the group. She turned and faced them. "This is ridiculous! I insist you stop immediately!"

Mrs. Sadler spoke. "We told you to stay at the inn, Miss Northrup. We know what we are doing."

"Someone take her back to the inn," Squire Biggers ordered. Mr. Sadler moved to obey.

The squire turned his attention back to Yale. He patted his blunderbuss. "Mr. Browne, I am also the local magistrate."

"It is a pleasure to meet you," Yale replied dryly.

"It's no pleasure for me, sir," the squire shot back. "We are all concerned for the reputation of Miss Northrup."

"Oh, I can't believe this!" Miss Northrup protested. She'd dug in her heels and wasn't making it easy for Mr. Sadler to remove her person.

Yale looked Squire Biggers in the eye. "I assure you her reputation is safe. I have done nothing untoward here."

"Do you call parading yourself naked in front of our women *nothing*, sir?"

Every man jack of them waited for Yale's answer, and he knew they wouldn't believe him, whatever he said. "It was a mistake. They have my sincerest apologies."

"Oh, it was a mistake, all right," the squire agreed. "And I have no doubt you've been in the company of Miss Northrup without your clothing, too."

Yale sensed a trap but he didn't know what kind. "If you have no doubt, then it is futile for me to protest it," he said cautiously.

"Not as long as you do the right thing, sir." Squire Biggers laid a loving hand on his blunderbuss.

"The right thing?" Yale asked.

"Aye," the squire answered. "We expect you to marry her."

Chapter 5

Hustled to the back of the crowd gathered around her kitchen door, Samantha heard the squire's words. Her knees buckled beneath her in shock.

Her stumbling caused Mr. Sadler to loosen his hold and she used the opportunity to twist out of his grasp, slip under his arm, and charge back into the house with a ringing, "No!"

She pushed her way past her neighbors to confront the squire angrily. "What do you think you're doing?"

He didn't even bother to look at her. "This is none of your affair, missy."

"None of my affair?" Samantha repeated incredulously. She shot a glance at Mr. Browne to see if he was as disbelieving as she was. He stood, his arms folded against his chest, his face a stone mask. He reminded her of the Sphinx of Ancient Egypt—except that he had the body of Apollo.

Funny she should notice that at this particular

moment, but then, any other man would look ridiculous wearing nothing but a sheet.

She faced Squire Biggers. "How dare you walk into my home, confront a sick man, and order him to marry me!"

There was a rustle of murmurs from the villagers. The squire was known for his quick, irrational temper. Few people dared question him.

Squire Biggers's eyebrows practically rose to where his hairline used to be and he pulled himself up to every inch of his short stature. "I dare," he drawled in his best patrician voice, "because you have *no one else* to speak for you, Miss Northrup. Because we have *standards* in our community, and we will not have some ne'er-do-well taking *advantage* of our dear departed vicar's daughter, God rest his soul."

"Mr. Browne has done nothing to take advantage of me," Samantha shot back. "None of this is his fault. He's been very ill. Since he wasn't conscious when we moved him from the inn, he didn't know where he was. Furthermore, I burned his clothes to prevent the spread of disease. The man had nothing to wear, he woke up in a strange place, and he didn't know the kitchen was full of women."

"What? He couldn't hear them?" Mr. Porter demanded. "I've never seen the lot of you get together without making a good deal of chatter."

"Mr. Porter, he did not know where he was," Samantha reiterated. These people were going to drive her to madness. "He'd been so sick, he didn't even know I'd undressed him."

"*You* undressed him?" the squire said, raising an eyebrow.

"Well, how do you think he got undressed?" she snapped. She glanced at Mr. Browne. He didn't appear to be attending the conversation but stared ahead, as if concentrating on something only he could hear or see.

"You know, you could be helpful in explaining all this," she told him.

"If they won't listen to you, what makes you think they'll listen to me?"

She hated his logic.

"It doesn't matter what either of you says," Squire Biggers insisted. "We are not questioning whether what you did saved this man's life or not. It did, we all agree. But now we expect him to do what is decent and marry you."

Samantha wanted to stamp her feet in frustration. "But he doesn't *have* to marry me. We did nothing *wrong*!" She spied a thin farmer hovering by the kitchen door in the back of the ever-growing crowd outside her house. "You, Mr. Hatfield. I helped you with the croup when it had left you so weakened you feared you would die. No one expected you to marry me, did they?"

"I am already married, Miss Northrup," the farmer answered.

She blinked and then cried out, "That's right!" seeing a new way out of this silliness. "And how do you know Mr. Browne isn't already married, Squire Biggers?''

"Because he told me he was not," Mrs. Sadler said. "When he signed the innkeeper's book, I asked him. I said, 'Do you have family in the area, Mr. Browne?' And he said, 'No.' And I said, 'Well, it is hard to travel away from one's family.' And he said, 'I have no family at all.' Just like that. Quick and short: 'I have no family at all.' " She looked to her friends gathered around her. "It is always good to know these things about your guests."

Her lady friends nodded agreement.

The squire smiled benevolently down at Samantha. "Then it appears the two of you can be married."

"No, it doesn't!" she argued.

But he continued as if she hadn't spoken. "Your father would understand the need for urgency. I believe a special license can be arranged. I'll send a lad on my fastest horse to the bishop. We should have it before dark."

Samantha watched the heads of her friends and neighbors agree with him. "This is lunacy. I will not marry this man. I don't know him. Besides, he is a drunkard," she added, in a flash of inspiration.

"Thank you," was Mr. Browne's dry response behind her.

"And he is sarcastic," Samantha finished without missing a beat.

Suddenly Mrs. Biggers charged forward, the

pheasant feathers on her hat quivering. "This is outrageous," she told her husband. "Why are you indulging the girl?" She confronted Samantha. "You are the most *ungrateful* woman imaginable. Do you not see what we are doing for you? Miss Mabel and Miss Hattie do not want you to live with them. They were only being kind, but now that they know you don't even blush over naked men, they are not even interested . . . are you, ladies?"

Miss Mabel and Miss Hattie stood side-by-side next to Mrs. Porter. When Mrs. Biggers had turned her attention to them, their eyes grew round.

"Well, no, we should not, should we, Mrs. Biggers?" Miss Mabel said.

"Of course not," Miss Hattie said. "Not if Mrs. Biggers says it is so." The sisters huddled together.

"Our village needs a new vicar, Miss Northrup," Mrs. Biggers said. "My nephew and his new wife deserve the benefice. Since your father's death, he has made the trek from Morpeth and back to say the Sunday service. It is past time for you to get out of the vicarage. No one wants to tell you this, but it is time for someone new to live here. And yet you, in your selfishness, stand in their way. Marry this man. Leave! You are a thorn in our side."

Samantha stared at the woman, stunned by her cruel words and yet hearing the truth in them.

For her part, Mrs. Biggers looked equally surprised that she'd said them. She burst out in loud, noisy sobs and was quickly surrounded by comforting friends.

Samantha stood alone.

Had she really believed that she'd been part of this small village? Every hope, every dream, even the reality she had assumed about her life melted away with nothing in their place.

Then a pair of strong hands came down on her shoulders. "I will marry her," Mr. Browne said.

The import of his words was slow to sink in. Samantha almost believed she'd misheard him—and then, when she realized she hadn't, the full circle of her shame was complete.

"No," she whispered. "I don't want—!"

The pressure of his hands on her shoulder warned her to silence.

Her protest wouldn't have made any difference anyway. The women squealed with excitement and the men grinned and made approving sounds.

Squire Biggers even offered to shake Mr. Browne's hand, but Mr. Browne made no move to take it. The squire withdrew his, pretending to straighten the coat cuff of his hand holding the blunderbuss. "I'll make the arrangements for the license."

"I expect you to," Mr. Browne said.

"Oh. Well, I guess we are done here," the squire said to his wife.

Her face tear-stained, Mrs. Biggers moved to

give Samantha a hug. But Samantha pulled back, finding herself in the protective embrace of Mr. Browne.

"Come, Mrs. Biggers," the squire said. "You must help the women make plans. We would not want it said that Sproule did not take care of Miss Northrup." Now as gentle and meek as a lamb, his wife followed him out the door.

Mrs. Porter and Mrs. Sadler came forward. "We are happy for you, Miss Northrup," Mrs. Porter said. "Everything will work out fine."

"I don't think we should leave her here, though," Mrs. Sadler said. "Why don't you come back to the inn with us?"

Samantha shook her head. She was too angry, too hurt.

"Later," Mr. Browne said. "Why don't you two help plan the wedding and you can come back and fetch Miss Northrup later?"

"Yes, that's a good idea," Mrs. Porter said. "Come, Birdie." She paused. "We'll also bring clothes for you when we come back."

"I would appreciate that," Mr. Browne said. "I have no desire to walk into a church wearing a bed sheet."

A few others came up and offered congratulations, but the majority of the villagers slipped away without speaking. Samantha waited until the last villager had gone out the door before crossing to it and putting down the lock bar.

She was alone with Mr. Browne. The kitchen was cold from having the door open for so long.

She crossed to the hearth and added more kindling. Once it had caught fire, she added a log and watched as the strong flame lapped at the hard wood.

"I don't care what they think or what they wish. I will not marry you." She rose and turned to face him, uncertain of his reaction to her words.

"Neither of us has a choice."

Not exactly a romantic reaction. She shrugged. "Forcing you to marry me makes a mockery of the sacrament."

He drew a chair up in front of the fire and sat. "Miss Northrup, no one is forcing me to marry you."

She laughed. "You can't mean you *wish* to do this?"

"Aye. I'm willing." He pulled another chair toward the fire and gestured for her to sit in it.

Samantha didn't. She didn't feel like sitting. She took off her cape and hung it on the peg on the wall and then paced the perimeter of the room, conscious of his patient presence.

"You can leave," she said. "Once we have clothes for you, you can sneak out of the house and escape."

"I do not sneak anywhere," he said with disgust, stretching his bare feet toward the fire. "Has it always been this cold in winter?"

"Have you been to Sproule before?"

He seemed to stiffen, as if she'd asked something he didn't want to answer. But when he spoke, his voice was relaxed. "I've passed through here."

"I don't remember seeing you."

"There is no reason you should have. It was years ago."

"Miss Mabel and Miss Hattie said the old duke of Ayleborough once had a tutor for his sons whose name was Marvin Browne, with an 'e.' "

"I wouldn't know him," came the stony reply.

She crossed her arms. "I don't want to marry you."

He turned to her then. "Because I drink?" He was teasing her. "I assure you, Miss Northrup, my drinking the other night was a momentary lapse into a bad habit I gave up years ago. You won't have a drunkard for a husband."

"That's not the reason I don't want to marry you."

"What is your Christian name?"

His change of subject was unsettling. "Why do you want to know?"

"Because I've asked." The steadfastness in his dark eyes was compelling.

Against her better judgment, she said, "Samantha."

"Mine's—" He paused. "Marvin."

"Yes, I know." She couldn't help but smile at the name. It didn't seem to fit him.

"Come sit here, Samantha." He patted the chair next to him.

Her name sounded differently on his lips than

she'd ever heard it sound before. "I'm fine here."

"Please."

She hesitated, then did as he'd asked.

They sat a moment staring into the fire, each lost in thought.

Then he spoke. "Would you leave Sproule if I didn't marry you?"

"Of course not. Where would I go? Why would I want to leave it even if we did marry?"

His jaw tensed with anger. "I will not leave you here, not with these people."

Samantha started pressing out one of the wrinkles in her dress with her hand. Her gaze didn't meet his as she said, "They are not bad people."

"No, just expedient," he replied with distaste. "Samantha, up until now, I haven't always done the right thing in my life. I have sinned, as you would so quaintly put it. Worse, I've made terrible mistakes for no other reason than my pride. But I have never turned my back on a person who needed help."

"I don't need help. It's just that—" She stopped, uncertain if she was saying the right thing.

"Just what?" he prompted.

She lifted her gaze to his. "I've spent the majority of my life making excuses for people. You're right. I'm deeply hurt that they want to be rid of me. But I've known it was coming. I've only managed to stay in the vicarage by my wiles. I thought that the people here valued my healing skills. They've always come to me and

I've always helped, even if it was in the middle of the night, or I'd have to stay for days. I felt I was one of them, and now, they've let me know differently. It's just that I can't imagine a life beyond Sproule.''

"There is plenty of life beyond Sproule," he said with feeling.

"What of *you*, Mr. Browne? Where did you come from?''

Again she had the feeling she'd asked a question he would rather not answer.

"I've come from here and there."

"But what is your profession, sir?''

"I do a little of everything, Samantha. You need never worry. I will take good care of you.''

"I will not marry you. Nor do I want your pity.''

"There you are wrong. I don't pity you, and you *will* marry me.''

She smiled at the autocratic tone in his voice. "Mr. Browne—"

"Marvin."

She rolled her eyes, but conceded, "*Marvin*. To hear you give me edicts, one would think you were a grand duke, but the truth of the matter is, it's not right for us to enter into the holy union of marriage just so that Mrs. Biggers's nephew can move into the vicarage.''

"It's also not right to hold onto the past once it is done and over.''

His voice had been soft—gentle, even—yet his words struck her with the force of a blow.

Samantha sat stunned.

"Is that what I've been doing?" she asked at last.

"I don't know. Only you can answer that."

She stared at him. Who was this man? He was no ordinary stranger who had just wandered into Sproule. But then, she had known that since the moment he'd asked for the keys to the Ayleborough vault.

"Who are you?" she asked once more.

"Marvin Browne," he replied smoothly . . . almost too smoothly.

"I don't believe you are good husband material," she baited him, wanting to slip past his guard.

He grinned, his teeth white and even. "You're right. I'm not. Nor will I change. I am a loner, Samantha. I need no one in my life." He reached for her hand and took it in his own. "But I will take care of you."

"Why?"

"Because you saved my life. The least I can do is protect your reputation. So, will you do me the honor of being my bride?" He paused before adding, "And the answer is yes."

Samantha studied her hand so much smaller than his. She could feel his calluses, a sign he wasn't afraid of hard work. She knew nothing about him. What she did know was a bit odd, such as his desire to visit the vault, his ravings about pirates, and his drinking.

And yet she trusted him.

"This is not the way it should be," she said slowly.

"Is anything?"

"I don't have a choice, do I?" she said.

"No," he answered.

"Then I guess my mind is made up for me. I will marry you, Mr. Browne."

"Marvin."

"Yes, Marvin." She tried to smile, but her lower lip trembled. This was a big step and she was very much afraid.

He gave her hand a reassuring squeeze. "You won't be sorry. I will take care of you."

Something in his promise reached deep down inside of Samantha to a place she hadn't even known existed. She wanted to believe his promise. It made her feel good that he would be there beside her in marriage. For a moment, at the thought of it, she couldn't even breathe.

A knock on the door brought her to her senses. She practically jumped out of the chair, pulling her hand from his.

With a guilty start, she turned to the door, but his hand recaptured hers. "We've done nothing wrong. Besides, we're betrothed."

She stared at him. He said that so easily, while her heart was beating as rapidly as if she'd run a great distance. She felt guilty for it and she didn't know why . . . except that her feelings toward Mr. Browne—no, she corrected, toward Marvin—were not as clear as they had been. Something had just happened between them.

She didn't know what, but she felt confused and a little giddy.

She didn't think he felt the same way.

She hurried to the door. Mrs. Sadler and Mrs. Porter stood on the step. She invited them in.

"We have clothes," Mrs. Sadler said. "They aren't the finest, but they'll do."

Marvin took them from her. "Thank you."

The innkeeper's wife slid him a glance that said she still had her reservations about him.

Samantha stepped in. "It is very kind of Mr. Sadler to share his clothes with Marvin."

"We will have a wedding breakfast after the ceremony," Mrs. Porter volunteered. "Squire Biggers has promised the license will be here before the wedding."

Samantha looked toward Marvin. His gaze met hers and she could see he hid a smile. She had to bow her head a moment. She knew enough about him now to know he probably had some dry, irreverent thought about the blustery squire.

"Also," Mrs. Sadler said, "we've prepared a room for you, Miss Northrup, at the inn. It's probably best we let Mr. Browne stay here the night before the wedding."

"But I would rather stay here," Samantha said.

Mrs. Porter stepped forward and put her hands on Samantha's arms before giving her a little hug. "We know that, dear, but tomorrow, after the wedding, Vicar Newell is moving right in. He and his wife have been living with his parents, and I understand his mother and his wife don't get along. He can't wait another day."

"Oh," Samantha said. She should have said more, something understanding or considerate—but all she could think was that she was losing the only home she'd ever known.

Marvin came to her rescue. "You'll need to gather your things."

"Yes, I will," she said, thankful that he had presence of mind when she felt completely numb. "It will take me a moment."

She walked from room to room, picking up the lace doilies her mother had tatted, the picture of the moors that hung on the parlor wall, the quilt on her parents' bed, her brown dress, her night-dress, and the stockings and kid slippers she wore to church.

Marvin had taken the opportunity to put on the breeches, the shirt, and the socks. She was surprised to find him in the kitchen, making small talk with the women. She'd assumed he would ignore them. Mrs. Porter was warming to him, but Mrs. Sadler was still suspicious.

Samantha entered the kitchen and set the smaller things in the wooden box she'd kept in a corner to stand on when she needed extra height to reach something. She added the teapot and the remaining two teacups. "I think I have everything."

"Let us help you carry them," Mrs. Porter offered. She picked up the quilt.

"I would still rather stay here," Samantha said.

The two women overrode her. "Come now. You'll need time to prepare for the wedding," Mrs. Sadler said.

Mrs. Porter linked her arm in Samantha's. "We'll help you. It will be so much fun."

Before Samantha knew it, they had her out the door and on her way to the inn.

Yale watched the women tramp across the layer of snow until they disappeared behind the huge hemlock at the edge of the cemetery.

He shut the door and raked his hair back from his face. What a devil of twist this was!

For something to do, he sat at the kitchen table and polished his boots with a rag he'd found in a basin in the kitchen. The polish was in a drawer of the sideboard.

Married!

He'd never thought he'd marry. But he would go through with it. He owed her his life.

However, their marriage would be one of convenience. She was already too upset to talk about the marriage rationally. He'd wait until after the ceremony. Then he'd explain that he had no intention of being a true husband to her. He couldn't. He had to return to Ceylon. But he would set her up in a house of her own wherever she wished. Of course, if he told her that now, she would refuse to go through with it, even if it meant being ostracized in this small village.

He wouldn't let that happen to her.

For a second, he allowed himself to consider what it would be like to be married. He'd never considered the matrimonial state before. The restrictions had never appealed to him.

Still . . . in spite of her baggy crow-black dress, something about Samantha Northrup attracted him.

She wasn't classically beautiful, but there was a freshness about her that he admired. Her willingness to forgive others was an interesting trait. How did a person become that good?

There was also the pull of something else between them, something Yale couldn't quite identify. Something he'd never felt before.

Perhaps he empathized with her over the unjustness of the villagers' treatment of her. He wondered if even one of them had stopped to think what would happen when she left tomorrow. Or did they think he would stay in Sproule?

The thought made him grin. If they believed that, then they were going to be sorely disappointed on the morrow.

Rising, he walked to the bedroom and set his boots on the floor. He stripped and climbed into bed. His strength still wasn't what it should be.

However, tomorrow, he would do something right in his life.

For a second, the thought that he was marrying her under a false name tickled his conscience, but he shrugged it aside. No one knew who he really was, and to explain would lead to complications he'd rather avoid.

Instead, he would marry the vicar's daughter and leave. He'd see that she had a fine home filled with beautiful things. Then he would return to his business affairs.

After all, a man like him didn't need anyone.

With that thought in mind, he slept soundly.

Samantha barely slept. She tossed and turned all night and didn't close her eyes until shortly before dawn.

Four hours later, Mrs. Sadler and Mrs. Porter woke her.

"Wake up! Wake up!" Mrs. Porter chirped happily. "It's your wedding day!"

Samantha buried her face in her pillow. "I don't want to marry," she mumbled.

Mrs. Sadler pulled her arm, half-dragging her from the bed. "Come now, no long face today, Miss Northrup. The decision has been made and the deed will soon be done. Your groom will be waiting for you in the church in less than two hours."

Now they had Samantha's full attention. She stumbled out of the bed. Catching sight of herself in the mirror, her first thought was, "My hair is a mess."

"Close your eyes," Mrs. Porter said.

"I just opened them when you woke me," Samantha said.

"No, don't close them completely," Mrs. Porter said, as if Samantha was being silly. "We have a surprise for you."

"A surprise—?"

Mrs. Porter covered Samantha's eyes with her cold hands. Samantha could hear the movement of feet. The door opened and closed and then the hands were lifted.

Mrs. Sadler and her oldest daughter stood by the window holding what had to be the most beautiful dress Samantha had ever seen. It was white and made of material so fine it seemed to float. A deep hem of flowers of every color was embroidered on ribbon stitched around the bottom of the skirt and on the ribbon separating the high-waisted bodice.

Samantha reached out and ran her fingers over the embroidery. "I have never seen anything so beautiful," she whispered.

"Well, try it on," Mrs. Sadler ordered.

Samantha turned to her in surprise. "It's for me?"

"It's not for your bridegroom, I can tell you that," Mrs. Sadler said. The women laughed.

Samantha pulled her hand back, suddenly shy.

"Oh please, Miss Northrup," Mrs. Porter said. "You deserve a beautiful dress on your wedding day. Mrs. Biggers had the material, and Miss Mabel and Miss Hattie had the ribbon, and all of us got together last night and made this for you. It's the latest fashion, even in London. See? Mrs. Biggers says they wear these little cap sleeves and this thin material even in the winter. Miss Mabel and Miss Hattie had the idea of sewing on the flowers. We wanted to make it special for you. We've been up all night."

Tears burned Samantha's eyes. "You have. All of you," she managed to say, and she hugged first Mrs. Porter, then Mrs. Sadler, and then her daughter Elmira.

"Careful now," Mrs. Sadler said. "We don't want to crush the material. It should fit. We tried it on Elmira. She's just about your size." Mrs. Sadler's daughter blushed.

"It will be perfect," Samantha declared. "I can't tell you what this dress means to me." She'd almost begun to believe none of them cared, yet look at what they'd done for her.

"Come, let us start getting you ready," Mrs. Porter said.

For the next hour, Samantha was pampered in a way she'd never been treated before. It turned out that Mrs. Sadler had a talent for hairdressing.

"I've been wanting to do this for a long time," she told Samantha, before twisting Samantha's hair up on top of her head. "Here, Elmira, hand me the pins."

Samantha didn't know what to think. She usually wore her hair braided or in a simple knot at the nape of her neck. This new style emphasized the line of her slender neck and gave her regal bearing. Of course, it took a lot of pins to hold her heavy hair in place.

"I should be so lucky to have so much hair," said Mrs. Porter.

"Yes, but yours is blond, while mine is a plain brown," Samantha averred.

"You've got a good rich hair color," Mrs. Porter said, "My blond is growing grayer and grayer every year."

"Now for the dress," Mrs. Sadler announced.

It took all of them to get Samantha into the gown. When at last it was on, Mrs. Porter pulled the laces tight while Samantha stared at her reflection in the mirror. The gown fit her to perfection.

The bodice was cut far lower than anything she'd ever worn. Still, the gentle swell of her bosom over the neckline was not too shocking and made her feel feminine, sophisticated.

The dress was even the right length and the flowered hem gave it just enough weight to hang nicely.

"It's beautiful," Samantha said.

"No," Mrs. Porter said, "*you're* beautiful. Every bride is lovely on her wedding day, and you are no exception, Miss Northrup."

She did almost look pretty . . . and she couldn't help but wonder what Mr. Browne would think.

There was a knock at the door and Mrs. Biggers entered without waiting for permission. "Is everyone ready for a wedding?" she trilled. She stopped in the doorway. "Why, Miss Northrup, you look quite handsome."

Samantha felt the heat of a blush. "Thank you."

Mrs. Biggers shut the door. "This is for you

from the squire and myself." She held out a shawl of the finest blue wool. "After we talked about the pattern for the dress, I feared it would be too cold. It is one thing for those belles in London to go traipsing around half naked, but tis another to do it so far north."

"Mrs. Biggers, I can't accept . . . it's too much."

"What nonsense!" She placed the shawl around Samantha's shoulders and leaned close to her ear. "The truth is, I regret my angry words yesterday. I shouldn't have been so blunt."

"You were upset. I understand."

Mrs. Biggers smiled. "I knew you would. Well, are we ready for a grand wedding feast? The squire and I also contributed to that. Someone has to act for your parents since yours are gone, God bless their souls."

"Thank you," Samantha murmured, overwhelmed by this sudden generosity.

Mrs. Sadler sent Elmira off to tell everyone downstairs to start for the church. "We're almost ready."

"Have you seen the bridegroom?" Mrs. Porter asked.

"No, I have not," Mrs. Biggers said. "But I will tell you this, I wish his name were something other than Marvin."

"I think the same," Mrs. Sadler said. "There isn't anything romantic about the name Marvin." She spit on Samantha's shoes before rubbing a shine with the corner of her apron.

"No, it's a strong name," Mrs. Porter declared.

"Alys, think about it," Mrs. Sadler said to her. "It's fine if you are saying, 'Marvin, come to supper. Marvin, wipe the mud off your boots.' But try—" She raised her voice to a silly falsetto, "'Marvin, take me!' It doesn't sound so good then."

The women burst into a fit of girlish giggles. Samantha was confused, but she didn't want to let it show. She'd been a midwife; she knew what happened between a husband and a wife. She thought that was what Mrs. Sadler referred to.

"Well, if every lad named Marvin looked like him," Mrs. Biggers said in a sly voice, "then I would not mind a romp or two between the sheets. Besides, it's not the name that matters but the man who wears it, and he strikes me as a very *capable* man."

Samantha stared in surprise at the normally correct and staid Mrs. Biggers. Even more shocking, Mrs. Sadler and Mrs. Porter snickered their agreement.

Mrs. Biggers gave Samantha a playful slap. "You should have a good time later on, missy, or else I'll begin to believe I've lost my eye for men."

During all her tossing and turning, Samantha had not considered the wedding night. How could she have been so naïve?

"Come, it is time to go," Mrs. Sadler said— and there was no time for Samantha's doubts.

Leaving, they had a bit of an argument over

whether Samantha should wear her heavy cape or just the shawl. Mrs. Biggers feared the cape would ruin the impact of the dress. Everyone else, Samantha included, feared she would catch her death of cold.

Samantha wore the cape. She reached in the pocket to put on her gloves, but Mrs. Biggers stopped her.

"For a dress like that, you should have long gloves," she said.

"I have nothing but these." Samantha held up her kid gloves that came to the wrist.

"Well, they will have to do," Mrs. Biggers said.

The day outside was cold, but the sky was blue and clear, a rare day indeed! The snow sparkled under the sun. Mrs. Biggers's sleigh waited outside the inn's front door. "I thought we should take the bride in style," she said.

Roddy served as the driver. He helped all the ladies up into the sleigh. As he took Samantha's hand, he said, "You look nice, Miss Northrup."

"Thank you, Roddy." His compliment was deeply appreciated.

As they drew closer and closer to the church, Samantha's stomach started to tighten into nervous knots, but she refused to let it show. She walked to the church with her head high.

St. Gabriel's was over six hundred years old. A small, simple church, there was no vestibule. Therefore, when Samantha stepped through the door, the heads of everyone inside turned to gape at her. It looked as if the whole parish had turned out to see her wed.

"Oh dear," she sighed.

Mrs. Porter heard her and gave her a quick hug. "You'll be fine. Oh, here, give me your gloves. I think they spoil the dress. I didn't marry in gloves, and Bert and I are doing fine." Samantha took off the gloves and handed them to her.

Squire Biggers waited to escort Samantha up the aisle. Samantha knew she should move forward but was so nervous, her feet felt as if they were glued to the floor.

Mrs. Biggers must have sensed her distress. With a flourish, she lifted Samantha's cape off her shoulders and repositioned the blue shawl.

Everyone in the church seemed to sigh in appreciation. It was just the thing to bring Samantha to her senses.

Squire Biggers offered his arm and she placed her hand on it. He started walking her to the front of the church.

And then Samantha stopped dead in her tracks.

Marvin stood waiting for her at the altar next to Vicar Newell, but this was not the man she remembered.

Marvin had shaved. His jawline was stronger than she had imagined it. He almost looked like a completely different man—a man with character and breeding. And incredible good looks.

His broad shoulders filled out the black home-spun jacket Mr. Sadler had given him as if it had been tailored for him. He'd managed to find a neckcloth to go with the white shirt and he'd tied it in a style that had a bit of dash to it. He'd even shined his boots for the occasion.

But the most disconcerting part was that he, too, stared as if truly seeing her for the first time. His gaze lowered slightly taking in everything from her low-cut bodice to the tip of her toes. When he raised his eyes, they were filled with obvious male approval.

For her! Of all people!

"Come, Miss Northrup," Squire Biggers said. "It is time to meet your destiny." He led her up the aisle.

Chapter 6

As Samantha walked toward the simple stone altar with its tatted lace altar cloth, images of endless Sundays spent in this church listening to her father's sermons crossed her mind. "Oh, Father, I wish you were here now," she said under her breath.

In answer, for the quickest of moments, something warm and comforting rushed through her. It was the same sort of feeling that she'd always had whenever her father had given the benediction at the end of the service. A sense of peace. A sense of hope.

And then she was standing beside her future husband.

He seemed much taller than she remembered.

He held out his hand. Samantha stared at it, uncertain. Squire Biggers took her hand from his arm and placed it in Mr. Browne's.

No, not Mr. Browne . . . Marvin.

Vicar Newell did an adequate job with the service. He lacked her father's resonant voice but she could still feel her father's strength here in this holy place.

She heard several women crying, overcome by emotion. Miss Hattie kept blowing her nose and Miss Mabel kept "shushing" her. It was like a hundred other weddings that Samantha had witnessed in this church.

But this one was *hers*.

She had trouble speaking her vows, finding herself more nervous than she'd anticipated. It wasn't until she'd finished that she realized how tightly she was squeezing Marvin's hand.

For his part, he repeated his vows in a deep, steady voice without any betrayal of emotion . . . and then they were married. He slipped a thin gold band over her ring finger. It felt strange, and yet right.

It had become the custom for the groom to kiss the bride at the end of the ceremony as a pledge of their troth. But Marvin did not kiss her. He tucked her hand in his arm and walked her down the aisle. She almost had to skip a step to keep up with him.

He didn't stop until they were outside, shutting the church doors behind them. She released her hold. "Why are we in such a hurry?"

"I would like us to take our leave," he said briskly.

"But the wedding feast—we can't leave now. Everyone has made arrangements at the inn."

He frowned down at her. "Are you saying you wish to stay for the wedding breakfast?"

Samantha didn't understand the accusation. "They planned it for *us* . . . it's all ready . . ."

He made an impatient sound. "Don't you realize what hypocrites these people are?"

At that moment, the doors burst open and the villagers poured out full of good wishes. Mrs. Porter thought to bring Samantha's cape, for which she was heartily grateful. Her dress offered no protection from the cold.

"We thought you had disappeared," Squire Biggers said, clapping Marvin on the back. "Congratulations, man! It's good to see another join the ranks of those of us who have the parson's noose around our necks."

Everyone laughed at his words—except Marvin.

"Come now," Squire Biggers said. "Just a joke. Here, let us go to the inn and I'll toast your health."

Samantha looked at Marvin, beseeching him with her eyes to let them go to the inn with everyone. It was important to her. So far, this whole morning had been like her fondest dream. She had to go the inn. Every bridal couple went to the inn.

His jaw tightened stubbornly. He was going to say no, and then his expression softened. "Of course, we will go to the inn."

Samantha had never felt so relieved. She received the congratulations and hugs in an almost euphoric state.

Squire Biggers's sleigh and horses took them

back to the inn with the villagers walking behind. Samantha didn't put on her gloves. She wanted everyone to see the shiny gold band on her left hand.

She was a married lady!

She still couldn't believe it.

"What is the matter with you?" Marvin asked.

His question surprised her. She raised her eyes from the ring to see him studying her. "Me? Nothing. Why do you ask?"

"Because you look inordinately proud of something."

She couldn't help grinning then, letting some of the happiness inside her bubble over into the day. "I wasn't expecting a ring."

He glanced down at the thin band and grunted. "It's not very much, but it is the best Sproule can do on short notice."

"It is enough."

His gaze held hers a moment. He appeared ready to say something, but then seemed to think better of it. It didn't matter, they'd arrived at the inn.

The wedding breakfast was just as it had been for every other wedding Samantha had attended, and she was overjoyed. They sat in front of the room, facing everyone.

The ale was strong and good and the toasts never seemed to stop. There was a whole keg of ale to be drunk before this day was over and everyone was in high spirits for it.

Of course, Samantha and Marvin would not

be there to see it dry. After the dancing, they would be escorted upstairs to the bedroom she'd used the night before and left there to consummate the marriage.

Samantha pushed her tankard aside, suddenly feeling she'd had too much to drink. Her heart pounded in her chest at the thought of being with Marvin in that way.

At that moment, his leg brushed against hers under the table. The brief contact was jolting. He must have sensed her restlessness, because he looked down at her with a question in his dark eyes.

She gave him a tight, reassuring smile . . . and then watched his gaze covertly drop and settle on her breasts swelling over the bodice of her dress.

She was tempted to raise her hand and cover herself, but instead she sat still, wondering if he found her at least a little attractive.

Secretly, she could admit she had never met a more handsome, more heroic man. He had rescued her from a life of obscurity. She was Mrs. Marvin Browne. Her hands in her lap, she ran her finger over the ring.

His glance shifted away. He smiled at something Mr. Hatfield said about husbands and wives, but beneath the table, he impatiently tapped his foot on the floor as if he was only biding the time until he could escape.

She didn't like that idea. She wished she knew what he was thinking.

At last the squire rose. He'd been drinking heavily, as was his habit. He raised his tankard. "I have something to say—"

"You always have something to say," his wife rejoined good-naturedly. Everyone laughed, although she was the only one who dared to talk to him that way.

Squire Biggers continued. "First a toast to our newest married couple, Mr. and Mrs. Marvin Browne."

Samantha blushed furiously as everyone said, "Aye," and lifted their tankards.

After they had drunk, the squire said, "Second, I want to offer Marvin a job. A good one. I could use a stablehand and I think he is suited for the position. I can always use a brawny man like you."

Everyone started to drink again—except Samantha and Marvin. She slid a look at him from the corner of her eye.

He was not smiling.

He pushed away from the table and came to his feet. Samantha stopped breathing as he picked up his tankard and raised it in the direction of the squire.

"I appreciate your offer," he said, his voice suddenly more cultured, more refined, the tones clipped and distinct. "However, I will take care of my wife as I see fit, and I must refuse. And now, if you will excuse us, we are going to leave." He drained the tankard, set it on the table, and offered Samantha his hand.

She had no choice but to take it. The whole situation was very awkward. The room had fallen into silence and she felt everyone stare at her.

He helped her to her feet, pushing the bench back to give her room. She had just taken a step toward the door when the squire stepped into their path.

"You will not take Miss Northrup," the squire said. "You can't. She is the only doctor of sorts we have."

"You should have thought of that before you married her off to a stranger," Marvin drawled.

"You will stay here," Squire Biggers said in a resolute tone. "If you don't like the job I've offered you, then perhaps I can talk to the duke of Ayleborough's steward. They might have something there for you to do. But you will not take Miss Northrup."

"Her name is Mrs. Browne," Marvin said. "And I'll do anything I damn well please."

Squire Biggers's nostrils flared with anger. "Aye, that you can . . . but only after the marriage has been consummated. Until that time, it can be annulled."

A gasp went up in the room. Samantha was one of those who had gasped.

Marvin took hold of her arm and pulled her behind him. "You'll do no such thing."

"I will do what I have to do to take care of what is mine," Squire Biggers said proudly.

"And there isn't a man in this room who wouldn't do the same."

As if on cue, all the village men, with the exception of Vicar Newell, stood up, a sign of solidarity with the squire. Samantha had seen it happen before. Traditions ran deep here and they all followed the squire. The only one who could gainsay him was the mighty duke of Ayleborough himself.

The air vibrated with tension. All earlier good humor vanished.

Samantha felt torn between the community she'd always known and this man who stood beside her. She turned to him. His expression was grim. He did not like the ultimatum—but then, to her surprise, his stance relaxed. He smiled even.

"You are right, Squire Biggers. I would be wrong to take my wife from this village. Perhaps a job in your stables would suit me."

A big smile split the squire's face. "Aye, it would, and happy we are that you have seen reason."

Samantha noticed that the smile of neither man reached his eyes. She sensed they were wary and waiting.

"Drink with me, then," Squire Biggers ordered, and Marvin dutifully held out his tankard for the serving girl to fill. He drank that one and several others, but Samantha did not see that drink had any effect on him. She was relieved to discover that he wasn't a drunkard. That doubt had lingered in the back of her mind.

The dancing had just started when Marvin took her hand. "Come."

"Where are we going?"

"To consummate our wedding." He didn't look at her but kept his gaze on the squire, who was dancing with his wife. His manner was far from loverlike.

He rose from the table, pulling her with him. They started walking toward the door leading to the outside hall and the stairs.

Mrs. Sadler saw them. "It's time! It's time," she shouted. Everyone stopped what they were doing and turned to the bridal couple.

Samantha froze. In her enchantment with being married, she'd forgotten the part of the ceremony when the villagers helped turn the bridal couple into the bed. Actually, she and her father had usually left before this part of the tradition, having no wish to see two people humiliated in such a manner. Many was the time the villagers had stripped the couple and tied them into the bed together.

Apparently Marvin knew of the custom because he squeezed her hand. "Run."

He didn't have to tell her twice. However, when they reached the door leading to the stairs and the hallway, he turned toward the outside door. Their clasp broke.

Samantha stared at him in surprise. He hadn't meant to take her upstairs.

The first villager almost made it to the door

when Marvin, acting quickly, shut it. "Where's the lock?" he shouted at Samantha.

"There isn't one."

"There isn't one?" he repeated, even as the door started to open.

There wasn't time to make an escape. He grabbed her elbow and directed her to the stairs.

Samantha was out of breath by the time they reached the top. The villagers shouted out their names along with crude jests and boasts. She ran into the her bedroom, Marvin on her heels, and they shut the door.

"Where's the lock here?" he yelled in exasperation.

"There isn't one!" she shouted back. She could hear the villagers laughing as they charged up the stairs. Her nerves were on edge. She wanted to scream. They couldn't come through the door. She would die of embarrassment if they did half of what she'd heard they'd done to other couples.

Marvin solved the problem by pulling the room's heavy chest of drawers in front of the door.

Someone pushed on the door but couldn't move the chest. Mr. Porter hollered, "Come on, now, we must have our fun."

"Go to the devil," Marvin told him.

They laughed at his response but stopped pushing on the door. Squire Biggers's voice said, "Come, lads, let us go finish that keg. We have them where we want them."

Samantha sank down on the bed, pressing her hand against her stomach as she heard them tramp back down the wooden steps. "That was close."

Marvin didn't answer her but walked over to the window and looked out it, his gaze studying something in the distance.

The room grew very quiet. Downstairs, the fiddler played a jig and the dancing had resumed. Samantha nervously tapped her toe to the music, all too conscious that they were alone—and for one purpose.

He swung open a narrow window. "I think I can make it out of here by climbing out this. I'll get the horse and sneak back in through another way besides the front door. What do you suggest? Does the kitchen have a separate entrance?"

Samantha shivered, but it wasn't from the cold air blowing freely through the window. Why was he so eager to leave?

She knew the answer . . . and it made her feel stupidly girlish. She! A woman of six-and-twenty. For one shining moment, she had naïvely hoped for a miracle, that he would fall in love with her and she with him and they would be happy ever after . . .

What rot.

She kept her voice as calm as she could. "You have no intention of honoring our wedding vows, do you?"

He shut the window, his brows coming together in concern, as if he'd just now thought of her. "Samantha, I . . ." He paused, whatever he'd been about to say abandoned. Instead, he said, "I'm a wealthy man. I don't need to work in a stable. I can set you up nicely, wherever you wish. You'll never worry for another thing for the rest of your life."

"But we won't have a marriage."

His hands dropped to his side. "I don't want you to feel tied down to me."

"Because you are leaving?"

"I have a life somewhere else."

She came to her feet, horrified by a new thought. "You aren't already married, are you? Mrs. Sadler said you told her you didn't *have* a family—"

"I'm not married, Samantha. You can be assured of that."

"Then why do you want to leave me?" She asked the question whose answer she most feared. She knew it would be because she was old and plain and too intelligent and forthright for her own good. "Why did you marry me at all?" she whispered.

"I married you because that is what you wanted most. And because I owe you for saving my life—"

"I expect no payment. And what makes you think I want marriage most in my life?"

"Because you told me. Yesterday, when you were crying."

Samantha remembered. Her cheeks flamed

with shame. Too embarrassed to look at him, she sat back down on the bed. "I was upset and tired. I shouldn't have spoken that way in front of you. Please, you are free to leave. I will not stop you."

Her fingers brushed the ring on her hand. She twisted it off. "Here. Now climb out the window and go to your freedom."

He didn't move to take the ring. "Samantha, I can't leave you here to face all of them alone."

She studied the stitching on the bedcover. "I will be fine." She didn't feel fine. She actually felt numb, as if her body was trying to protect her from pain.

The mattress gave as he sat down beside her. "I'm not going to leave you."

She didn't try to speak. If she did, she would cry. How could she have shamed herself and admitted her innermost thoughts to him?

He hadn't married her to be gallant; he'd pitied her.

She doubled up the bedcover in her fist without realizing it and then had to force her hand to release it.

"Samantha, look at me. We must talk of this."

A lump had formed in her throat. It hurt to speak. "There is nothing left to say."

He was not happy with her answer. She could sense his exasperation, but she could do nothing for it. She wanted him to leave—the sooner, the better.

Outside this silent room, she could hear Squire

Biggers's voice above all the others, singing with the fiddler. They were having a grand party in her honor.

She should hate Marvin . . . but she couldn't. All she could feel was disappointment, as if something expectant and hopeful had died within her.

"Please, Samantha, don't be this way."

She didn't know what he meant. How did he expect her to act?

He raked his hair with fingers, a gesture she noticed he did whenever he was irritated or frustrated.

Downstairs, the fiddler changed his tune. The dancers were "whooping" with rowdy joy.

And then Marvin placed his hands on her shoulders, turned her bodily to face him, and kissed her.

Samantha had never been kissed before by someone other than her parents, and this completely surprised her. His lips felt hard and unyielding. His hands were on her shoulders. Her hands were flapping in the air.

Her eyes were wide open.

He opened his.

She went cross-eyed staring into his gaze.

He jerked back, the kiss broken. "Samantha, when a man kisses you, you aren't supposed to stare at him."

She raised trembling fingers to her lips. "I didn't know what to do."

The corner of his mouth twitched. "Obviously."

His dry sarcasm hurt her already wounded ego. "I thought you were leaving."

"I am, once I've convinced you to come with me."

"And how are you going to do that?" she asked.

"I am going to kiss you again," he said doggedly.

Samantha jumped to her feet and backed toward the door. "I don't want you to. I didn't like it." The noise of hand-clapping drifted up from downstairs. The wedding party was still going strong.

"Oh, Sam," he said, with exasperation.

Sam. No one had ever shortened her name in that manner. She liked it; she shouldn't like it.

He rose from the bed and began walking toward her. "We're going to try it again."

"Why?" she asked, moving around the room away from him. "Because you feel sorry for me?"

"No. Because I want you to come with me."

He stopped.

She stopped. Her back was to the bed.

"Give it a chance, Sam," he said quietly. "Try and be something you are not for just a little bit and you may find you enjoy the new freedom."

She wasn't sure what he was talking about, but this time, when he took the three steps to stand directly in front of her, she did not run.

"Your dress is pretty," he said in a rough voice.

"The villagers made it." Her tone was more clipped. She inwardly winced to hear it.

"They did a fine job."

She could only nod. When he stood this close and his purpose was so intent, she found it hard to breathe, let alone speak.

"Sam, give me your hand."

She shied away, but her legs hit the bed and she could move no farther. "Why?"

"I want to hold your hand."

It seemed like an innocent request. She held up her hand. He took it in his much larger, stronger one.

"For being such a strong woman, you are a petite thing." The flats of his fingers gently traced the tips of hers. He stood so close that if she leaned forward, her breasts would rub his coat.

He carried her hand up to her chin and used it to tilt her head up. "This time, I want you to close your eyes."

"This time?" she echoed breathlessly.

He placed her hand on his shoulder. "Aye, this time."

He bent over to kiss her and her eyes fluttered shut.

This time his kiss started off tentative, respectful. But when she offered no resistance, it changed. It became insistent, even demanding. He nuzzled her with his nose and tickled her bottom lip with his tongue. She parted her lips in surprise and his lips opened to match hers.

Samantha discovered herself kissing him as if it were the most natural thing in the world to do. She lifted her head higher, the better to let him kiss her, and he took full advantage.

His lips were no longer soft and yielding, but hungry, with a hunger she found in herself.

She made a soft noise of anticipation and his arms came around her to fit her to him. The kiss deepened.

Being this close to another human felt good. When he pressed his hand flat against the small of her back, she scooted nearer still until their bodies seemed to line up—her breasts against his chest, her thighs against his thighs.

She could taste him now. He used his tongue and she didn't even flinch because it all felt so very right.

No wonder poets wrote about kissing! It was far better than any description she had ever read. It made her feel warm, real, alive . . . and when Marvin stroked her tongue with his in very slow, deliberate movements, her toes curled and she pressed herself against him for more.

He accepted her surrender with a low growl of satisfaction. Before she even realized it, he was pressing her back on the bed. He lay down beside her, still kissing her.

His lips left hers and worked their way along her jaw to her ear. His breathing was deep and heavy.

Hers was too.

"Sam." His voice hummed in her ear and seemed to go through her body.

"Yes," she breathed.

"You are a good kisser."

She almost laughed, his praise pleasing her. "You are too."

Against her neck she felt his lips curve into a smile. "I'd like to make love to you."

She almost melted into the bedcover. She struggled for common sense. "I . . . don't . . . know."

"Ah, Sam. You want it too. See?" His hand caressed her breast and her nipple tightened into a hard bud. It felt good to have him touch her this way.

She attempted to rise, but he leaned over her and kissed her again.

This time, he didn't have to tell her to close her eyes. Between her legs, she felt an answering tug when his tongue began stroking hers.

She didn't know what was happening to her. She no longer recognized herself. Her arms were up around his neck and she was pressing herself closer to him.

When he broke the kiss, she made a soft moue and then he ordered, "Sam, unfasten my breeches."

His command should have shocked her, but it didn't. If anything, she wanted to know more. His kiss had opened a Pandora's box of new and exciting feelings. She was an eager student.

Her fingers began fumbling with the buttons. They were almost impossible to twist open with him outlining her ear with the tip of his tongue.

He didn't seem to be having the difficulties she was. His fingers deftly unlaced the back of her dress. He nuzzled the neckline down over her breasts and pushed aside her light camisole. He pressed his lips over the tight nipple.

Samantha cried out.

She no longer heard the sounds of dancing and clapping downstairs. She could not imagine the bed, or the inn, or even the village. Her whole being centered on this man and what he was doing to her body.

He sucked first one breast and then the other. His hands slowly pressed the dress down her arms so that she was more fully exposed to him. He began untying the tapes of her petticoat with practiced ease.

She felt wanton. Wicked. Sensual.

She began pulling at his coat, wanting his clothes removed too. He paused to help her, tossing the coat over the side of the bed and ripping at the knot in his neckcloth.

She tugged his shirt from the waist of his breeches. She started to work on the buttons again, but he said, "Wait."

He stood and removed his shirt. He then sat on the edge of the bed and yanked off first one boot and then the other. He dropped them on the floor, where they landed with a *clomp.*

Then he stood and began unbuttoning his breeches.

Samantha watched wide eyed.

He grinned, hooked his hands under the waist, and pushed them down, taking his socks off with them.

When he straightened, her lips parted in surprise. She'd never seen a fully erect man before and she was impressed. Her body ached to feel him beside her. And yet—

"Is something wrong?" he asked.

Samantha hesitated and then admitted, "I am not certain how this all works."

He laughed, the sound sure and knowing. "I'll show you."

He knelt on the bed and began undressing her. He took his time, keeping her warm with his kisses. He kissed places she'd never imagined anyone had ever *thought* of kissing, and she could do nothing but sigh with pleasure.

When she wore nothing save her stockings tied with garters, he leaned over her and began nibbling the inside of her thigh.

She squirmed. This was too much.

He raised his head and smiled wickedly. "You're not ready for that yet, are you?"

She didn't know what *that* was, but she wasn't sure she wanted him to stop—and then his fingers brushed the downy hair between her thighs, before dipping lower and touching what seemed to be the very core of her being.

Samantha reached for him, lost in a world that

centered on this man and what he was doing to her body.

She placed her hands around his shoulders, feeling the smooth skin of his back. Her legs parted, giving him fuller access to the deepest reaches of her.

"Marvin," she repeated again and again, his name a plea, a cry, a benediction.

She ran her hands down his back and along his side. Her fingers brushed his erection and she was startled that he could feel so soft and yet so hard at the same time.

"That's the way, Sam," he cooed to her. "Touch me."

His hand covered hers and he taught her to be bolder.

"It feels good, love, when you touch me," he whispered.

He had called her "love." The endearment almost brought tears to her eyes.

He shifted, and she felt him against her. Strong, poised, ready.

She was eager for him. She felt as if she hovered on the threshold of the meaning of life. Other women knew it and now she would too. This act between a man and a woman was sacred. They were going to become one, joined in the great mystery of life.

His tongue traced the bottom line of her lip before he nipped it lightly. "Sam, love, look at me."

Slightly dazed, she opened her eyes.

"This may hurt a bit," he warned. "If it hurts too much, say so, I'll stop if I can."

"Oh, Marvin," she said, smiling. "Stop talking." She pulled his head down to meet her lips, felt his body slide into hers, and knew she would never be the same.

Chapter 7

$$\curvearrowright\!\!\curvearrowright\!\!\curvearrowright$$

At that moment, Yale had two immediate thoughts: *this is heaven!* And *there is going to be the very devil to pay for this bit of business.*

He went still. With what little reason he had left, he wondered how he could be making such a fatal error . . .

And then her muscles tightened around him— and reason evaporated. Dear Lord, she was delicious.

"Sam." He breathed her name on a sigh as he buried himself deep within her.

He knew little about virgins. He'd never actually been with one before. He'd heard that some girls cried out for their mothers, while others broke into tears. Then there were those who screamed in pain.

Sam did not do any of those things. Instead, she wiggled—and almost sent him over the edge.

He moaned in ecstasy.

"Have I hurt you?" she whispered in surprise.

"No . . . it's all right . . . now," he gasped, struggling to put a check on himself. After all, he was the experienced one. He should be in control.

He nuzzled her neck, drinking in the soft, warm scent of her, and praying fervently for mercy.

"Now?" she echoed. "Did I do something wrong earlier?"

He could feel her throat move as she spoke. He brushed his lips against it.

She certainly didn't seem ready to scream or burst into tears . . . or give in to unbridled passion.

Yale lifted his head. Her bright, curious eyes met his. She appeared uninvolved in his love-making.

Below stairs, a man bellowed out a tone-deaf solo.

"It's the squire," she explained, as if he'd asked. "He always gets the urge to sing when he's in his cups."

Yale nodded absently, not giving a damn about the squire. "I haven't hurt you, have I?" he asked, bringing her back to the topic of what the two of them were doing together.

"It was nothing. It just felt tight, like a pinch, and any discomfort is gone." Her brows came together. "So, that was it? I mean, I thought there would be more, what with the poets going on about dying for love and all that."

Yale stared at her, slowly letting the meaning

of her words sink in. She thought they were done? No, it was worse. She was *ready* to be done.

And then the ridiculousness of the moment took hold of him and he laughed.

Astonishment lit her golden brown eyes. "I felt you laugh. Deep inside of me." Her voice softened. "It feels good."

Yale pressed his lips against her smooth cheek, tasting her, and whispered, "I do not think I have ever met a woman quite like you before."

She stiffened slightly. "Is that bad?"

"No. It's good." He pulled himself back and then thrust, deeper this time, enjoying the feel of her, before adding, "Very good."

"I felt that, too."

"And this?" He stroked her again.

Instinctively, her body arched to receive him. "Yes," she said breathlessly.

He stroked her again and she whispered, "Oh, this is so much better."

Yale laughed in triumph. "Oh, Sam, you are a find. A real treasure."

"A treasure," she repeated, her body starting to move against his.

Yale nipped her ear. "A pearl beyond compare." Then he couldn't talk, because she was meeting his thrusts with a movement all her own—and it was very good movement.

His sweet Sam was an eager learner. Who would have expected such a hot-blooded woman in the guise of a vicar's daughter?

The fiddler played a sprightly jig. The sound of it seemed to come up through the walls and Yale caught himself moving to the rhythm of the music.

They were dancing, an intimate dance as old as time. He watched the changing expressions of her face, awed by her fresh, unguarded response to him. The music faded as Yale lost himself in the magic of her body.

She set the pace now, rising eagerly to meet his thrusts. It was everything he could do just to maintain control—and then he felt her tighten and knew she was there, at the pinnacle. She cried out in surprise, hugging him close to receive all of him.

At last, Yale sought his own release, and none had been sweeter. Thoroughly spent, he collapsed on top of her.

Slowly the world came back to order. Squire Biggers still bellowed downstairs. In fact, he now had a chorus singing behind him.

A chill tickled Yale's backside while the heat of this willing woman beneath him kept his front toasty warm.

He opened his eyes. Her eyes were closed. Dear Lord, he must be crushing her with his weight. He started to roll off but her arms tightened and cradled him closer.

"Sam?"

She opened her eyes. They were dreamy with satisfaction. "That was the most incredible ex-

perience." She rubbed her breasts against him.
"Is it always like that, Marvin?"

"It's never been like—" He broke off abruptly;
her use of his fake name signaled a return to
common sense.

What had he done?

Yale practically bolted off her. He sat up on
the edge of the bed, trying to collect his scattered
wits.

Her hand caught his. "I'm cold." She smiled
at him sleepily—and Yale thought he'd never
seen a more beautiful woman than his vicar's
daughter. A few pins still held a lock or two of
her hair in place, but the rest was pleasantly
mussed. Her lips were swollen and red from his
kisses.

Suddenly, his doubts were unimportant. What
was done was done.

He pulled the bedcovers out from underneath
her and stretching out beside her, covered them
both. He cupped her breast with his hand. She
had lovely breasts. They were full and tight. He
longed to kiss them again.

"No," he admitted, "it's never been like that."

She sighed with satisfaction and snuggled her
nose against his chest. "And will it always be
like that?"

Yale gathered her close and promised, "The
next time, it will be even better."

She kissed his shoulder. "You smell like au-
tumn, with its fresh winds and changing leaves.
I like it."

Her description flattered him. "You smell of the spring, of ripe opening buds, and a rich blue sky." He'd never been a man given to poetic words, but Samantha Northrup inspired him.

Her arms came around his neck. She pressed against him. "When can we do it again?" she purred.

Yale grinned self-consciously. "Sam, you have to give it a little time—"

He broke off. She'd started nibbling the sensitive skin beneath jaw and he felt himself stirring again.

Still, he had to think about her. "We'd, ah . . . we'd better wait." But his body didn't want to wait. He was already as stiff as an iron pike. Worse, she knew it.

She touched his nose with the tip of hers. Her lips curved into a smile. "Must we?"

"Sam, it would be best for you."

She reached down between them and ran her finger experimentally up the length of him. "It's amazing, isn't it? I'd never imagined. I knew people liked to do it and now I understand why."

He captured her errant hand before she explored farther. "It's too soon for you."

She tried to pull her hand free, her legs brushing against him. "But Marvin, I ache." She rubbed against him. "Inside of me I feel a need."

Oh, and he hungered for her too. "I don't want to hurt you."

Her eyes widened. "Does it hurt you?"

"No, it doesn't hurt me at all."

"Then I don't think it is going to hurt me." She kissed him.

He knew they shouldn't. He started to push her away, but she turned slightly and his hands came down on her breasts . . . and his will to resist disappeared.

After all, what man could resist such a sweet invitation—especially since he was definitely ready for it?

Positioning himself on top of his wife, Yale reflected that perhaps marriage wasn't such a bad thing after all.

"I do not think the name Marvin suits you," Samantha said. She lay on her back, her head on his flat stomach. It was late evening and she felt sated and content. She wore nothing. She didn't think she'd ever wear clothes again.

The poets had been right! Love was worth dying for. They'd made love three times this afternoon. She now knew what bliss was. It was the feeling of her husband's body joined with hers.

The hand he had idly been running back and forth along her arm paused. "Why do you say that?" he asked.

She rolled over and lifted her head to look up at him, tossing her hair over one shoulder. "Because it doesn't."

His eyebrows came together in a frown. To her surprise, he got up from the bed, the movement sudden. He reached for his breeches on the floor and started to pull them on.

"Marvin, is something the matter?"

For a second, she didn't think he was going to answer. Then he smiled. The expression seemed forced. "I'm hungry. Are you?"

He didn't wait for her response but opened the door and shouted for the innkeeper to deliver their supper. Samantha dived under the covers, pulling them up to her neck. "What are you doing?"

He leaned against the door frame. "We've got to eat, don't we?"

She frowned at his flippant reply. "I don't want them to know what we've been doing."

His teeth flashed in a grin. "I think they have an idea."

"No! They couldn't have," she returned in a horrified whisper.

His expression turned suddenly serious. "Do you have any regrets?"

His question surprised her. "No, no regrets."

They might have said something else to each other, but at that moment she heard the maid coming up the stairs. In a second she appeared in the short hallway, a tray loaded with food and drink, leftovers from the wedding breakfast.

Samantha pulled the covers up over her head. She might not have regrets, but she was blushing down to her toes with embarrassment.

"Thought ye'd never call," the maid said, once she came into the room. "If ye'd taken much longer, I would have come up and pounded on the door. Mr. Sadler says I can go home once I deliver your supper. He and everyone else are off to their beds or over at the smithy's, wagering who can drive an iron spike into the ground with one blow."

"Who do you think will win, Emma?" Marvin asked, surprising Samantha in that he knew the maid's name.

Emma snorted. "It's hard to tell. They are all drunk as lords. Squire Biggers is the worst of his lot, but his nephew, the new vicar, drove him and his wife home."

"Well, thank you, Emma, for staying for us." He flipped her a coin that he'd pulled out of his pocket.

She bit the coin to see if it was good and grinned. "Y'er a gentleman, sir. Call me in the morning when ye want yer breakfast. I'll bring it to you." She paused in front of Marvin and lowered her voice. "Mind ye, I think Mr. Sadler will expect the two of ye out before the sun rises too high."

"We will be gone before then," Marvin answered. "By the way, put all this on Squire Biggers's tab. He owes us a wedding gift, don't you think?"

Emma giggled, thoroughly charmed. "Aye, yer right. And if ye can get him to pay, I'll have more respect for ye."

They both laughed like old cronies and then Emma left the room.

Samantha waited until Marvin had shut the door. "How do you know her name?"

He walked to the tray of food. "From when I was here before. She's the one who brought me the first bottle of brandy." Pulling a leg off a roasted capon, he offered it to her. When she shook her head no, he took a big bite out of it.

Sitting up in bed with the sheet covering her breasts, Samantha plucked at the bedcovers, not wishing to reveal her jealousy—and she was jealous of Emma's familiarity with her husband. The maid hadn't done anything wrong, but Samantha had felt a strong possessiveness about Marvin. She hadn't liked the two of them sharing a jest, even such a small one.

"Sam?"

She didn't answer, too busy sorting out her confused feelings.

The bed ropes bounced as he threw himself down on it beside her. He grinned up at her, a foolish, unself-conscious smile full of teasing— and it went right to her heart.

Her husband was a handsome man, but his rugged good looks were no longer the only thing she found dear about him. No, what pulled her to him was something special and unique to him alone. That, and the fact that he had done so much for her. Because of him, she felt like a complete person.

The idea surprised her. But it was true. She'd been waiting for something in her life and now, here he was.

"Would you like a glass of ale?"

She shook her head no.

He leaned closer. "Sam, why are you so serious?" He slipped a finger beneath the sheet she held over her breasts and attempted to tickle her.

It was an invitation . . . and she wanted to answer it. She wanted him more than food and drink. More than anything she had ever known.

She reached up and captured his wandering hand, her fingers closing over his.

His hand was so strong and capable. A small white scar stood out on one of his knuckles. She touched it.

"Did you receive this while fighting with pirates?"

He went suddenly still. "Fighting pirates?" he asked cautiously.

She gave him a reassuring smile, surprised he would be so upset she knew. "When the fever was at its worst, you imagined you and your friend Billy fighting pirates. Was that true? Did you do that?"

He looked off a moment. "Did I say anything else during the fever?"

She shook her head. "You talked in several languages, but I didn't understand them." She waited, hoping he would elaborate on the pirates.

When he didn't, she prompted, "Who was Billy?"

"Just a lad I knew."

"Where does he live?"

"He doesn't. He was killed off the coast of Africa. He was young and he was stupid." His lips twisted in a rueful smile. "He thought he was a swordsman. He found out differently." He added after a long, thoughtful moment, "He was my one *true* friend."

His admission touched her deeply. She wondered if she had ever had a true friend.

But now she had Marvin.

He started to pull his hand away, but she tightened her grasp. Raising her eyes to his, she said, "I just want you to know that I . . . I am growing very fond of you."

He smiled. "And I'm fond of you."

Samantha swallowed, almost frightened of what she was about to say. She noticed his eyes weren't completely black. This close she could see the pigments of brown, a complex pattern of color. As complex as the man beside her.

"It may be more than that, Marvin. I think I may be falling in—" She paused. "I'm falling in love with you."

She immediately wished she could call the words back. But she couldn't . . . because she had spoken the truth. The bright, shining truth.

He stared at her as if he had not heard her correctly and she sat paralyzed, waiting, holding his hand as if she'd never let it go.

With his other hand, he ran his fingers through his thick hair, pushing it back from his forehead.

"You need a haircut," Samantha said self-consciously, needing to say something to fill the sudden silence.

"You can't love me, Sam." His voice was sad, quiet.

She felt like laughing; she felt like crying. "I already do."

He gave a half-laugh of disbelief. "You don't know me. If you did, you wouldn't say such a thing."

"I don't have to know you. I only have to know what I feel. Here." She touched her breast over her heart.

He shook his head to deny her words. "I'm a selfish, worthless fellow. I'm not worthy of your love. Or anyone's."

He meant those words. She could hear his conviction and a fierce protectiveness rose up inside her. "No, that isn't true. You're a kind man. You didn't have to marry me. You could have left me and not given a care about what happened to me here in Sproule, but you didn't."

"Sam, you had saved my life! What would you have me do?"

She came up on her knees, heedless of her nakedness. Her hair tumbled down around her shoulders. "No! It's more than that. I don't know if I believe in fate, but I do know that my life started to change from the first moment we met in the graveyard."

He rose, pulling his hand from hers. "Sam, I'm not what you think I am. You can't have feelings for me."

"I already have them," she said simply. When he didn't speak, she went on, "I know you may have done some terrible things, but that is in the past. We have a future together. Trust me. Trust me as I have trusted you."

He stared at her as if he had turned to stone. Silently she willed him to do her bidding.

But she was impatient. "What were you doing in the graveyard that night?" she prodded. "Why did you want in the vault? Answer those questions."

The corners of his mouth turned down. "Can't you leave well enough alone? Isn't it enough we enjoy each other?"

"No. Not anymore."

"I don't want to talk about it, Sam."

A knot seemed to form in her stomach. She shrugged apologetically, almost wishing she had never approached the subject. "But I've already started it."

"Then leave it be. Now."

She placed her hand on the warm skin of his bare chest and felt his heart racing beneath her flat palm. "You aren't wanted by the authorities or the tax man are you? I mean, you haven't committed any crimes?"

He tilted back his head and laughed, the sound bitter. "No, none that I've been caught at."

"Then what is it?" she dared to press. "Tell me."

"Ah, Sam, leave it be," he begged softly, and

taking her hand, he lifted her fingers to his lips. He kissed their tips and then brushed his lips along her palm. She could feel the roughness of his whiskers. His hand cupped her buttocks, pulling her toward him. The cotton texture of his breeches scratched the soft skin of her belly. He brought her hand down between them.

He was already hard for her.

His hand over hers, he slipped the first button from its buttonhole. Samantha knew he wanted her to touch him, but she hesitated. "Marvin? Trust me, please."

Placing his hands on either side of her face, he forced her to look up at him. "Leave it be," he whispered, and then his lips came down upon hers.

And because he knew her body better than she did herself, because he was in her blood like a narcotic, because *she loved him*—she did as he'd asked.

They made love, but this time there was a difference. She tried to communicate to him through the only means he would allow—her body—the strength of her love. *I will be there for you. I will honor you. I will love you.*

Perhaps he didn't have the same feelings she had, but someday he would. She knew that. Squire Biggers had said Marvin was her destiny. Now she believed those words.

And if the only way she could hold him was through her passion, then so be it.

He was her white knight. The man who had

rescued her from a life of obscurity and uncertainty. He was the man she loved.

In the dark hours of the night, Yale sat against the headboard of the bed, Samantha asleep in his arms. His conscience bothered him too much for sleep.

He was in a devil of a fix. Why hadn't he told her his real name when she was begging earlier for the truth?

Because he feared what she'd say when she discovered their marriage was a fraud. Marvin Browne's name was on the special license, not Yale Carderock's.

And because he didn't want to see disappointment in those trusting eyes of hers. Right now, he was her hero . . . and, damn, it felt good.

He had agreed to this hell-born marriage out of righteous anger. The villagers had no reason to treat Samantha with such callous disregard. And he'd meant the part of his wedding vows promising to keep her safe.

Of course, since he hadn't been able to keep his bloody hands off her—and he refused to regret a moment of it!—his plans of installing her in her own cottage with her own income, before riding out of her life were not going to work.

He bent down and kissed the top of her hair. It smelled of wood fires, fresh air, and their love-making. His dear, dear Sam.

Why did she have to say she loved him?

For a second, he toyed with taking her with

him when he returned to Ceylon, but then ruthlessly rejected the idea.

He wasn't worthy of her love. Nor did he need it, he assured himself. Besides, what did they know of each other? He wasn't a naïve, love-struck fool who believed passion between the sheets could last a lifetime. He was her first. Of course she would think she loved him. But sooner or later, they would grow bored with each other. It was the way of things. He'd had many mistresses over the years and that was how it had gone.

Once, he had been like Sam and believed love was important, that it mattered. That was before Sally, Lady Garrett. She'd taught him that money and power mattered. Love was a means to achieve an end.

What a fool he'd been! Even now, he could conjure Sally's face in his mind. Golden blond hair, laughing green eyes . . . the most beautiful woman in London.

But it hadn't been love. She'd refused to see him once he'd been disinherited. It had been lust.

"Just as this is lust," he told the sleeping Sam.

But then, Sam was no Lady Garrett. She was a country girl, a vicar's daughter whose clear-eyed thinking saw the world in black and white. Shades of gray had not invaded her safe corner of the world—yet.

Nor did he want to be the one to introduce them.

Confessing he'd married her under a false

name would destroy the trust she had in him.

And Yale discovered he couldn't do that. But his ship was waiting for him. His shipping empire could not wait much longer for his attention. Every day was an opportunity to make money . . . and he was wasting precious time in the small village of Sproule.

For a second, he could almost hear his father's stern voice. What would the old man say about this current scrape his least-favorite son had embroiled himself in?

But what if he *didn't* tell Sam his real name? What if he kept the marriage as it was?

The idea had merit. He shifted her weight, cradling her close to him. He could set Samantha up as originally planned in a small cottage of her choosing. That way she could continue to be Mrs. Browne and he could see her once or twice a year and pretend to be Mr. Browne.

Many couples lived that way and she'd never be the wiser.

Now all he had to do was think of a convincing story . . .

"You are a sailor?" Samantha said with surprise.

They sat across from each other at one end of a table in the far corner of the Bear and Bull's common room. Marvin had insisted that they come down and join the others for their breakfast. Mr. and Mrs. Sadler had greeted the newlyweds with jovial good humor.

Samantha was wearing her brown dress. She felt dowdy after wearing the beautiful wedding dress that hung in their room. She was nervous, excited, and a bit giddy all rolled into one. The time had come for her and Marvin to start their married life together.

He'd waited until Emma had set beefsteaks and tankards of ale in front of them before telling her what he did for a living.

"What of the squire?" she asked. "You told him yesterday you would work in his stables."

"I had to tell him something to avoid trouble. But the sea is in my blood," Marvin said regretfully, before taking a healthy drink of ale. He wiped his mouth with the back of his hand. "You do understand, don't you?"

Samantha ran a finger along a crack in the table before admitting, "I suppose. I—I have trouble picturing you with a tarred pigtail."

He laughed. He'd been in great humor since he'd awakened her by making love to her. Her husband was a lusty man. But then, she found herself a good match for him.

"There is many a sailor who does not sport a tarred pigtail," he told her.

"None that I've ever seen. And you dress well. Too well for a sailor."

"These clothes aren't mine, remember?"

Samantha smiled at him as if he teased her. "Of course I remember, but I also recall what you were wearing when you first arrived in Sproule. I would never have thought you a sailor, Marvin." *Marvin*. She'd even become accustomed to his name. It was a good, strong name. An honest name. She was proud to be Mrs. Marvin Browne, with an "e" on the end.

"Well, I am a sailor," he said decisively. He leaned across the table, reaching for her hands. His voice dropped a notch. "The problem is, I can't take you with me, Sam. Not when I'm out sailing, but I'll come home to you between voyages."

Samantha pulled back. "Come home to me?"

"Aye. Today you and I are going to start a new life. We'll leave Sproule forever."

"Where shall we go?" she asked cautiously.

"Wherever you wish. You can stay in Northumberland, preferably closer to the sea, or even go to London, if you like."

Samantha studied him a moment. He was smiling ... but something didn't seem quite right. She pulled her hands from his, folding them on the table in front of her so that he couldn't see them shake. She traced her wedding band with her thumb. "How often would I see you?"

"Anytime my ship is in port. But you won't have to worry about anything. I'm a wealthy man. You'll be well taken care of. We can hire a companion for you so that you won't be lonely."

Her smile seemed fixed on her face. "I've never known a sailor who was wealthy." She waited for his reaction.

It was very subtle. If she hadn't been watching

closely, she might have missed the slight hesitation, the hint of annoyance in his eyes.

"Ah, Sam," he cajoled, in a low, warm voice. "It's all for the best, you know. If you had me around all the time, you'd grow bored with me sooner or later. This way you will always be happy to see me."

It wasn't the words that hurt; it was the carelessness with which he'd said them. "I would be happier to live with you."

"Yes. But it's not possible."

Samantha drew a deep, steadying breath. She stared at the meat growing cold on her plate. "I meant what I said last night about loving you. I know you don't love me . . . but you should give me a chance." She raised beseeching eyes to him. "Certainly there are ships that have women on them."

The lines of his face hardened. "It's not the life for a lady. I will not endanger you in that manner."

"But if I wanted—"

"*No.*"

The finality in which he said that one word doused her hopes. The only thing left was to save face. She picked up her fork and pushed a piece of meat on the plate. Tears threatened, but she would not let them fall. He would not appreciate a scene. "I will miss you," she said at last.

He came around the end of the table to sit beside her, placing his arm around her shoulders.

"Sam, don't look so glum. I'm not leaving right away. We have to find a cottage for you and we'll have more time together." His breath brushed her ear. "It may be weeks before I can pull myself away from you."

He made "weeks" sound as if it were a lifetime, whereas to her, they seemed mere minutes until he would be gone . . . and she would be alone.

"Sam?" he prompted.

She set the fork down and stared at her hands in her lap. "Last night, I dreamt we had a baby together."

His arm left her shoulders. "Baby?" He made the word sound foreign.

"Well, it could happen, considering what we've been doing since yesterday afternoon."

He didn't speak.

She felt the heat of a blush stain her cheeks. "I hadn't had time to think about this, but when I woke after the dream . . . and you and I were so close . . . I realized I want your baby." She raised her gaze to his. "But if you are at sea, our son will grow up barely knowing his father. He'll have a lonely childhood."

"Son?" The word sounded as if it had been strangled out of him.

"Yes, a son. That was what the baby was in my dream." Every man wanted a son, didn't he? A baby was also the one way she could bind Marvin to her.

But she never heard his response, because at

that moment there was a terrible commotion at the entrance of the inn. Booted heels clumped on the Bull and Bear's wood floor. Through the common room door, Samantha caught a glimpse of servants in a familiar burgundy livery, and one of them wore a snowy white bagwig.

She leaned close to her husband. "I recognize the man in the bagwig. He's Fenley, the duke of Ayleborough's personal servant."

"Ayleborough?" Marvin repeated. He rose slowly to his feet.

Mr. Sadler had gone out into the hallway at the first sound of new guests. They now heard him say, "Your Grace, it is indeed an honor for you to visit my humble establishment."

The duke was here in Sproule! What an unexpected surprise.

Now Samantha too came to her feet, as did everyone in the room. "This is very exciting," she whispered to her husband. "The new duke rarely returns to his seat and has never come all the way to Sproule since his father's funeral."

"Exciting," Marvin echoed the word, but he didn't sound very excited.

At that moment, His Grace, the duke of Ayleborough swept into the room. He was a balding man of medium height with a rather strong nose. Squire Biggers followed behind him, so close on his heels he almost tripped when the duke stopped to speak to Mr. Sadler.

"I was passing through on pressing business and I stopped by to see the good squire because

I heard there was a wedding in Sproule yesterday. My steward informed me that one Marvin Browne—that's Browne with an 'e'—was staying here and married the vicar's daughter. Is that correct?"

Everyone in the room glanced at Samantha and Marvin. Mr. Sadler bobbed up and down and said, "Aye, Your Grace, it's true."

Samantha nudged her husband. "Does the duke know you?"

Marvin didn't answer.

"Amazing," Ayleborough said. "Marvin Browne was my tutor. I was very fond of him."

Again there was mention of the tutor. Something was not quite right. Samantha glanced up in question at Marvin, but he wasn't attending her. Instead, his gaze was on the duke.

"But I seem to remember the vicar's daughter as being a young woman, is that not so?" the duke said. "Mr. Browne must be well over eighty if he is a day. A good man, though. I had thought he'd passed on years ago, but I must be mistaken." He tugged on his glove. "Where is he? I'd like to see him."

Mr. Sadler shot a look at Squire Biggers, who shrugged. "He's here in this room now, Your Grace," Mr. Sadler said, and then stepped back.

"In this room?" the duke demanded, anxiously scanning the room for Marvin Browne.

Everyone was staring at them now, except Ayleborough.

And then the duke's searching gaze reached

her husband. His mouth dropped open and he appeared to have a sudden problem breathing.

She started forward, fearing he was having an apoplectic fit, but Marvin's hands came down on her shoulders. He gently but firmly held her to his side.

"It can't be," Ayleborough said slowly. "It's impossible."

Her husband drew a deep breath, straightening his shoulders. "Yes, brother, it is I."

"But we thought you dead," Ayleborough said.

Marvin opened his palms like a magician showing he played no tricks. "I'm not."

Chapter 8

Confused, Samantha looked to her husband, not understanding. *The duke was his brother? But Alyeborough's family name wasn't Browne.*

She expected the duke to deny the relationship, but once he had recovered from his initial shock, he said in a clipped, polite voice, "I think it best we continue this conversation in private."

"As you wish," Marvin answered, equally formal. He could have been addressing a stranger.

"Fenley," Ayleborough said to the bagwigged servant. "Make arrangements for a private room." Fenley pulled Mr. Sadler aside and the two men stepped into the hall.

Marvin turned to Samantha. "I must talk to my brother. It will take only a few minutes. Do you wish to stay here and finish your breakfast, or go up to the bedroom?"

She could scarce believe her own ears. "You're not jesting, are you?"

"About your going to the bedroom, or about

157

the duke being my brother?" he asked, expressionless.

Samantha made an impatient sound. "The duke."

"No."

She rocked back on her heels as she digested this new information. She cast a quick glance around the common room. Mrs. Sadler, Squire Biggers, the duke's servants—all watched her as if witnessing a play unfold.

Only Ayleborough and her husband seemed not to notice. Then, for the briefest second, the duke's gaze met hers. He looked away quickly.

Marvin must have seen the exchange. He took her hand. "You know I'll always take care of you. You understand that, don't you?"

She searched his grim face, feeling more uncertain than before. He stood so close, she could see the texture in his eyes. This morning, she had teased him about how dark they were, claiming he must be hiding a black soul to have such unfathomable eyes. She had been lying on top of him, naked, happy, satiated. Her teasing had brought a flicker of copper light into his eyes and she had declared him not completely unsalvageable. He'd laughed then and had rolled her down onto the bed, where he'd tickled her, and when she'd begged for mercy, he'd held her in his arms and kissed her tenderly.

Even sitting here in the middle of the common room with everyone staring at them, her body ached for his touch . . . while her pride, and what

was left of her common sense, warned her to be-
ware.

"You're not really a sailor."

He shook his head. "Not here, Sam. I'll answer
all your questions, but not here. There are too
many people watching."

She nodded dumbly. Nothing made sense—

A blinding flash of insight caught her unawares. She forgot his warning. "You aren't really
Marvin Browne. You couldn't be and also be the
duke's brother."

The line of his mouth flattened. But he didn't
deny her accusation.

And she had her answer. The realization
shook her to the core.

Fenley informed the duke that a private room
was ready. Ayleborough looked to her husband.
"I'll be back shortly, Sam. We'll talk then."

Samantha started moving with him. "I will go
with you. I must hear everything."

"It would be best if you waited," he said.

She nodded to the small crowd watching
them. "I'll go mad waiting. I want to be there."

He hesitated, but changed his mind. "Then
come." He tucked her hand in the crook of his
arm. It was a possessive gesture—and yet as she
followed him across the room toward the duke,
she felt as if she walked beside a complete
stranger.

Her legs felt like two rickety poles which
could barely support her weight. Head high, she

managed to avoid the curious and wondering eyes of her friends and neighbors.

However, at the door of the inn's single private room, her husband stopped. "Samantha, wait for me inside. I have something I must attend to."

Ayleborough already waited for them. A flash of irritation crossed his face. "Yale, you can't leave now."

Yale. Of course. She felt stupid that her befuddled mind was taking so long to put all the pieces together. "You are the prodigal? The one who died at sea?"

He frowned at her use of the word "prodigal." "I will explain everything, but I need one moment." Without further explanation, he left her alone with the duke of Ayleborough.

"Please come in," Ayleborough said in a kind voice. "It's Miss Northrup, Vicar Northrup's daughter, isn't it?"

Samantha nodded mutely.

"Well, sit here in this chair, my dear. My brother has always had his own priorities." He guided Samantha to one of the four chairs sitting in front of a cheery fire burning in the hearth. Gratefully, she sank down onto the hard wood chair seat. She felt cold, very cold—but her chill wasn't from the weather and the heat of the fire could not help her.

"Fenley, fetch something for Miss Northrup to drink," Ayleborough said. The servant hurried to comply. The door shut behind him.

Samantha raised her eyes to his. "I'm not really married, am I?"

"Married?" This news seemed to surprise the duke more than discovering his brother was alive.

She grasped her hands in her lap. "Yes, Marv—I mean . . ." Her voice trailed off. "I don't know what to call him," she confessed.

The duke drummed his fingers on the table. "Don't call him anything for now. Just tell me what happened."

Samantha told him of the marriage in a low monotone. She kept her emotions firmly in check. In reality, she was afraid of feeling anything. Afraid of the truth. When she'd finished, she forced herself to ask, "Is he the one everyone thought had died at sea?"

The duke clasped his hands behind his back. "Yes."

Samantha was thankful she was sitting, or she might have swooned. She'd unknowingly married Yale Carderock. *The prodigal . . . the rakehell . . . the scoundrel!* She'd called him as much the night they'd met.

The door opened without a knock. Her husband came back in the room, closing the door firmly behind him. She stared at her hands lying uselessly in her lap, listening to his steps walk the wooden floor toward her.

His booted feet stopped in front of her. "Sam, I'm sorry you heard the truth this way."

"Which is?" she asked carefully, needing him

to explain all—yet fearing the explanation.

"I'm not Marvin Browne."

There. He'd admitted it. "With an 'e,'" she added softly.

His hand came down on her shoulder, but suddenly she could not bear his touch. It sparked too many memories, too many questions.

She shook his hand off and came out of the chair, practically fleeing to the other side of the room. She would have run further if she could have. Instead, she crossed her arms protectively against her chest, waiting.

Fenley interrupted them with a tray of drinks. Understanding that his presence was not wanted, he placed the tray on the table and backed out of the room.

The duke took command. "Yale, tell us what happened. We're both shocked. After all, everyone in England has believed you dead for years."

"I survived the storm," Yale said curtly. "I don't know how you received news of my death. You would know more about that than I."

"But why didn't you contact us? And why have you returned now, after all these years?" Ayleborough asked.

For the span of a heartbeat, Samantha thought she saw regret in her husband's dark eyes, but his voice revealed no emotion as he said, "I came to see Father."

"You're late," Ayleborough said crisply.

"I gathered that," came the dry response.

For the first time, seeing the two men standing

together, Samantha was struck by the uncanny resemblance. Yale towered almost four inches over his brother and had dark hair and eyes, yet both shared lean jawlines and strong noses. Worse, they shared the ability to look right through a person. They were doing so right now to each other. Stubborn, resolute, arrogant . . . it was a quality born into them and more telling of their paternity than a certificate of birth.

She also sensed they were more strangers than friends.

She cleared her throat and dared to ask, "Why didn't you tell me your real name?"

"Yes," Ayleborough agreed. "Why didn't you tell her who you really are? Or have you no pride in your family name?"

"Damn you, Wayland," came the low, dangerous growl from the man she'd married. "I owe an explanation to her, not to you. Father disinherited me . . . or have you forgotten?"

Ayleborough's blue eyes flashed with anger. Samantha doubted if anyone ever talked to him in that manner. "I have not forgotten," he answered, but then he paused, the stiffness leaving his body. "It was the one thing in our father's life he truly regretted. Yale, he'd sent runners out to look for you. He realized he shouldn't have done it almost the moment it was done. He hadn't really planned for matters to go so far. It was all a mistake."

"A mistake?" Yale shook his head. "He posted the announcement in the papers, Wayland. He turned my life upside down. My friends refused me and all doors were shut to me. He left me with nothing. And now you tell me it was a mistake."

"He only wished to point out to you the error of your ways," the duke answered, defending their father.

"Well, he did that," Yale answered. "It was a bitter lesson. I wouldn't have wished it on my worst enemy."

Ayleborough shifted uncomfortably. "Yes. Well, you know how our father could be." Almost as if for Samantha's benefit, he added, "He expected much from his sons."

"And I was a far cry from what he thought proper," Yale injected crushingly. "He couldn't wait to turn me out."

"Yale, that's not it. Perhaps if you'd done better in school," the duke said, as if picking up the threads of an old conversation.

"It was more than that, Wayland, and you know it." He looked to Samantha. "It's true I was a poor student, the bane of my tutors. Father hated imperfection in any form ... especially when he had perfection in Wayland."

"Yale, I was not—"

"Nonsense, brother. You were—and are—the very image of our father. He couldn't help but admire you more."

Ayleborough turned toward the mantel, staring into the fire a moment before saying in a quiet voice, "I'm also different in many ways."

"Yes?" Yale drawled with a lack of interest. "That remains to be seen, doesn't it? So far I'm unimpressed."

Samantha drew in a sharp breath. She'd never heard anyone even dare to speak of the powerful duke of Ayleborough in this manner.

Nor was the duke accustomed to it. His eyes narrowed on his brother as if he studied a disagreeable insect. "You will remember my station."

Yale smiled, his expression cynical. "I have never been allowed to forget it. After all, I was the one too unworthy to be the son of the duke of Ayleborough."

Ayleborough pounded his fist against the mantel. "Damn you, Yale. You never were one to listen to reason. Can't you see what a devil of a fix you are in? I'm the only one who can release you from it. Once those villagers realize you've married Miss Northrup under false circumstances and played a prank on all of them, they'll want to see you hanging from the highest tree in Sproule."

Yale's fists doubled at his side. He stood ramrod straight, towering over his brother. "My marriage to Miss Northrup is not a prank. Nor do I need or seek your help. We would have been gone from Sproule by now, except for your appearance."

"Oh, pardon me for inconveniencing you."

Ayleborough's voice dripped sarcasm. "By the way, what were your plans for her? Were you just going to drag her here and there like a wandering gypsy?"

"She'd be with me," Yale said.

"To do what? To go where?"

"That is none of your bloody business . . . *Your Grace*."

"Oh, but it is now. I'm the head of this family—"

"And I'm not a part of it. I was given the boot, the sack. I have no claim on the house of Ayleborough, and it has no claim on me!"

For a long moment the two men squared off, their eyes alive with anger. Samantha didn't know what to think. She resented their talking about her as if she were nothing more than a sack of wool—yet she felt she was witnessing a clash of titans.

Then the duke hit the table with his fist so hard it jumped. "Damn you, Yale. You are the most infuriating person. You never would listen to reason. Eleven years has done nothing to change you!" He paced the floor in silence.

Samantha glanced at her husband. He was completely unmoved by the duke's outburst.

She broke the silence. "Were you ever going to tell me the truth?"

With a start, both men turned to look at her. It was as if they'd forgotten her.

Yale took a step toward her. "Sam . . . I don't want you to think the wrong thing."

"Then what is the right thing?" she asked, her voice a quiet contrast to their shouting. "I want to hear the story from your lips."

For a moment she feared he wouldn't answer her. And then he spoke. "Seeing my own grave in the vault that night shocked me. I'd come to Sproule because I'd been told my father was dead. I didn't believe it. Childish of me, wasn't it, to think he would live forever? But then, Wayland will tell you Father possessed that sort of charisma."

"I can understand your reason for using the false name at first, but once you knew we were going to marry, why didn't you tell me your real name?"

His lips curled derisively. "After you gave me the lecture over what a profligate son I had been? Are you saying now you would have changed your opinion?"

Samantha remembered telling him of her father's sermon on the prodigal son and her cheeks burned. "Still, you could have told me your real name at half a dozen different opportunities."

"And would that have made you happy, Sam? Would it have changed anything, or only caused you to distrust me more? I didn't ask to get sick, or for you to be the one to care for me. It was happenstance, one of the cruel tricks of fate that life plays on us. Before I realized it, it was too late to confess the truth."

"But you married me under a false name."

"I wasn't going to leave you behind to face the

censure of these selfish villagers. You didn't deserve it. You'd done nothing wrong." He shot a quick glance at his brother before confessing, "And I didn't want my family to know I had been here. Perhaps it would have been different if Father had been alive."

"Why did you come to see Father?" the duke asked with sudden interest.

Yale ignored his question. Instead he took a step toward Samantha. "I wasn't going to leave you, Sam. I was going to take care of you."

She shook her head sadly. "But you were still going to leave me behind."

"In your own house, with your own living."

But I'd still be alone . . .

When she didn't answer, he prodded, "Sam?"

She turned her head away, not wanting to speak of it anymore. She wished she could curl up into a little ball and disappear.

Yale refused to let her be. He crossed the space between them. "Talk to me, Sam. Don't close up on me."

She didn't answer. It hurt too much.

"I'll make it up to you. I never meant to hurt you." He reached out, but she jerked away, moving closer to the duke. Tears threatened, but she would not cry. She would never cry over him.

A knock sounded on the door. Yale almost rushed to answer it. In walked Vicar Newell and Squire Biggers.

"What are you doing here?" Ayleborough

said, as irritated as Samantha by the interruption.

"I asked the squire to fetch the vicar," Yale said. "I need to remarry my wife."

Samantha's mouth dropped open, but before she could discover her voice, he launched into a very credible explanation to the vicar for the present state of affairs. Samantha listened in shock as he explained how he'd been surprised that his family had thought him dead and had assumed a false name so that he could tell his family first of his existence and not have them learn of it through gossip.

He made it all sound plausible—innocent, even.

"Unfortunately, I became ill. I was confused by the illness and thought it better to keep my real identity quiet until after I had gotten in touch with my family. You are aware that I was disinherited?"

Squire Biggers and the vicar nodded.

"Then you can understand my concerns," Yale said. "However, now that I have seen my brother and have received his blessing, I can marry Miss Northrup under my real name. Vicar, will you perform the service?"

"Now, Mr. Browne? I mean, Mr.—ah, er . . . ?" The vicar looked at confusion to Squire Biggers.

"Wait!" Samantha said. She wasn't about to remarry this man, but no one paid attention to her.

"You will address my brother as 'Lord Yale,' "

the duke said, his voice overriding hers.

"I don't want a title," Yale said abruptly. He nodded to Vicar Newell. " 'Mr. Carderock' is fine."

" 'Lord Yale,' " the duke corrected, almost through clenched teeth.

"I was disinherited, remember?"

"I've already informed you the disinheritance was a mistake," his brother said, smiling tightly.

"Nevertheless—"

"Nevertheless, I am reinheriting you."

Yale faced his brother, the set of his jaw stubborn. "I don't want to reinherited."

Ayleborough stared at him a moment before turning to the squire and the vicar. In a pleasant voice, he said, "Would you gentlemen please give us a moment of privacy?"

They didn't dare disobey him and moved back out the door. The minute the door closed behind them, Ayleborough whirled on his brother. "You don't contradict the duke of Ayleborough in public."

"I'll do whatever I like."

"This is a family matter, Yale. We don't air family business to anyone other than family. You *will* accept a title." He jabbed the air for emphasis. "You have no choice but to depend on me for a living. You have a wife now."

"I shall take care of my wife *my way* and I have many, many choices."

Ayleborough straightened, his hands behind

his back. "She is part of the family. She will live in a style befitting a Carderock."

"Damn you, Wayland. You sound exactly like Father."

"And you are as headstrong and flighty as your mother!" his brother shot back, his words reverberating in the room.

To Samantha's surprise, Yale went very still, the color draining from his face. Then she remembered that the two brothers had different mothers. The duke's mother had been the beloved first wife. Yale's mother had been the much younger, and very foolish, second wife.

"I want nothing from you," Yale said.

Ayleborough glared at him. "If that is the way you feel, why did you return?"

Yale walked over to his brother until less than a foot stood between them. "I returned to prove to Father that I wasn't the scapegrace he thought me."

The corner of the duke's mouth lifted in grim amusement. "So, you married the vicar's penniless daughter under an assumed name and planned to abandon her. Oh, that would have convinced Father."

Yale pulled back as if his brother had hit him.

Immediately Ayleborough recognized his error. "I shouldn't have said that. It was wrong of me, but you must see that is how it looks. We have to take care of her, Yale. As a family. Otherwise it doesn't appear good."

"And you don't believe I can?"

The duke's glance ran over his brother's home-spun outfit. "I feel it best if I help you."

Yale laughed, the sound without mirth. "You jump to conclusions, brother. I am not as bad as you believe. I have one hundred thousand pounds to my name and own a fleet of ships that ply the trade between here and the Orient. I did that on my own. I don't need your money. I don't need *the family*."

If the duke was surprised by this news, his face didn't betray him. Instead, he answered quietly, "Father's dead, Yale. You can't prove anything to him."

The anger immediately left Yale. The hardness in his eyes softened. "I should have come back sooner."

"What? To throw his actions in his face?" Ayleborough placed his hand on his brother's shoulder. "Yale, I will repeat it and repeat it until you believe me. Father wished he had not acted so rashly. He wanted you back."

Yale turned and walked to the window. He stood there, but Samantha doubted he saw the view of the hillside beyond the inn. He was lost in his own world.

Something inside Samantha longed to comfort him, but she ruthlessly quashed the emotion. She would have nothing to do with him.

Instead, it was his brother who went up to him. "Come back to the family. Bring your wife and let us make amends for the past. We are your heritage. We're your children's heritage."

"I wish you would stop talking as if I'm part of this plan, Your Grace," Samantha said. "I'm not going to leave Sproule *or* go anywhere with this man."

However, he ignored her. Yale flicked a glance in her direction, and then said, "Call in the vicar."

Ayleborough clapped his hand on his brother's back. "I knew you would see reason. Welcome back, brother."

Yale shook his head. "Don't kill the fatted calf yet, brother. I'm only doing this for Sam."

"For me?" She wanted to scream at the two of them. "Don't reconcile with your family on my account. I don't want to marry you," she told Yale flatly. "I didn't want to the first time, and I certainly don't now."

"Sam," Yale said reasonably, walking toward her.

She warded him off with her hand. "Samantha is my given name, but I'm *Miss Northrup* to you."

"You're my wife to me."

"Not legally!"

"We are going to rectify that momentarily," he answered.

"I-don't-think-so," Samantha said, speaking carefully so he could understand exactly what she was saying. "I won't go through with it."

He shrugged. "You have no choice. The marriage has been consummated. We must make it legal."

She cast a look at the duke for support, but he

was pretending to study the flames licking a log in the hearth. She drew a deep breath, lifted her chin, and said, "No, *we* don't."

Ayleborough gave a sharp bark of laughter. "This is excellent. My brother has finally found someone as stubborn as he is."

Frowning, Yale went to Samantha's side and took hold of her arm. She didn't want him this close. It reminded her of the intimacy they'd shared, the way she'd craved his touch, the way he'd made a fool of her.

She pulled on her arm and he released it, but he did not step back. "Sam, you must marry me. If you don't, there will be no place for you, not in Sproule. These people are too narrow-minded. The only way I can safely steer you away from the threat of a scandal is if we marry. Otherwise, you will be ostracized. I've had that happen to me and I will not let it happen to you."

She didn't speak; she couldn't. She felt as if a heavy weight rested on her chest, making speech impossible.

He placed his hand on her shoulder, his thumb resting on the pulse point between her chin and neck. "Ah, Sam, I'm sorry to drag you through this, but it will work out for the best. I really am a rich man. I can buy you whatever you wish."

"Whatever I wish?" She almost laughed. "I wish I'd never laid eyes on you. I wish you hadn't humiliated and embarrassed me. I wish you'd had the decency to tell me the truth from the beginning! Can you accomplish that now?"

His eyebrows rose. "No."

She sidled away from him, but still he followed. "What happened to the lass who said she was falling in love with me?"

She shot him an angry glance. How could he use her words against her at this time? The sting of tears burned her eyes. She blinked them back, reminding herself that he wasn't worth it. "It was lust," she managed to choke out. "I mistook it for love."

Her words caught him off guard. The teasing light in his eyes died. "Sam, I didn't mean to hurt you."

"You didn't mean to be honest with me, either."

"Touché," he answered softly.

And so that is it, she thought sadly. They were done with each other. She hugged her waist and waited for him to leave, refusing to look at him, refusing to think of her future.

He walked across the room to the door. She heard it open and held her breath. In a second, he would be gone from her life forever.

Instead, he said, "Vicar, we are ready for you to perform the ceremony."

"What?" Samantha said, spinning around.

Yale didn't even bother to look at her as he answered, "We are going to marry."

Squire Biggers and Vicar Newell entered the room. Samantha stepped into their path. "Would you please leave?" Samantha said to them. "There will not be a marriage."

The two men looked at Yale. "Yes, there will," he said solemnly. "You see, Miss Northrup doesn't know what is good for her, so you and I must help her. Otherwise, she will insist on staying in Sproule."

"She can't do that," Vicar Newell said. "I just moved my missus into the vicarage and she's happy." He confided to Samantha, "We're also going to have a wee one in a few months."

"You don't have to worry," Squire Biggers assured his nephew. "She won't be moving back into the vicarage."

"Then I'll stay with Miss Mabel and Miss Hattie!" Samantha exclaimed.

Miss Mabel's head popped into the doorway. "Did someone say our name?" She entered the room, followed by Miss Hattie, Mr. and Mrs. Sadler, and what seemed to be everyone in the village.

Samantha gasped. She should have known a crowd would gather.

She faced Yale. "I won't marry you. I won't answer the questions when asked, or say 'I do'! Do you hear me? I refuse to speak a word!"

"Aye, I hear you," Yale said grimly. "But the marriage will go on. And these good people will witness it."

Samantha could hear the squire explaining to Mrs. Sadler what had transpired. Samantha was surprised he hadn't already spread the word while he cooled his heels outside the door. Mrs. Sadler made a soft sound of surprise and then began whispering in Miss Mabel's ear. Soon the whole village would know of her humiliation.

Somehow, in some way, Samantha vowed she would learn to live with the disgrace. But she would not marry him.

The Porters had arrived and pushed their way into the room. The duke of Ayleborough motioned for Fenley to make arrangements for drinks for everyone.

"If you are related to the duke, then you must be very rich," Miss Hattie said to Yale.

"Yes, very," he answered, and she turned in wonder at her sister.

"How lucky you are," Miss Mabel said to Samantha. "You are going to be part of the Carderock family. This is most romantic."

"This man has deceived me," Samantha practically growled. "He's deceived all of us. There is nothing romantic about it."

"But he wants to make it right," Mrs. Sadler said, and the other women around her nodded. Even a few men agreed.

Then the duke spoke, "I have one condition before giving this remarriage my blessing, brother." Everyone went silent.

"And that is?" Yale asked.

"That you come to London with your wife, at least until she is properly settled."

"I will," Yale said firmly. "I'll do it for Sam."

The women in the room oohed their approval.

Samantha harrumphed her thoughts. She turned her back on him.

Emma and Fenley appeared with tankards of ale. More villagers crowded into the room. Glancing over her shoulder, Samantha realized that Yale was on one side, she on the other. Vicar Newell stood lost in the crowd somewhere in between.

"Let us get this ceremony done with," Ayleborough announced, taking a tankard for himself. "I am eager to be on the road to London to see my family."

"Well, then," Squire Biggers said. "Let's start the ceremony, else my nephew will find himself without a house again."

That was all the impetus the mousy Vicar Newell needed. He started reading the words of the marriage ceremony out of the *Book of Common Prayer*.

Samantha kept her back turned to all of them, amazed that they should so completely ignore her wishes. Well, she wasn't going through with this. She wouldn't!

She listened to Yale repeat his vows. He sounded more sure of them than he had the day before.

Her jaw hurt from clenching her teeth to keep herself from crying. As he earnestly promised to keep her to him until death, she wanted to rage at him like some Greek harpy.

Then it was time for her vows.

"Samantha Northrup," the vicar said. "Wilt

thou have this man to be thy wedded husband?"

Samantha stared at a crack in the plaster wall in front of her. She would not say one word.

Miss Mabel nudged her. "You say 'I will' here."

Samantha ignored her.

The crowd shifted uncomfortably. Then Mrs. Biggers's overbearing voice came from the doorway, "Oh, pother! I'll answer for her. She will!"

Samantha turned on one foot. "I do not!"

"You already have," Mrs. Biggers said. She looked at her nephew. "She took these vows yesterday. There's no reason to say them again. After all, she married him using her real name."

"Yes, that's true," Vicar Newell said, pushing his spectacles up the bridge of his nose.

"Aye, what difference is it whether she said it yesterday or today?" Squire Biggers said impatiently. "Let's get on with it."

And to Samantha's horror, the vicar did exactly that. "Will thou love him, comfort him, obey him?"

When she didn't answer, Mrs. Biggers and the other women did for her, their voices speaking in unison, "She does."

"No, I won't!" Samantha protested.

"Wilt thou honor and keep him, in sickness and in health?"

"She will!" The men joined in this time and the sound was much louder.

"No!" Samantha stamped her foot, so angry she could burst into flames.

"And wilt thou forsake all others, and keep thee only unto him, so long as ye both shall live?"

"She will!" everyone answered, absolutely jovial by now.

Before Samantha could protest again, the vicar said, "ThenIpronounceyoumanandwife." He closed the prayer book and smiled beatifically. "Those whom God hath joined together, let no man put asunder."

The crowd responded, "Amen," and hoisted their tankards to drink to her health.

Stunned, Samantha stared at them, people she had known and trusted all her life. They didn't care about her—finally she understood what Marvin, no, what *Yale* had been trying to tell her.

And then the hairs on the back of her neck tickled, as if someone watched her. She shifted her gaze and met Yale's. The expression on his face was one of sympathy touched with regret. He knew what she was thinking.

She gave him her back.

Chapter 9

Yale watched cynically as the villagers rushed forth to congratulate Samantha. Mrs. Biggers droned on and on about how wonderful it was "our dear Miss Northrup is now related to the duke of Ayleborough."

Miss Mabel and Miss Hattie cried noisily, while Mrs. Porter and Mrs. Sadler both bragged that they'd known there was something "special" about Mr. Browne.

"I knew the moment I clapped eyes on him that he wasn't just a nobody," Mrs. Sadler declared.

"Aye, I felt the same," her husband agreed.

Yale remembered their first meeting differently. When he'd paid for his room in advance, the innkeeper and his wife had practically bit his coin in front of him to see if the metal was good.

He was glad he was taking Sam away from them; they were all such hypocrites. They didn't deserve a person as fine and giving as she was.

Wayland's voice was heard over the crowd. "I

hate to spoil this splendid party in honor of my brother and his new bride, but we must be on our way. I plan to make London by Tuesday night."

"By Tuesday night, Your Grace?" Squire Biggers said. "That's a spanking pace in this weather."

"It is, but I will do it," Wayland answered, pulling on his gloves, while Fenley placed a heavy greatcoat sporting no fewer than five capes around his shoulders. "I have my own teams waiting between here and London. I promised Her Grace I will be there, and so I shall. I don't like to be away from my family any longer than I must." He gave his brother an indulgent smile before adding, "But then, it was a good thing I made this trip, no?"

Yale wanted to answer, "No, it was not." If Wayland hadn't appeared, he and Samantha would be on their way and she would be as content and happy as a cat. As it was now, he'd be lucky if Sam thawed toward him by spring.

But his answer wasn't necessary. Mrs. Biggers was busy fawning all over his brother. "Oh, yes," she trilled. "And you have a new baby, too. It has been years since we've seen the other boys. When you return to Braehall, do bring them to Sproule!"

"Yes, I should," Wayland agreed. "But Her Grace doesn't enjoy traveling. Not with the children so young."

"It is hard," Mrs. Biggers said, and Yale

wanted to snort in derision. He doubted the woman had ever been more than five miles from Sproule in any direction.

Then Wayland started for the door and Mrs. Biggers and her husband and all the others hurried after him.

Yale looked across the room. Samantha had already been forgotten.

Fenley had her cape. Yale had out his hand and nodded for the servant to leave them.

They were alone.

He crossed the room toward his wife, uncertain of his reception. The cape in his hands was practically threadbare. He would buy her a new one, but not black. He would buy her a bright red one made of the finest wool. Perhaps that would sweeten her temper.

He placed the black cape over her shoulders. She accepted it without looking at him.

"We must go," he said. "I had Fenley pack for us."

"Including my mother's things?"

"Yes." He offered his arm to escort her to the waiting coach, but she didn't take it.

He waited.

"I don't consider us married." Her eyes flashed with defiance. "Regardless of what happened between us last night and this morning."

He had expected such an ultimatum. His wife adhered to strong moral principles and rules. In the short time they'd been together, he'd managed to offend or break every one of them.

Yale drew in a deep breath and released it slowly before saying, "Sometimes, Samantha, it is not what we think that matters but how other people perceive us. Whether you like it or not, we *are* married."

"I wonder if you even know what the word means, sir."

"That question could be asked of any man."

She rejected his claim immediately. "My father valued his marriage, and his family." With a thin smile she added, "Of course, he was completely honest about his intentions from the moment he met my mother."

"Yes," Yale said. "And he died leaving his daughter penniless and alone."

He regretted the words the moment they left his lips.

If he had struck her with his hand, he could not have landed a more fatal blow. Her face paled. Then her anger rose with such force, her voice shook as she said, "I will never forgive you for saying that."

"Ah, Sam—"

"My name is Samantha," she said, refusing to let him speak. "And you are a stranger to me. What happened between us last night was . . . was not love or caring or any form of commitment. I shall not make the same mistake twice. Do not expect it!" She turned on her heel and almost ran from the room.

Yale watched her go, and then sat on a chair. "How did you make such bloody mess of things?" he asked himself aloud. The question echoed in the empty room.

It's England, he concluded. He was a success anywhere else in the world; he should never have returned, or involved himself in the affairs of the vicar's daughter. He had been better off alone.

From the front of the inn, he could hear Squire Biggers's laugh. It was a hearty and good-natured but false sound.

Yale wondered if Wayland ever tired of boot-lickers like Biggers following him so closely they almost had their noses up his arse. Of course, that was one of the advantages to being a duke—everyone toadied up to you.

Perhaps Sam would have toppled into his arms if she'd found herself married to a duke, instead of to the ne'er-do-well younger brother.

He pulled a wry face. No, she wouldn't.

And that was one of the things he liked about her. That and the fact that she was an enjoyable little piece in bed. Too enjoyable. Even thinking of her made him hungry for her.

Fenley's voice from the open doorway interrupted his musings. "Excuse me, Lord Yale, but His Grace wishes you to join him. He is ready to leave for London."

Yale rose to his feet, feeling weary before the journey had begun. "*Mr. Carderock,* Fenley. I have no use for all that nonsense."

"Yes, my lord," Fenley answered dutifully. He

held the wide-brimmed hat Yale had worn from London.

Yale sighed. He missed the freedom of the sea and being his own man. At the doorway, he paused in front of Fenley. The servant had been with the family since Yale's grandfather's days.

He took the hat. "Fenley, you've seen a great deal in your life, haven't you?"

"I believe so, my lord."

"Tell me, do you understand women?"

A twinkle sparkled in Fenley's rheumy eye. "No, my lord."

"That's what I feared," Yale answered. "There isn't a one of us that stands a bloody chance." With those words he sauntered down the hallway to go to London, the stage of his youthful humiliation, with a brother who didn't know him and a wife who despised him.

Life promised not to be dull.

The duke of Ayleborough did not travel light. Besides the ducal coach with his coat of arms painted on the door, there was a second coach just for luggage and servants. Each coach came with a driver and footman, to keep the passengers safe.

A footman held the coach door open for Samantha, but she hesitated. Once she climbed into this coach, she would be leaving everyone safe and familiar.

The duke took her hand. "You take one step at a time," he counseled her in a low voice. "And don't ever forget, you are one of us now. My name and my family protect you. Hold your head high."

The man was kindness itself. How could he be so different from his brother?

"Thank you," she murmured. "I am in need of a friend."

"You'll do fine," he assured her, and helped her up into the coach.

She'd never seen anything like the interior of this vehicle. The emerald green seats with their gold tassels were more springy and soft than a feather mattress. She'd never sat in anything more designed for comfort.

The duke took the seat opposite her as Yale climbed in behind him. Samantha wished she'd had the foresight to insist the duke sit next to her, but now it was too late.

Her husband was a big man and his long legs didn't quite fit inside the confines of the coach, especially once Fenley joined them. Still, she wondered if it was necessary for him to scoot quite so close to her.

His arm brushed her breast and her nipple tightened instinctively to his touch.

She pushed back into the corner of the coach, crossed her arms, and wondered how long it would be before she could erase the memory of his lovemaking from her mind.

Focus on his faults, she told herself. Certainly that would keep her mind busy all the way to London!

Ayleborough leaned his head out the window to say a few last words to Squire Biggers. He pulled it back in. "Is everyone ready?" He didn't wait for an answer but knocked on the roof, signaling the coachmen.

With a shout at the horses, they were off. Because everyone in the village still crowded around the coach, they could not go fast. Samantha waved farewell to Miss Mabel and Miss Hattie. Mrs. Biggers practically chased the coach waving her good-bye.

Mr. Porter stepped out behind his fire at the smithy to watch the two coaches go through the village. His wife had joined him and she used a corner of her apron to wipe away a tear.

The coach rolled by the church and the vicarage. The vicar's wife stood in the open kitchen door. Many a time Samantha had stood in that very place to watch the goings-on in Sproule.

They passed the cemetery, the Ayleborough vault, and the graves of her parents. Samantha said a silent prayer to the souls of her parents, asking their blessing on this new turn her life had taken.

Someone nudged her elbow and she was surprised to see the duke holding out his handkerchief. She accepted it and thanked him profusely, aware that the more she went on about his small kindness, the deeper Yale frowned.

Ayleborough glanced at his brother's scowl and smiled at her. She returned the smile. She liked him. She might even trust him.

Yale cleared his throat as if to remind them of his presence. Beneath her lashes, she slid a look at her husband. He was staring out of the opposite window, but she knew he was aware of everything. He shifted, his leg rubbing against hers. Ignoring the erratic beat of her heart, she very deliberately moved her leg away.

"Yale, tell us what you've been doing these eleven years." Ayleborough asked.

"A little of this, a bit of that," came the infuriating answer.

Samantha's gaze met the duke's and she rolled her eyes heavenward. He openly grinned back at her.

Yale caught the grin. "What is so funny?"

"Nothing, brother," Ayleborough said.

"Perhaps since he doesn't feel like expanding on your *very reasonable* question, Your Grace," Samantha said in her sweetest voice, "would you tell us about your new son?"

She'd hit the topic closest to Ayleborough's heart. He launched into a description of each of his three sons. He was a proud father. Nor did he hide his affection for his wife, Marion. He quite adored her and said as much. They'd named the new baby after her father, Charles.

From the moment Ayleborough had started speaking, Yale had closed his eyes, but Samantha was certain he feigned sleep.

"What are the other boys' names?" she asked.

"John and Matthew," Ayleborough answered. "I had no desire to give them outlandish names like Wayland and Yale. Our father was a renowned Anglo-Saxon scholar. Silly names, if you ask me. Our sister's name is Twyla. You will meet her in London, too."

"Does she have children?" Samantha asked.

"Two girls, Louise and Christine, and two boys, Arthur and Douglas."

Samantha couldn't resist saying in Yale's direction, "I had no idea you were an uncle, Yale." The name still sounded foreign to her.

He pretended to snore.

Ayleborough winked at Samantha and the two of them laughed. Even Fenley smiled.

Yale pretended to wake. "What is so funny?"

Samantha shrugged her shoulders. "Nothing in particular. Is that not right, Your Grace?"

"A small jest. It wouldn't interest you, Yale, and, Samantha, please call me Wayland when we are in private. May I also say, I'm well pleased with my new sister-in-law."

"Why?" Yale said baldly. "Because she asked about your children?"

"Actually, I find her intelligent as well as lovely. I can't wait to introduce her to Marion."

Samantha didn't know who was more surprised, Yale or herself.

"Thank you, Your Grace," she managed to whisper.

"Wayland."

She smiled. "Thank you, Wayland. I appreciate the compliment. I am also pleased with my brother-in-law."

"You're pleased. He's pleased," Yale interjected crossly. "What about you, Fenley? Are you pleased, too?"

"With all due respect, my lord, Lady Yale appears to be a superb catch," Fenley answered dutifully, but with a smile tugging the corners of his mouth.

"Mrs. Carderock, Fenley. *Mrs.*, *Mrs.*," Yale chastised. He made a show of trying to situate himself better in the coach. However, this time when his leg brushed hers, he was the one who pulled away. "Haven't we all something better to talk about?"

"We could discuss my earlier question," Wayland said.

"Which question was that?" Yale said, stifling a yawn of boredom.

"The one where I asked what you had been doing with yourself these past years."

Yale crossed his arms, stretched out his legs as much as he could, and stared out the window. Samantha had almost begun to think he wasn't going to answer his brother at all when he said, "I've been building a shipping company."

"Your own company?" Wayland asked with interest. "Tell me about it."

"There isn't much to say."

"Come on, man," Wayland said impatiently. "What is the name of the company?"

"Rogue Shipping."

Wayland's eyes widened. "Rogue Shipping?" He gave a sound of delighted laughter. "You are the one behind Rogue Shipping. Why, that's most opportune!" He looked to Samantha. "It's a small company, but it's well run. There are those who predict it will become the foremost shipping firm in the Orient next to the East India Company."

"We contract with them sometimes, too. More and more lately," Yale answered laconically.

The duke sat back in the corner of the coach and gave his brother a stare of utter amazement. "For a shipping magnate, you should see to your tailor."

"Do you doubt me?" Yale asked, his voice silky with challenge.

"No," Wayland said bluntly. "Every wealthy man dresses in well-worn garments almost ten years out of date."

"Actually, the village gave him those clothes," Samantha said, feeling a need to speak in Yale's defense. "I burned his other clothes."

"You did?" Wayland asked, his eyebrows coming up in interest.

"To prevent the spread of disease," Samantha added, once she realized her words could be misconstrued. "I had reason to burn them."

"You don't owe him an explanation," Yale said protectively.

"But it would be nice," Wayland countered. "The squire told me the marriage was in a bit of haste."

"There was no scandal involved," Yale said.

Wayland frowned his disbelief.

"I saw her and fell head over heels in love," Yale said, answering the unvoiced doubts, and surprising Samantha. "But I feared giving my real name because she would think the worst of me. Which she does."

Wayland looked from his brother to Samantha and back. "Well, if you are the head of Rogue Shipping, you are richer than a nabob," he said, obviously thinking it was time to change the subject. His voice still held a hint of doubt. "When we get to London, we'll see about your wardrobe. I will send you to my tailor."

"Correction, brother," Yale said. "I will see to my wardrobe. I have no need of your tailor."

"Stubborn to the end, aren't you?" the duke said.

"Aye," came Yale's response.

The conversation died after that, each person keeping his own counsel. Samantha had been startled that Yale would declare himself madly in love with her. It was a gallant but silly gesture. People would notice soon enough when he left her what his real feelings for her were.

After a while, Wayland, Samantha, and Fenley amused themselves with a card game until it was too dark to play. Yale stared out the window, lost in his thoughts.

Shortly after the sun had set, they arrived at the first posting house of their journey to London. The innkeeper was expecting the duke, and a good hot meal of roasted leg of lamb cooked in a brandy sauce awaited them in a private room.

The inn was a popular one and very busy. The innkeeper informed them there had been a horse race only that day. There were no other rooms to be had, but when Yale held out a gold sovereign, he managed to find one for Samantha.

She was tired and could barely eat a bite of her meal. The day's traumatic events and her lack of sleep the night before had all conspired to make her so tired she almost fell asleep in her plate.

Yale was the first to notice her nodding off. "Go on upstairs to bed, Samantha."

Fenley, who stood guard at the door supervising the duke's personal footmen and the inn's servants in serving the dinner, quickly moved around the table to pull out her chair for her—but Yale had already done it. Samantha smiled at Fenley. He had bustled around from the moment they had arrived to ensure their bags were delivered to their room and that matters were as the duke liked them.

"I do not know how you do it," she told him. "I'm tired almost to death."

Fenley smiled, pleased with her compliment. "I have had years of practice, my lady."

Yale took Samantha's arm. "And he is tougher than an old rooster."

"As you say, my lord," Fenley said with a bow.

Samantha noticed that Yale had stopped correcting Fenley every time he referred to Yale as "my lord." She didn't know how she felt about being "my lady." The day had been too full of surprises for her to worry about it. Tomorrow she would consider this startling change in her importance.

Yale escorted her out of the room, placing her hand on his arm. Once the door was shut behind them, Samantha removed her hand.

"I can see my own way from here."

"Oh, Sam . . . antha," he added at her cross look. "The inn's crowded. It is no place for a gentlewoman to be wandering about alone." As if to punctuate his words, the sound of male laughter came from the taproom.

"I am more worried about being accosted by you than by complete strangers," she said briskly, heading for the stairs.

In three long strides he placed himself in front of her. "Samantha, I have to do what is right."

"Oh? How amazing of you finally to remember that." She stepped around him, lifted her skirts slightly, and started up the stairs to her room.

Behind her she heard him mutter something about exasperating females. It pleased her.

The steps were winding and narrow. A gentleman was coming down and she had to move to the side to let him through. As the man passed, he glared with a touch too much familiarity at Samantha's bosom—that is, until Yale placed a protective hand on her waist.

"So sorry," the gentleman muttered.

Yale practically growled a response, and Samantha had to concede that perhaps he was right and should escort her to her room. Either way, it didn't appear she was going to dissuade him. And he thought *her* stubborn!

At the top of the stairs, they walked down the hall in silence. This inn was five times the size of the Bear and Bull. Samantha had never thought inns could be so huge, and she suddenly realized what a country mouse she was.

Yale opened the door to her room and stepped back. Samantha started to walk in and then stopped with a gasped cry.

He was right behind her. "Sam, what's wrong?"

"There is someone in here," she said, backing out.

Yale glanced in the room and then suppressed a laugh. "Sam, it's the maid."

Samantha stopped. "The maid?"

He pushed her forward and said to the girl in the room, "You're the maid Fenley arranged, aren't you?"

The girl bobbed a nervous curtsy. "Yes, my lord. The master said there was a lady here without her maid and sent me to tend to her. Did I startle my lady? The master said I should wait for her." She bobbed another curtsy.

"Everything is fine now," Yale replied easily. He placed his hand on the small of Samantha's back and attempted to push her covertly into the room.

Samantha hung back. "I know nothing about maids," she whispered to him.

"Excuse us a moment," he said to the maid, and closed the door, leaving them out in the hall. His voice low, Yale said, "You don't have to know much about maids. *They* have to know everything. You just stand there and let her do her job."

"What *is* her job?" she asked him desperately.

"She'll brush your hair, help you take off your dress, and tuck you into bed."

"I don't need anyone to do that. I've been doing that myself for years."

There was genuine sympathy in his eyes as he said, "You have, Sam, but you're a lady now, and you will soon learn that what you wish doesn't matter to the duke of Ayleborough. We have appearances to uphold. When we arrive in London, you will be assigned a maid of your own and you'll never get to brush another hair on your head or lace up your own frock again."

"But I *like* doing those things."

"Yes? Well, now you are Someone Important."

"Someone Important?"

"You know, a person whom all the village watches and gossips about."

"I was that as the vicar's daughter."

"But now you are related to an important title and are rich. And in the interests of family harmony, let's not argue about it tonight. The girl will receive a more than handsome tip for her services, so let's not disappoint her, shall we?"

Samantha considered his words a moment before saying, "She probably thinks I am a fool for crying out when I saw her."

He rubbed the side of her cheek with the back of his fingers. "No, she knows she startled you. It will be fine."

"It's just so different than what I'm used to."

He tilted her chin up with one finger. "Sam, you are going to find that London is a far cry from Sproule. There will be things that are different than what you are accustomed to, matters that will make you anxious. Just take a deep breath and realize there are no dragons anymore. You will make mistakes, but you will thrive. I know that."

She looked into his dark eyes a moment before saying, "Is that why you haven't left me yet? You want to make sure I'm not eaten by dragons?"

His face was so close she could see the line of his whiskers even in the muted light given off by an oil lamp on the hall table. "I have an obligation to see you taken care of properly."

"It's not necessary, you know. I can take care of myself."

"So you keep telling me."

"It's true!"

"Sam . . . Samantha, we're tired. Let's not argue now. I'm seeing you to London and I will make sure you're set up, and I don't care what you say. I'm not as rackety as everyone remembers."

She could have argued that point with him, but he was right. She was tired. She withdrew her hand from his. "Well, thank you for your advice. I try to heed good advice, no matter the source."

"Challenging to the end, aren't you?"

"Did you expect less?"

"No."

She smiled at his quick reply and turned the handle of the door. "Good night."

Actually, Jenny, the maid, turned out not to be a dragon at all. She was a sweet, simple girl who knew little about what was expected of a lady's maid. She and Samantha got along very well. It was nice to have someone else brush her hair until it shone and to ensure a hot brick had been placed between the sheets.

In less than an hour, Samantha was dressed in her comfy flannel nightdress and tucked in for the night beneath toasty warm bedclothes, a nice fire burning in the hearth. It was nice to be treated as Someone Important.

"Good night, my lady," Jenny said at the door. "I'll see you on the morrow."

"Thank you, Jenny," Samantha said sleepily. The maid shut the door.

Samantha closed her eyes and snuggled under the covers. Bed had never felt better. These sheets were much cleaner than those at the Bear and Bull and made of fine linen. Jenny had told her that the duke of Ayleborough always traveled with his own sheets.

Yes, it was very nice to be Someone Important.

She was just about ready to drop off to sleep when the door opened.

Samantha rubbed her nose against the pillow. "Jenny? Have you forgotten something?"

"It's not the maid," came Yale's voice. "It's your husband. I'm here to spend our wedding night."

Chapter 10

Samantha bolted up into a seated position. "I thought that door locked."

"It does," Yale answered. "See?" He locked the door with the key and held it up for her.

"I do not want you here," she said brutally. "I made that very clear at the inn this morning. I do not consider us man and wife."

"Yes, you made that very clear," he replied without heat. "However, there is no other place for me to sleep. The place is overflowing with guests. People are even sleeping on the benches in the taproom." He sat on the corner of the bed by her feet and leaned against the bedpost, yawning sleepily. "Besides, my brother, the one you were so cozy with all afternoon, would imagine me guilty of all sorts of notorious acts if I wasn't in bed with my wife."

"There's plenty of room for you to sleep in the stable. Your wife does not want you in bed with her," she told him succinctly, then added, "And what do you mean, I was cozy with your brother all afternoon?"

"One concern at a time, Samantha." He rose from the bed and stretched before shrugging off his coat. As he hung it on the back of a chair that sat before a small desk, he said, "To answer your first question . . . the stables are full of all sorts of vermin. Would you really want me in the coach with you and Lord only knows what else? We'd be itching all the way to London."

Samantha itched just at the thought of it.

"Second concern," he said, pulling his shirt tail out from his breeches. "My wife doesn't want me to sleep with her." He paused a moment as if considering the matter before tugging the shirt over his head. At the sight of his bare chest, the room suddenly felt several degrees warmer to Samantha. She avoided his eyes.

He again sat on the edge of the bed and began pulling off his boots. "Of course," he continued conversationally, "I could remind her that yesterday, she said her vows of her own free will, and I do have conjugal rights."

Samantha forgot maidenly modesty and glared at him. "You wouldn't dare."

"Challenging me, Sam?" he asked. He let the boot drop to the floor. "Don't worry. I've never forced a woman yet and I'm not about to do it now."

"Oh, I am sure they all *beg* to tumble into your bed," she said sarcastically.

He nodded. "Usually."

Samantha folded her arms against her chest. "Well, now you've met one who won't."

"So you keep telling me." He started working off the other boot.

His unruffled response angered her. "You know, you are a far cry from your brother."

That jab hit home. His movements froze and he shot an annoyed look toward her. She couldn't hide a smile of satisfaction.

"Yes," he said grimly. "I am a far cry. And you'd best remember it." He tossed his boot on the floor and rolled down his socks.

She shook the bedclothes with a hard jerk, as if to shake him off the bed. "Why don't you just go on your way? Leave me and be done with it. I've had enough of this farce you've been playing about accompanying me to London. *And would you please stop undressing?*" There was something very intimate about a man's bare feet.

Yale tossed his socks on top of his boots and rose. "I don't sleep in my clothes. Not even for you."

Then, to her horror, he began unbuttoning his breeches. First one button, and then a second.

Samantha stood up in the bed, almost beside herself with outrage. "Out!" She pointed to the door.

"I'm not leaving. I'm staying here." He unbuttoned a third button and she felt a wild sense of desperation. What would she do if he pressed her?

She doubled her fists, shaking with indignation. "Is there no limit with you? I thought at yesterday's *and today's* wedding you had humiliated me enough, but you seem to have a number of other tricks up your sleeve!"

"Sam, I have no tricks," he said.

"*And my name is Samantha*! Sam is a different person, a person who *trusted* you. Samantha is wiser. She's not a fool!"

Then, as suddenly as it came, her anger left her. She sat on the bed, facing the opposite wall. She had never lost her temper, ever . . . and yet she did over and over with him. Perhaps the man was driving her to madness? He had her so angry and confused she didn't know herself anymore.

She felt his weight move across the bed. Immediately she started to rise, grabbing for her pillow. "I will sleep in the stables. You can have the bed."

But before she could move, his hand caught her wrist and pulled her back. She landed on the edge of the bed, her back against his chest, his legs on either side of her.

"Let me go!" She wrestled to pull her wrist free.

His arms came around her, holding her prisoner. "Samantha, stop struggling. Come, love, stop it. I won't hurt you."

"I thought you never forced yourself on women!" she ground out.

"I'm not, Samantha. I'm just trying to calm you down."

"Well, this isn't calming me!" she shot back, but she stopped twisting and turning.

"I'm sorry," he whispered into her hair. "I was only teasing you."

"And is that teasing?" she asked archly, wiggling a bit so that he knew she was aware of his erection pressing against her backside. He still wore his breeches, the top three buttons undone.

"That cannot be helped," he muttered. "Damn, Sam, I'm a man, after all. When your eyes flash fire and your chin gets that determined set and your hair is down around your shoulders, you remind me of an affronted princess. So beautiful and yet so distant."

Beautiful? Had he called her beautiful?

She shook her head, warning herself to be wary. He was a passionate man who liked women. He'd say anything to bed her. "Then I shall change my personality. I'll become sweet, complacent, and boring so that you will find me ugly."

He chuckled. "Yes, but then, I like your *sweetness* best. Nor are you completely indifferent to me. Your nipples are hard." He flicked the tip of one with his thumb.

Samantha felt the movement all the way to the core of her being.

He cradled her closer. "We were so good together," he whispered into her ear. "So very good."

"I do not feel anything for you," she attempted to deny.

"Um-hm," he said noncommittally.

"I don't!"

"Did I say I didn't believe you?"

She practically growled her vexation, but she didn't move. It didn't feel bad being close to him like this. "You don't have to say it. I hear your laughter in your voice."

"I didn't realize I was so readable. I shall have to give up cards."

She caught a glimpse of them in the cheval glass in the corner of the room. They appeared to be a couple. Yet such were their differences there might as well be a chasm between them. "I will not be intimate with you," she said carefully.

"I understand."

"Do you accept that?"

He sighed, the sound heavy. "I meant what I said about not forcing you, Sam. I'd make love to you all night if you let me, but it is your decision, not mine."

She lifted her chin. "I decide no."

His eyes met hers in the mirror and one corner of his mouth quirked into a smile. "So you keep telling me."

"Then what are you going to do?"

"Pretend I'm a eunuch?"

"Be serious."

He released her then and leaned back on his elbows. "I'm going to stretch out right here on the bed and get a good night's sleep."

Samantha came to her feet, facing him. "I don't believe that is a good idea."

He made an impatient sound. "Why?"

"Because you'll want more than sleep. I know you too well."

"Oh, Samantha, you don't know me at all," he said, with genuine irritation. He buttoned his breeches before scooting over to his side of the bed and punching the feather pillow in place. "I stayed alone in your cottage for how long? Two or three days, and I didn't ravish you."

"But you were sick."

"Sam, I'm not a rutting stag. I can control my impulses. Now, come to bed."

He gave her his back. His body lay on top of the covers.

Samantha stood staring at him, willing him to leave.

He didn't move. Several seconds later, she heard his deep, steady breathing.

He'd gone to sleep!

Here she was, her body tingling with awareness, and he'd gone to sleep. In less time than it took for her to snap her fingers, no less!

She looked at herself in the cheval glass. She appeared completely ridiculous and she did feel a bit silly for all her posturing.

But she was tired. Her weariness returned with an incredible force. The bed had never looked so inviting.

She picked up the pillow that had fallen down

to the floor. She placed a knee up on the bed. Yale didn't stir.

She eased her other leg onto the bed and lay down, pulling the bedclothes on top of her. Yale slept on.

Slowly she began to relax. She could even laugh at herself a bit. She must have looked funny standing up in the bed the way she had. What was it about him that made her act in ways she had never thought herself capable of before?

She mulled over that thought as at last she gave in to the pull of sleep.

He rolled over in the bed and placed his hand on her breast and his lips over her mouth.

For a second, she thought she was dreaming. His hand caressed her breast and she stifled a soft moan of pleasure against his lips. Her mouth opened and he kissed her the way she liked.

It felt good. So very gooood—

Samantha came to her senses with a start. This was no dream. Yale was kissing her! And fondling her breast! And worse, she was liking it!

She sat up in bed. The firelight caught the flash of his straight, white teeth as he gave her a self-deprecating grin. "I guess I'm not a good eunuch."

Rage surged inside her. With a strength she didn't know she possessed, she rolled him bodily out of the bed. He hit the floor with a thump.

"Ouch," he said, but there wasn't a great deal of pain in his complaint. He hoisted himself up on one hand to see over the edge of the bed.

"Come, Sam, admit it. You liked it just a little, didn't you?"

"You are a *beast*," she said, reaching for a pillow and throwing it down on top of him.

"Ouch," he complained again.

"Here is the bedspread," she said, tossing it over the side of the bed. "I pray you suffocate in it."

On those words, she lay back down, and surprised herself by quickly falling asleep.

Yale was gone the next morning when Jenny woke her. The bedspread again covered the bed. The pillow he'd used was beside hers.

Heavy-lidded and still tired, Samantha suffered Jenny's best ministrations in silence. The maid did have a talent for hairdressing. She twisted Samantha's hair up into a knot. The extra height emphasized the line of Samantha's neck and made her eyes look larger.

She wondered what Yale would think before mentally chastising herself for giving more than a half penny's thought to him. "It's very nice, Jenny. I'm pleased."

"Thank you, my lady," she said with a curtsy. Samantha almost curtsied back, but caught herself in time. She didn't think she'd ever grow accustomed to being a "lady."

She went downstairs to the duke's private room. The inn was very quiet at this early hour.

She found the duke sitting down to breakfast.

He and Fenley were pleased to see her. Fenley pulled out a chair.

"I trust you slept well, Samantha," Ayleborough said.

She glanced at him, uncertain if he knew what had happened between her and his brother last night. "I did, Your Grace, thank you," she replied.

"I've told you, please call me Wayland. We are family now. Speaking of which, where is that errant brother of mine? Is he up and about, or still hugging his pillow? He was always so lazy. However, I want to be off within the hour."

Samantha thought many things of Yale, but she would never have called him lazy.

Fortunately, Fenley saved her from having to answer. "Lord Yale was up early this morning," he said. "He expected to be back before you were ready to go, Your Grace." He placed a plate of eggs and sausages before Samantha.

"He's not here?" Wayland said with annoyance. "Where the devil did he go at this hour? It's barely daylight."

Fenley answered, "He went to buy a horse."

"A horse?"

"Yes, Your Grace. He found the coach too confining and wished to ride today. He promised to be back before we left."

"Why didn't he hire one of the nags from the inn?"

"I don't know," Fenley replied judiciously,

and then surprised Samantha by giving her a conspirator's wink.

She wondered what Fenley would think if he knew that she had even less knowledge of Yale than the duke did.

"What the deuce kind of horse can he buy at dawn in Darlington?" Wayland wondered.

Both of them found out shortly. Just as they were ready to board the coach, Yale rode up on a spirited black stallion. He was hatless and the ends of his overcoat flapped behind him.

He grinned at them, his eyes sparkling with enjoyment. "He's a great one, isn't he?"

Even Samantha could tell this was a magnificent horse. Wayland stepped forward and ran his hand along the chest and up the neck.

"He is," he said with appreciation. "Where did you get him?"

"Bought him from the local squire up the road. I heard some of the men talking about him in the taproom last night."

"I daresay he cost you a pretty penny," Wayland hinted.

Yale shrugged. "He's worth the price. After all, they say it pays to wager on a dark horse."

His brother frowned. "Where is your hat?"

"I lost it when I put him through his paces on the road back there."

"A gentleman always wears a hat," Wayland said stubbornly.

Yale dismissed his words with a wave of his hand. "I'll buy one at the next town." Then, with a sly smile in Samantha's direction he said, "I'm naming him Beast. I hope you approve."

She caught the reference to the night before. "It's the perfect name for him," she replied curtly, and climbed into the coach. Wasn't it just like him to poke fun at everything?

Before the footman could close the door, Yale guided the horse up next to the coach. "I also brought you this, my lady." From inside his overcoat, he pulled out a single red rose.

Samantha was surprised to see the bloom in the dead of winter. "Where did you find it?" she asked, taking it from him. Already the edges were curling from the cold, and she wanted to protect it.

"The squire had a hothouse. Growing roses is one of his hobbies. It cost me almost as much as the horse." His gloved fingers closed over hers. "I hope you like it."

Their gazes met—and she read in his an earnest plea for forgiveness.

He leaned closer and spoke so that only the two of them could hear. "I shouldn't have teased you last night, Sam."

She nodded, not trusting her voice to speak. She didn't like him when he behaved in such a conciliatory manner. His behavior made it hard to keep the walls up between them.

She pulled back and Yale released her hand. The footman shut the door.

Wayland rapped on the wall and they were off.

Samantha slowly twirled the rose stem. She wished she could remove her gloves so that she could feel the velvety petals, but she would not do so in front of Wayland and Fenley. There was a danger of such a gesture being misinterpreted.

Wayland broke the silence. "I'm disappointed Yale decided to ride. I was hoping to have this time to talk with him."

Curious, Samantha asked, "About what?"

"I do not know if he told you, but we do not know each other very well. I am twelve years older. We rarely spoke when we were boys. I was always off at school while he was growing up. By the time he started school, I was out and gone."

Samantha glanced at Fenley, surprised Wayland would talk so freely in front of him.

The duke smiled. "Don't ever worry about saying anything in front of Fenley, Samantha. He can be the wisest counsel a person can have in times of indecision. I value his opinion tremendously. He knows all the Carderock family secrets and we'd trust him with our lives."

"Thank you, Your Grace," Fenley said, pleased at the compliment.

A certain familiarity having been established, Samantha approached a question that had bothered her from the beginning of the trip. "Why is it that you wish Yale to come to London—or myself, for that matter? I admit to a bit of nervousness. I really am nothing more than a country mouse. I would have been happy to stay back in Sproule."

Wayland shook his head. "Come, Samantha, there is no reason for you to be nervous. As a member of my household, it is only right that you be introduced properly in Society. Marion will see that you are presented at Court. She's very smart about all that."

"Presented at Court?" she repeated weakly.

"You will do fine in London, Samantha. You have my name to protect you. As to my reason for wanting both you and Yale close, well, you're family. Do you have much family?"

"No, I was an only child and have no living relatives."

"Well then, I imagine you realize how important family can be?"

"There have been times I've wished I'd had brothers and sisters."

"I'm a parent now, and I cannot imagine the pain of losing one of my sons. Father really did regret his actions. Learning of Yale's death made him age almost overnight. I want my brother back in the fold. Family is important. Almost more important than money or prestige. I will not let Yale leave again."

They could hear Yale outside the coach, laughing with one of the outriders.

"He always laughed that easily," Wayland said. "Always so devil-may-care, and without a hat, no less!"

He fell into silence then. Samantha took a

small nap. When she woke, the three of them passed the time playing cards. They did not talk about Yale again.

That night at the inn, Samantha wondered if her husband would join her as he had the night before. After being ignored by him all day, she perversely anticipated another encounter with him.

He did come, but it was after she was asleep, and he left before she woke. She knew he'd been there because she could smell his shaving soap in the air. Looking over the side of the bed, she spied a pillow and sheet on the floor.

They had no private moments between them except for right after breakfast when they met by chance in the hallway. "Yale?"

He stopped. "Yes?"

"Your brother would like to spend time with you. I hope our differences don't prevent you from pleasing him in this small way. He'd like for you to ride in the coach."

"Why would he wish to have me near?"

"Because he is the head of the family, and because you are important to him."

Yale snorted his opinion, but later that day, he did spend some time in the coach. He even answered without rancor the questions his older brother put to him about his business interests.

Samantha found it informative too. Yale was not only rich, but a very shrewd businessman—one who had still not bothered to purchase a hat, much to his brother's continued impatience.

That night, Samantha lay in bed wide awake, listening for Yale. He slipped in the door close to what she thought was midnight. He smelled of the rich aroma of tobacco. He must have been in the taproom.

She listened as he quickly undressed. He was reaching for the pillow when she said his name.

Yale gave a startled oath and stepped back. He was bare chested but wore his breeches. "Samantha?"

"Yes?"

"You scared a year off me. I didn't expect you to be awake." He threw the pillow on the floor. "Mind if I take the bedspread?"

"Please do." So, he wasn't planning another seduction attempt. She didn't know if she was pleased, or a bit piqued.

She waited until he was settled before saying, "Your brother appreciated the time you spent with him."

"Glad to make him happy," he answered, his voice ending in a yawn.

"He's older than you."

"Um-hm."

Samantha shifted restlessly. "He said you didn't know each other very well."

Yale's head popped up by the side of the bed. His brows came together in irritation. "What is this, Samantha? An interrogation about my family?"

"I am just curious," she said defensively.

"You are, hm?" He considered her a moment

and then sighed. "Actually, you might as well know about the lot of it, since you will be spending a great deal of time with them. Then you'll realize how absurd Wayland's protestations of a close family are."

He lay down, his hands cupping the back of his head. Samantha positioned her pillow close to the edge of the bed to hear better.

"The truth is, none of us are close," Yale began. "My mother was Father's second wife. He married her to give Wayland and my sister Twyla—you'll meet her in London, no doubt— a mother. But he also tweaked his own vanity a bit by marrying a much younger woman. My mother was the daughter of an improvised baronet but had enough looks to be the toast of the Season."

Having known the old duke, Samantha was not surprised. He'd always had an eye for the ladies.

"You favor her, don't you?" she asked.

"Yes, something that didn't work to my advantage. The marriage was a disaster. Father and Mother could not agree on anything. Wayland wasn't set against Mother, but Twyla hated her. She must have been about seven or eight at the time of the marriage. Worse, my mother was the sort of chit who never matured into a woman. Even I could see that. Someone always had to take care of her. Of course, she had servants— wait until you see the house in London. Even the servants have servants—but she demanded Father's constant attention and he got so he couldn't stand her silly prattle."

"But hadn't he fallen in love with her?"

"Love? What a queer notion." And then he paused. "Ah, yes, I forgot . . . you believe in love."

"Don't you?"

"I rarely believe in anything I can't touch, taste, or see."

She moved restlessly. "But what of feelings?"

"Feelings lie, Sam," he replied brutally. "Remember when you thought you loved me?"

She did . . . and she had to agree he was right.

Hugging the pillow closer, she said, "Finish your story."

"There isn't much else to say. Father hoped for more sons. Mother gave him one, and since he valued reason and intelligence, and she had none of that, she bored him. After I was born, he ignored her until she died of typhus when I was six. End of story."

But Samantha heard what he didn't say. "It was hard losing my mother last year. I can't imagine losing her when I was a child." By now, she was close enough to the edge of the bed to see over it.

He shrugged, studying the fire burning in the hearth. "I lost more than a parent. I was summarily shipped off to school. Father didn't want any memory of his marriage underfoot. Besides, I was never what he wanted me to be."

"And what was that?"

"What else? The image of Wayland. Wayland always did whatever Father asked of him and never questioned him once."

"Whereas you questioned him often?"

Yale grunted his response before adding, "Experience has finally taught me it is never wise to tweak the tiger's nose in his lair. Of course, now that I'm older, I understand Father better. He was right about many things, especially those concerning me."

He smiled up at Samantha. "He called me a dreamer. It was the worst thing a person could be, to his way of thinking. He always used to say dreamers are fools."

"But that's not true." Samantha came up on one elbow, tossing her hair over her shoulder. "I envy the dreamers. They are the people who can imagine things and see the world as a better place. My father was a dreamer. I've always been the sort who does the right thing. No matter how hard I try, I can't be anything but practical."

"People can change, Sam. It's hard, but it can be done. After all, look at me. I'm a right bloody pragmatist."

"And you no longer dream?"

"Not that I would admit it."

"Was it hard, being on your own?" she asked.

" 'Lonely' is a better word. When Father printed the disinheritance letter in the papers, all my friends vanished. My landlord turned me out. Even my mistress gave me the boot."

Samantha ran her finger along the edge of the

mattress. "That's how I felt when the people of Sproule wanted me out of the vicarage. I'm still angry at how they treated me. How did you cope?"

"I got drunk and signed up on a merchantman headed for the China Sea. Something I don't recommend you do."

She smiled. "I can't see me working before the mast, either."

"Nor could I back then. When I sobered and realized what I had done, I tried to leave the ship and got a sound beating for my endeavor."

At Samantha's sympathetic gasp, he shook his head. "It was the best thing that could have happened to me. I was an idealist who didn't understand how the world worked. That night, as I was nursing my wounds, I vowed I would prove everyone wrong about me. I would make my own way in the world, and so I have."

Yawning, he rubbed his face with his hand, but she felt wide awake, mulling over his words in her mind.

She rested her chin on her hand. "Why did come back to England?"

"What do you mean?"

"Why now? Why did you return now?"

For a moment, she didn't think he was going to answer her, but then he said, "To show my father I was a worthy son." His lips curved into a smile. "I was going to sail my ship up the Thames and invite him on board. I wanted him to see me as a wealthy man and know he was wrong about me. But it was all for naught," he added softly. "None of it matters, now that Father is dead."

Samantha reached out and touched his arm. His skin felt warm and smooth. "He was proud of you," she whispered. "He deeply mourned your death and often came to the vicarage and talk to my father about you. I overheard them."

Yale stared at the ceiling. For a second, she thought she saw tears well in his dark eyes. Then he said, "Go to sleep, Sam. Tomorrow we'll drive until we reach London. It will be a long day."

But Samantha didn't want to go to sleep. She'd liked sharing confidences with him. She sighed.

"What is it, Sam?" came his low, irritated voice.

"How did you know I was still awake?"

"Your squirming is about ready to drive me to madness." Again he yawned, only this time, she echoed it. "Why aren't *you* sleeping?" he asked.

"I can't stop thinking."

He gave her a slow, knowing grin. "I know of one way to take your mind off your worries."

She pulled the bed clothes up around her chin. "You can stay on the floor."

He laughed. "Tell me what you were worrying about."

She wasn't about to tell him she just liked talking with him. He would think her silly.

"Is it London?" he asked.

His suggestion sounded plausible. "Yes," she answered. "I've never even been as far as Morpeth. I can't imagine what it is like."

"Then let me tell you about it. Or at least as I remember it."

He began speaking, his deep voice low and soft. He started off talking about the streets, especially the ones leading to Penhurst, the duke of Ayleborough's city residence. He took her through the front door and showed her the marble foyer and the heavy chandelier that held a thousand candles. He talked of the last ball he'd attended there, one given in honor of his brother and Marion, shortly after they were married.

She smiled. "You make it sound lovely. I wonder that you ever left it all."

"Ah, but then, you don't know the wild beauty of Ceylon."

"Tell me," she said.

She was the first person since he'd set foot on British soil who had asked about his other life.

"It's an enchanted place," he started. "Older than Britain itself, and yet so backward it's frustrating." He described to her the rock fortress of Sigiriya with its great carved lion's feet guarding the entrance.

"The lion's feet are taller than two men, one standing on the shoulders of the other."

"Who would build such a thing?"

"I don't know the complete history," he said. "But Ceylon is an ancient country full of mysteries."

He contrasted the fortress with a story of his swimming in a pool surrounded by a tropical forest and fed by spectacular waterfalls. ''There are three of them,'' he said. ''One larger than the other.''

''It sounds lovely,'' she whispered.

''It is.''

''And it is warm enough to swim all the time?''

''Year round.''

Slowly, her lids grew heavy, lulled by the sound of his voice.

Yale watched her eyes close and knew when she'd fallen asleep.

Funny, but he'd never really spent time just talking to a woman before. Women had had only one place in his life, but now his vicar's daughter was changing all that. Whether he liked it or not, he valued her opinion.

The first day of their travels, he had been almost insane with jealousy over her preference of Wayland's company over his own. That was the reason he'd bought that damn horse, to show both of them that he did have wealth, that he was a man of substance—and to exert his independence.

The problem was, he had no use for a horse. Any more than he had use for a wife.

Unfortunately, he was growing attached to both.

He reached up and lightly touched her relaxed and curled fingers. They flexed at his touch and he wondered if she attracted him because she challenged him. Or was she a challenge because of his attraction for her?

Yale lay back down, bunching the pillow under his head, uncertain if he wanted to know the answer.

Chapter 11

Samantha woke the next morning with her face snuggled in the feather pillow Yale had used the night before. She drew a deep breath. All too well she recognized his scent. Masculine. Distinct. Unmistakable.

He was already up and gone. It had been his closing of the door that had awakened her. The bedcover was also back on the bed.

She lay there, imagining him tucking the cover around her.

A sharp knock sounded at the door. Langston, the maid assigned to her the night before, entered without waiting for admittance.

"It's time to be up and about, my lady," Langston prodded with authority. "His Grace wishes to leave at first light. He is most anxious to arrive in London."

Samantha nodded and put her feet over the side of the bed. *My lady.* She didn't know if she'd ever become accustomed to the form of address.

She felt like a fraud. Not really a wife; not really a lady.

Or perhaps her husband's stubborn pride on being a plain commoner was rubbing off on her.

Langston sniffed as she took Samantha's black dress from its peg in the wardrobe. She didn't say anything, but Samantha knew heavy black cotton wasn't what a lady of means wore. Samantha had sewn it herself last year, right before her mother's funeral. Even to her unsophisticated eye the dress was hopelessly dowdy.

She was tempted to wear her wedding dress, but common sense warned her she would freeze in it.

"When you arrive in London," Langston said, as she brushed out the dress, "you will wish to petition the duchess for a new wardrobe. Her Grace travels in the best circles. Go to a seamstress on Oxford Street, Madame Meilleur. You may use my name."

Samantha's stomach tightened. If the servants were this haughty, what would a duchess be like? She wished she had the pleasant Jenny with her instead of Langston, who was so very aware of all of Samantha's shortcomings.

"And there is another issue, my lady," Langston said, while helping Samantha on with her dress. "You come from the north, and sometimes women have an unfortunate accent. It will make you a laughingstock of polite society, who do not admire the Scots or the northern accent."

She smiled as Samantha shook her skirts down

around her ankles. "I say this only for your benefit. Do you wish me to style your hair in the latest fashion, my lady?"

"Um, yes, please," Samantha mumbled, suddenly self-conscious of her speech. She sat down in front of the vanity.

Langston deftly divided Samantha's hair with a comb and wound it into two big buns, one over each ear. She began pinning it in place.

Samantha stared at herself in the mirror, horrified by the style. "Wait, please, I don't know what I think about this."

"It's the latest fashion, my lady," Langston replied. She pushed the last pin in place. "You don't want to be *out* of fashion, do you?"

Samantha met the maid's challenging gaze in the mirror. "But doesn't it look a bit silly?" she suggested timidly. She reminded herself of nothing less than a woolly ram.

"You do not like the latest fashion?" Langston asked with patent disbelief. "I think you look more sophisticated."

Samantha didn't know what to do. She stared at her reflection. "Well, perhaps once I become accustomed to it . . . and it is the fashion?" She looked to Langston for confirmation.

"I am certain the duchess of Ayleborough wears her hair in this style," Langston said.

Samantha had met the duchess only one time, at the old duke's funeral. The duchess had said a few words to her and her father. Unfortunately, she'd been swathed in a dark black veil

of mourning and Samantha didn't have any idea
what her face looked like, let alone her hair. But
she was all the villagers had talked about for
days.

Samantha wanted to make a good impression
on her new sister-in-law in spite of her home-
made clothes. She tilted her head. Actually, the
style wasn't *that* bad. "Thank you, Langston. I
appreciate your guidance."

"Perhaps, my lady, you will recommend me
to the duke. I am presently in search of good
position."

Samantha stared at the proud lady's maid and
felt a touch of panic—until she noticed how
Langston's gaze didn't quite meet her own, and
the stiffness in Langston's shoulders. Here was
another woman alone. Samantha immediately
recognized the fears. But the thought of Langston being assigned to her permanently was intimidating. Yet she couldn't turn her back on a
soul in need. "Ah, perhaps."

Apparently that was all Langston had expected her to say. The tension in her shoulders
eased and she bossily ordered Samantha to
hurry to meet the duke.

Samantha gathered her cape and bonnet,
thankful to escape the woman's presence.

When Langston said, "I will escort my lady to
the breakfast parlor," Samantha assured her she
could find her way, feeling a need to separate
herself from the maid's self-seeking service. She

slipped out the door before Langston could comment.

She had to walk carefully down the hall to the stairs because her hair was so heavy the pins felt as if they would fall out at any moment. Fortunately, the inn was quiet at this hour of the morning. In fact, it was so quiet that as she came down off the last step, she could hear arguing coming from the duke's private room where they'd eaten a hasty dinner the night before.

Wayland was shouting, "You have responsibilities here in England! You have no right to even talk about dashing off and leaving it all to me!"

She paused outside the door, her hand on the handle.

"I was disinherited," Yale answered. His voice lacked the heat of his brother's. "I have no life here. My home, my work, everything is in Ceylon."

"Perhaps at one time. But now you are back."

"Wayland, I don't *want* to stay in England."

"Then why the bloody hell did you come back, if you didn't plan to stay?"

"I returned to see Father. But I'm leaving, Wayland. I have my own money, my own life. I make no claim on the title for my living. My share was spent years ago getting me out of debt."

"You are a damn stubborn fool!"

"Well, on that point, we may agree," Yale said pleasantly. Samantha didn't realize how close he was to the door until he pulled it open. She still held the door handle and stumbled into the room, catching herself before she landed sprawled on the floor.

Her cheeks flamed with embarrassment to have been caught so ignobly eavesdropping.

"Good morning, Sam," Yale said, as if he hadn't just dragged her into the room. "Styled your hair differently. I don't like it. You look ridiculous."

Her earlier good humor with him vanished. She held her head high. "It is all the fashion in London."

"Ah, yes." He paused and slid a glance at his brother. "I was never one to follow fashion. I'm going to see to Beast. I'll wait for the two of you outside."

Without another word he left.

Standing in the middle of the room, Wayland stared after him, hands on hips, his mouth set in disgust. Samantha wanted to say she hadn't really been eavesdropping . . . but that would have sounded stupid, so she remained quiet.

Fenley shut the door, taking her hat and cape from her. "Would you care for grilled sausages and eggs, my lady?"

"Yes, please," she said quickly, and took a seat at the table.

Wayland didn't speak, but threw himself down in the chair opposite hers. Lost in thought, he stared at the pattern in the carpet.

Fenley set the plate in front of her and Samantha busied herself with her breakfast. She sliced off a piece of sausage and was just about to put it in her mouth when Wayland blurted out, "He is being ridiculous, you know."

Samantha shot a glance at Fenley, who told her with a raise of his eyebrows that he didn't know what to expect, either.

"No matter what he thinks he has built for himself," Wayland continued, "I'm offering him a great deal more. After all, we are his family." He looked to Samantha for confirmation.

Realizing he expected an answer, she murmured, "Yes, that's true."

Wayland came to his feet and started pacing the perimeter of the room. "It's not like I'm asking too much. He has an obligation to help carry the family responsibilities. But does he realize that? No! He insists on living his own life. Taking off whenever he wishes and leaving me with the majority of the burden."

Samantha chewed the sausage slowly, uncomfortable with the topic.

Wayland looked at her. "Being a duke isn't that much fun," he said candidly. "I could use help, especially from someone who knows what he is doing, like my brother. Imagine, Yale is the owner of Rogue Shipping. He may have botched his boyhood Latin lessons, but he possesses the keen sort of business savvy we need in this family."

She swallowed the sausage. "What of your sister? Isn't she married? Can't her husband help?"

"That twit!" He immediately regretted the words. "Don't tell her I said that. She thinks the world of him, but I don't trust him. His eyes are too small. Besides, Samantha, it has to do with blood. Yale can't turn his back on me. We're blood. Can you understand that?"

"It's not a question of what I understand, Your Grace, but of what Yale believes."

"Yes," Wayland agreed. "But what I fear most is that once he leaves a second time, he will never return." He lapsed into a glum silence, his hands behind his back.

Samantha's appetite left her. She set the fork down on her plate.

It would have been easier to accept the inevitable if she and Yale had not talked last night. Part of her wanted still to think of him as a scoundrel.

The other part of her had carefully packed the hothouse rose in tissue paper.

The duke's voice interrupted her thoughts. "Samantha, you and my brother do get along reasonably well, don't you?"

She looked up at him, suddenly wary. She was conscious that Fenley's ears, too, had perked up. "Do you mean, in spite of his misrepresenting himself when we married and his planning on leaving me?"

"Oh, that," Wayland said dismissively. "Yes, well, the two of you may not have gotten off to the best start, but things are *close* between you, aren't they?"

Samantha sat back. "I'm not certain what you mean."

Wayland sat in the chair across from her. He leaned across the table, pressing the palms of his hands together. "Close. You've been close, haven't you?"

Samantha felt the blood rush to her cheeks. She cleared her throat. "We get along." She wasn't going to confess more than that.

Wayland lifted a skeptical eyebrow. "Oh, come, Samantha, you do a bit more than just 'get along.'"

"I do not know what you mean," she said, attempting to be obtuse.

"Squire Biggers said the two of you literally shook the floorboards."

Samantha's mouth dropped open. She was astounded the duke would say such a thing. She glanced over her shoulder at Fenley, who seemed inordinately interested in a speck on one of the silver dishes. "It wasn't quite like that," she hedged.

"They could hear the two of you."

"Hear what?" she asked, almost frightened of the answer.

"Apparently, either you or Yale were quite loud in your enjoyment." Wayland shrugged. "It happens."

The walls of the room seemed to close in on Samantha. She moved her mouth, but no words came out.

Wayland reached across the table and took her

hands. "Here now, I've embarrassed you, and that was not my intent. I merely wish to speak frankly because I am going to approach a delicate subject."

"I don't know if I can take much more frankness, Your Grace," Samantha replied honestly.

He looked over at Fenley and signaled with his eyes for the servant to leave the room. Once the door had closed behind him, Wayland asked, "Have you and my brother—" He paused as if considering his words, "made love on this trip? You *do* understand what I'm asking now, don't you?"

The breath left Samantha with a soft *whoosh.* She should have pulled her hand away, but he held it fast.

"I—I don't think I shall answer that."

One corner of Wayland's mouth turned down. "You haven't. *Damn*, that's what I suspected."

"And why did you suspect that?" she asked with genuine surprise.

"There is an energy about my brother, a restlessness, that's made me wonder if he was, ah, fulfilled or not."

Samantha didn't need an explanation of what "fulfilled" meant. Did all men have nothing but one thing on their minds?

Releasing her hand, Wayland sat back in his chair. "I was newly married once. I well remember the intense desire of new lovers. I offered Yale the privacy of the coach yesterday, but he turned it down."

"The privacy of the coach?"

"Yes. You haven't made love until you've done it in a well-sprung coach." He smiled at the memory.

Samantha's senses reeled at his bold words. She came up out of the chair. "Perhaps you shouldn't be so frank."

Wayland also rose to his feet. "Oh, wait, I've put your back up, and that wasn't what I meant to do. I forget how sheltered your life has been."

"Being sheltered has nothing to do with it! You may be the head of the family, Your Grace, but I don't believe what happens between Yale and myself is your business."

He gave her a quizzical smile. "When you talk in such a manner, you sound exactly as high-handed and independent as my stubborn brother."

Samantha changed the subject. "Isn't it time we left?" She moved for her cape and bonnet hanging on a peg by the door, but he stepped into her path.

"It is time—but first I have a favor to ask of you, Samantha, and it is so important, the horses can wait a moment longer."

"What is it?" she asked, fearing his answer.

"Sit down, please," he begged her, and refused to say another word until she had honored his request.

He knelt down beside her chair. "If anyone has any influence over Yale, it is you."

She almost laughed out loud. "He wishes to

leave me behind as much as he is determined to leave you, Your Grace."

"But you can change all that." He took her hand in his. "You see, I think Yale would like to be *close* with you."

"Yale would like to be close with anything in skirts," she countered tartly.

"Don't deceive yourself, Samantha. He is far more discriminating than that. Always has been."

"Yes? Well then, why was he disinherited?"

Now it was Wayland's turn to look ill at ease. "That is another story for another day, my dear."

Samantha tilted her head, studying him a moment. "I'd always heard there were women involved."

"Yes, but what do you care if he chased a brigade of them? All that happened years ago. Besides, Father didn't disinherit Yale for his interest in the fairer sex. He would have disinherited me if that had been the case. No, Father was upset with the money Yale squandered. But my brother has mended his ways. He couldn't have built his own shipping company if he hadn't."

She digested this a moment, having to shift her picture of her brother-in-law. She had trouble seeing Wayland as a ladies' man.

"I know you and Yale are not a love match, but I don't share your opinion that he is indifferent to you."

Now he had Samantha's complete attention. "Why do you say that?"

"Because I've seen him watch you, Samantha. I'm a man. I know what he's thinking. He wouldn't be making this trip to London if it weren't for you."

"But I can't influence him to stay. He told me the morning after our wedding that he was going to leave. He has not changed his mind."

"But he has not left yet," Wayland said pointedly. He lowered his voice. "I believe that if you tried, Samantha, you could convince him to stay."

She looked down at her lap. She was pressing pleats into her skirt with her fingers. "I don't know."

Wayland's arm came around her chair. "I admit, it wasn't a good trick that he played, marrying you under a false name and all that. But he does have a plausible explanation. And you must understand *my* position. I wish to keep my family intact. I've already spent years without my brother, and I refuse to spend more. I need him. The estate needs him."

Still holding her hand, he traced the back of it with his thumb before saying, "I'm going to ask a favor of you, and I fear, knowing what I do of your character, it will be a difficult request. But for the good of the family, I'm going to ask it anyway."

She held her breath.

"I want you to get my brother to fall in love with you."

Samantha almost fell out of the chair. "Have you gone mad?" she managed to sputter. "Yale is the last man I could imagine being led around by his nose."

"Oh, no," Wayland differed with a superior laugh. "We can all be easily led with the right enticement. And unless I miss my guess, my brother is enamored of you. You seem to have aroused in him a sense of chivalry. It would not take much more than a little warmth on your part to make him listen to reason."

"Warmth?"

Wayland's steady gaze met hers. "You know, make the floorboards shake."

Samantha came to her feet before he could stop her. She marched halfway across the room. "Do you realize what you are asking?"

"Nothing more than what you have already given," he responded plainly. "In fact, I believe the Church considers it your duty."

She faced Wayland. "I can't. It's about principle and values. From listening to you speak about your wife, I thought you understood those things."

Wayland came to his feet. "I do, I do . . . but this is about family. Yale is a far cry from the wayward youth he was at nineteen. He's a man to be respected. I want him to stay in England. He doesn't need Rogue Shipping or anything else. Not really. However, the Ayleborough estates and all the business, enterprises, and responsibilities that go with them are vast. Yale can help me ensure the family's future for generations to come. My sons need him. *Your* children need him. I will do anything to keep him from leaving England."

Samantha placed the flat of her hand against her stomach. Children. She could already be carrying Yale's child. What would she say to that child when he grew old enough to ask where his father was? Wayland had a valid point. The Carderock name would be part of her child's birthright.

And yet she had her pride. Her principles.

"What I understand, Your Grace," she said, her voice shaking slightly with emotion, "is that you want me to compromise myself on the altar of your wishes. Your request makes a mockery of the sacrament of marriage. Yale did not mean the vows he took with me. His intention has always been to leave me. I will not beg him to stay. Or seduce him."

The duke's lips pressed into a thin line. He seemed to weigh what she had to say and then walked over to her. "Samantha, your highstrung sense of honor is, however admirable, a bit of an irritant. I am not accustomed to being refused when I make what I consider a reasonable request. I'm opening my home to you. I've embraced you as a sister. Your refusal to help my family in return is—" He paused as if to consider the right word. "Distressing."

Samantha felt as if her heart had stopped beating. "I must be true to myself."

"Nonsense. Everyone is asked at one time or another to make a sacrifice for the good of the whole."

"And what if I discover I cannot honor your request?" she asked faintly.

"Why would you want to refuse me?" Wayland countered politely, but Samantha could sense a chasm growing between them.

He said, "My role in this family is to keep it together. That has been the duke of Alyeborough's role for succeeding generations. My father was a shrewd man. His wise investments built the family coffers to what they are today, but once Yale left, he considered himself a failure. If my brother leaves a second time, I will consider myself a failure, too. Can you understand that, Samantha?"

She nodded, not trusting her voice.

"Family is important, Samantha. It is the only reason any of us is here. Without it, life would be a cold, lonely existence." He turned and left the room, closing the door behind him.

Samantha stood rooted to the floor. Life was lonely without family. After the past year, she knew that all too well.

Of course, Yale had offered to buy her a house of her own. She was not without resources. She did not have to sacrifice her principles.

Then she thought of Yale's description last night of Penhurst, the duke's London residence.

She thought about the possibility that she could be with child . . . and did not want the child ostracized by its uncle, the great duke of Ayleborough.

Or that she would be alone. Again.

His words had been couched as a request, but there had been a ducal command behind it. He was not a man to be crossed.

Slowly she raised her hands and began pulling the pins out of her hair. It tumbled down around her shoulders. Without the aid of a mirror, she plaited it into a single braid . . . and felt a bit more like herself—plain Samantha Northrup, the vicar's unwanted daughter.

She pulled her gloves on and then, picking up her cape and worn bonnet, left the room.

Outside the horses were stamping impatiently. Yale waited astride the Beast. His and the animal's breath came out in small puffs of frigid air. Fenley stepped forward and helped her don her cape.

"Sam, I was beginning to fear you were not coming!" Yale greeted her. The duke was already inside the coach.

She took a moment to tie the ribbon of her bonnet. "Of course I was coming. Where else do I have to go?" If she thought he wouldn't notice the slight sarcasm in her voice, she was mistaken.

With a kick of his heels, Yale urged Beast close to her. He jumped down. "You and Wayland took your time coming out." He touched her cheek with the back of his fingers. "Is anything the matter?"

For a moment, she was tempted to tell him . . . but what purpose would that serve, except to set Yale against his brother? "I had to change my hair."

He smiled at her and lightly touched her braid. "I like your hair down. This is how I saw you when I first woke from my illness. If I had my way, you'd wear it thus all the time."

His thumb stroked her neck before he pulled his hand back. Where he'd touched her, her skin tingled.

"Come along!" Wayland shouted from the coach window. "I want to make London before midnight. You're wasting time."

"Don't mind him. He is a surly brute in the morning," Yale whispered, in a voice loud enough for Wayland to hear.

The duke grunted and closed the window with a snap. Yale opened the door and helped her inside.

She paused on the step. "You won't be riding with us?" she asked, aware that Wayland was listening.

Yale studied her a moment. She wished she could read his mind. When he spoke, his voice was light, "No, I'm enjoying the cold wind. It helps me keep my perspective."

She wanted to ask him what he meant but lacked the courage. Instead, she took her seat. Fenley followed her into the coach and Yale signaled the coachmen it was time to leave.

The atmosphere inside the coach was far from the congenial camaraderie of the previous days. She gave her back to Wayland and huddled in her corner, lost in thought. For a moment, she wished she was a man and didn't have to be dependent upon others for every morsel she ate, every thread of clothing she wore, everything she touched.

Her father had always told her that her one sin was her pride—and it was hurting very much indeed. She was a wife, and under the law she was not even considered a person in her own right, but her husband's property. And her husband didn't want her—except for one thing.

For a moment she entertained the notion that Yale might have put his brother up to his request. But she dismissed it. The argument she had overheard earlier had been too bitter to have been staged.

Worse, part of her missed the intimacies she'd shared with Yale. If she closed her eyes, she could almost remember the feel of his strong body joined with hers. The rock and sway of the coach, combined with Wayland's earlier salacious observation, served to heighten lustful memories that would be better forgotten.

Her doubts and worries circled each other with every turn of the coach wheels. At last she took refuge from her misgivings and fears in sleep.

They made few stops. The closer they rode to

London, the more anxious Wayland was to be reunited with his family.

He did insist, upon spying a hat shop in one of the villages they passed through, that Fenley get out of the coach immediately and buy Yale a decent hat. "We can't have him riding into London hatless."

Fenley hurried to obey his command. Yale rolled his eyes heavenward and led Beast to a drink of water.

"You should go with Fenley and try on the hat," Wayland prodded.

Yale ignored him.

When Fenley returned, he carried a very handsome curled-brim beaver. Yale had already remounted. He reached for the hat, thanked his brother profusely for the gift, and then slapped it on his head so hard it almost came down over his eyebrows. He proceeded to ride out of the village that way.

"He thinks he is a damn clown," Wayland muttered under his breath. He knocked on the side of the coach and they were off.

It wasn't until after dark that the coachman announced he could see the lights of London.

Heedless of the cold, damp air, Samantha pulled down the window and craned her neck, hoping for her first glimpse of the metropolis. The coach rolled to a stop on a small rise and there, in the distance, she saw hundreds, thousands of tiny lights. The air smelled of chimney smoke.

Yale reined Beast in beside her. He wore the infamous hat the right way now, but with a rakish tilt to it. He looked very handsome.

"There it is, Sam," he said in a low voice. "London, the center of the civilized world." The planes of his face were golden in the light of the coach lamps. He looked very serious . . . and very handsome.

"You have nothing to fear," he promised her, misreading her silence. "Be your own courageous self and London will be at your feet."

"I want to believe that," she whispered.

"If it is in my power, I shall make it so."

For a moment his gaze lingered on her lips, and she thought, he could kiss me now and I would let him.

But when he leaned forward slightly, she pulled back, conscious that they had an audience.

If Yale noticed or if a kiss had been his intent, he didn't say, but put his heels to his horse and rode on ahead.

The coach followed him.

Samantha pulled her head back into darkness and raised the window.

"Do you still wish to pretend he has no feelings for you?" Wayland's voice asked behind her.

Samantha didn't answer.

"I only ask that you try, Samantha—nothing more. As a favor to the family."

Did a person ever refuse a duke anything? she wondered bitterly, as the coach drove her closer and closer to London and a new life.

Chapter 12

Travel weariness left Samantha the moment she set foot into the stone and marble foyer of Penhurst, the city residence of the duke of Ayleborough.

It was exactly as Yale had described it and much more. The chandelier hanging in the middle of the room was large enough to hold a thousand candles, although none of them were lit. Instead, the burning candles from no fewer than twenty wall sconces played against its crystal prisms.

Gold scrolling across the ceiling framed a classic scene. She gawked like the country girl she was at the chubby satyrs who chased long-haired nymphs through an imaginary forest. The colors were vivid—the forest greener than anything real, the nymphs' lips red and inviting, their naked breasts in full display.

"My great-grandfather had a sense of humor," Yale commented dryly in her ear.

She felt the heat of a blush burn her cheeks.

"I've never seen anything like it. You didn't tell me about *that*."

"He spent almost more than the cost of the rest of the house on the ceilings. Mother hated them, especially this one, and would cheerfully have painted over them if Father had let her. But no man in his right mind would paint over such buxom beauty. Not even Father."

He spoke without thought, and his obvious masculine appreciation only heightened her uncomfortable awareness of him as a man. A handsome man.

A man who'd taught her the meaning of pleasure in bed.

"Welcome home, Your Grace, Mr. Fenley," said a man who could, by his formal attire and dictatorial manner, only be the butler. Yale had been correct about even the servants appearing as if they had servants. No less than a score of footmen and maids swarmed around them, carrying in luggage, taking their coats.

"Good to be home, Timothy," Wayland said. "I've brought guests with me. Please see to their things."

"Yes, Your Grace."

There came a shout. "Papa!"

A young boy of six or so ran down the carpeted steps that curved down into the foyer. He paused on the last three steps only long enough to launch himself at Wayland, who caught the child in his arms.

"John, my boy," Wayland said, and unashamedly gave the child a huge hug.

"We are glad you have returned," a woman said from the stairs, and they all looked up to see Marion, the duchess of Ayleborough, standing on the landing. She was a tall, regal woman with blond hair and intelligent blue eyes. Beside her stood another boy of about nine years of age. Samantha recognized him. He was Matthew, the marquess of Danforth, Wayland's oldest son and heir.

Wayland bounded up the stairs two at a time to reach his wife. "I'm glad to be home also." He kissed her hand. It was a formal gesture, but his lips lingered. A silent communication passed between husband and wife, and Samantha felt a stab of jealousy.

She slid a look in Yale's direction. He wasn't even paying attention to the tender moment. Instead, he watched Matthew and John with a bemused expression.

Wayland set John on his feet beside his brother and now young John aped Matthew's serious demeanor. Matthew put him in his place with an elbow in the ribs. John jostled back, waiting impatiently for his father's attention.

Samantha wondered what Yale was thinking.

Wayland tore his gaze away from his wife and bowed to his oldest son. "Matthew."

The boy bowed back, accepting his father's hand. "Father." For all his solemnity, he couldn't resist a triumphant look at his younger brother.

John's lower lip turned down into a pout.

"Have you been taking care of your mother and brothers while I have been away?" Wayland asked.

"Yes, Father, I have," the child answered.

"Good, then. I am proud of you." Wayland placed a hand on Matthew's head and embraced him. The boy grinned unself-consciously.

John tugged on his father's coat.

"Did you bring any treats, Father?"

"Ah, not now," Wayland chastised him. "Not until I've had a chance to sit down. You know the rule." He turned to his wife. "How is our Charles?"

"Cranky," Marion said. "He's cutting a tooth. Nurse is worn thin from being up with him all night, and he didn't nap today, either. We just got him down and she warned me that you are not to wake him up."

"And I won't," he promised. "But first, I have a surprise for you." Taking her by the shoulders, he directed her down the stairs to Samantha and Yale. "Now, be ready. This will be quite a shock." He stopped her in front of Yale. "Here."

Marion smiled at both Yale and Samantha. "You've brought guests. That's very nice. Welcome to Penhurst. I'll have Mrs. Witchell prepare rooms for you."

"No, Marion, look closely," her husband said. "They are not just any guests. Do you not recognize them?"

She stared and then blushed. "Miss North-rup . . . from Sproule, no?"

Samantha curtsied. "Yes, Your Grace, although I am surprised that you remembered."

Marion held out her hand. "This is an unexpected pleasure. I hope you enjoy your stay with us."

"Thank you, Your Grace."

"Yes, yes, yes," Wayland said impatiently. "But she is not my surprise. Look closer at *him*."

The two boys had come down the stairs, too, and they now stood beside their mother, staring up at Yale.

Marion shook her head. "I'm sorry, sir. You seem familiar but I can't place you. Have we met before?"

"It's my brother Yale," Wayland whispered in her ear.

"Yale!" Marion almost collapsed. She stared in confusion at Yale and then rounded on her husband. "How can it be? We were told . . . we thought . . . I don't know—"

"It's him," Wayland confirmed.

Marion turned back to Yale and took a step toward him. Her hands came up to touch his shoulders, the side of his face. It was a motherly gesture, kind, reassuring. "You live."

Yale took her hand and kissed it. "Yes, alive and well."

Tears formed in her eyes, and Marion threw her arms around him. "We've missed you so much. Twice we've mourned for you. Once when you'd left, then the other when we'd heard you were killed in that storm. I can't believe you are back with us."

"I knew it would be a grand surprise," Wayland said with satisfaction. "I could have sent a message, but I wanted to deliver the news to you myself. I wanted to see the expression on your face."

Marion swiped at tears rolling down her cheeks. "I should give you a severe tongue-lashing for springing him on me this way," she told her husband, and then held out her hands for her sons. "Come, Matthew, John, meet your uncle."

The boys took a cautious step forward. Their expressions were so serious, Samantha wanted to hug each of them.

Even the servants had stopped to watch the unfolding drama. Several maids dried their eyes on their aprons.

Matthew held out his hand just as he had with his father. Yale took it. The corners of his mouth twitched, but he hid his smile before making his bow.

"It is good to meet you, sir," Matthew said.

"And I you, my lord marquess," Yale said. "In fact, it is very good."

Then John, mimicking his brother, also offered his hand. "We are glad you are not dead," he said with a child's open honesty, and Yale laughed.

"I am glad, too," he admitted. "But Wayland and I have another surprise."

"I do not think I could stand another one like that last one," Marion said. She was still crying and tried to dry her cheeks by pressing the back of her hand to her face.

"But this one is a happy one," Yale promised. He pulled Samantha forward. "Miss Northrup is my wife."

"*You* are married?" Marion blurted out before she could stop herself. Her face turned red with color. "I am so sorry for that way that sounded, Miss Northrup—"

"Samantha," Wayland corrected.

"Yes, Samantha," his wife amended warmly. "I never expected to see Yale again, let alone to see him married. But this is a blessing." She embraced Samantha, whispering, "Welcome to the family."

Family.

The word brought tears to Samantha's eyes. Reading her thoughts, Wayland's gaze met hers . . . and she understood what he felt was at stake—

He did not want Yale to leave again.

And he expected her to see that Yale didn't.

"Come," Marion said, hooking her arm with Samantha's. "I have sandwiches and wine waiting for you. Wayland is always hungry when he returns from travels, aren't you, darling?"

"I thought I'd take the boys back up to the nursery and check on Charles," her husband said. "I'll catch up with the three of you."

"Do not wake the baby," she said sternly.

"I won't," he promised, heading up the stairs with his sons. "Here, who wants a piggyback ride?"

"I do!" John said immediately.

"I'm too old for that stuff," Matthew sniffed.

"Your loss, then," his father replied, and bent down for John to hop from a higher step onto his back. He glanced at Matthew. "John and I'll race you to the nursery."

Obviously Matthew wasn't too old to race, for without another word, he went tearing up the steps. John and Wayland charged after him.

Yale stared after them, his eyebrows raised. "Was that my brother who just pretended to be a horse?"

Marion laughed. "He dotes on his sons. He visits them every day for no other reason than to play. I keep telling him that Matthew is old enough to be sent to Eton, but Wayland insists on keeping him one more year at home."

"How different from Father."

Marion nodded. "We both wanted our children raised with more affection than what our parents had given us. Of course, most of our friends think we spend too much time with the boys . . . but they grow so fast. I shall miss them when they are on their own."

She turned her attention to the housekeeper, giving her instructions on which rooms to ready for the guests. "Samantha, did you bring a maid?"

"No, she didn't," Yale said smoothly. "And I have no valet."

"That poses no problem," Marion answered. "Mrs. Witchell will assign a member of the staff to each of you." She then led them into a richly appointed sitting room off the main hall.

This was more luxurious than the foyer. Fine portraits hung on walls covered with green Genoese cut velvet. On the ceiling, half-dressed young girls were swinging while handsome men knelt at their feet.

A maid brought in a plate of small sandwiches and offered it to Samantha. She accepted it gratefully. Wayland had refused to stop longer than to change the horses on their trip that day.

"I can't stop looking at you, Yale," Marion said. "You left here a boy and have returned a man."

"I thought I was grown up when I left."

"So you did," she agreed, a sad note in her voice. "It is good to see you again. Now tell me, where have you been?" She offered Yale a glass of wine. "And how did you meet Samantha?"

"I've been in the Orient and met Samantha in Sproule, where she saved my life," he answered dutifully.

Marion's eyes widened. "Tell me everything," she demanded.

"I went to Sproule and came down with influenza. My blood has apparently grown too thin from living all these years in a tropical climate. The English cold just about killed me."

Marion, sitting gracefully on an upholstered couch, indicated for Samantha to do the same before asking, "You nursed him?"

Sitting on the very edge of the couch, Samantha cleared her throat, still uneasy to find herself accepted and moving among people who had for years been like storybook characters to her. "Yes, Your Grace, I did."

"I remember what a fine job you did with the old duke. And please address me as 'Marion.' Wayland and I are not formal. Not with close family. He will have to give you a title, Yale. Lord Yale is not enough."

"I am happy as I am, sister."

"Are you? What a wonder. Then you are the only one who is. Wayland has such trials with the other family members," she confided. "Seems everyone wants something of him. But finish your story, Yale. Did you wake up from your illness and find Samantha nursing you? Was it not love at first sight?"

"It was indeed," Yale agreed gallantly, his words catching Samantha in the middle of taking a sip of wine. She almost choked on it.

"A love match," Marion said with a happy sigh.

Samantha rose and started to correct the misinterpretation. Her honest nature demanded it, but Yale had anticipated her move.

Before the words could come out of her

mouth, he said outrageously, "Yes, we are." He threw a careless arm over Samantha's shoulder and gave her a warning squeeze.

"That is so romantic," Marion said. Again, tears of happiness welled in her eyes.

Samantha drained her glass of wine.

The chimes of the mantel clock struck ten.

Marion shook her head. "Look at me, I'm prattling on and you are both probably fatigued unto death. Come, I'll show you your rooms. Mrs. Witchell has had time to ready them."

"Who is Mrs. Witchell?" Yale said, as they followed Marion out of the room.

"The housekeeper."

"What happened to Mrs. Limkin?"

"She suffered from apoplexy about five years ago. She didn't last long after that, poor thing." Marion led them up the stairs. "I'm putting the two of you in the set of rooms Uncle Roscoe and Aunt Louise used. I had them completely redone after they died."

Yale stopped on the stairs. "They're dead?" There was a quietness in his voice that caught Samantha's attention.

"Years and years ago," Marion said. "Shortly after you left, Roscoe started wasting away. The doctors didn't know what ailed him and could do nothing to cure him. It was very sad. One night he quietly passed away. Louise didn't last more than a year after that." She glanced at Samantha. "Listen to us, with all this talk of death. They were in their seventies, Samantha, and such lovebirds, even at their age. I believe Louise died of a broken heart.''

She turned and climbed the last few steps to a corridor running the length of the house. The hall was lit by candles in brass wall sconces. The fact the duke could burn as many candles as he wished impressed Samantha more than the thick carpets and painted ceilings.

Even the doors were special in this house. Scrolls to match the plaster ceiling had been carved into them, and the handles appeared to be made of gold featuring the same design work.

She'd heard that the duke's Northumberland estate, Braehall, was even more magnificent.

"Wayland and I wanted to model our marriage on their example," Marion was saying softly to her brother-in-law.

"Instead of Father's," he answered.

She nodded sadly. "Unfortunately, your father was not a happy man. Our marriage was arranged, but we have been blessed. I fell in love with Wayland almost the moment I clapped eyes on him." She smiled at the memory. "You have not asked about your sister," she said, smoothly changing the subject.

"Oh, yes, how is she?" he asked, without enthusiasm.

Marion laughed. "She hasn't changed much over the years." She dipped her head low to Samantha. "Twyla has very strong opinions and doesn't hesitate to express them. I will send a note to her first thing in the morning. I'm not going to shock her with your presence the way Wayland did me. He probably anticipated my reaction all the way from Sproule. He loves to catch me off guard."

She stopped in front of a door. Before opening it, she said, "What we should do is have a small family dinner tomorrow evening to introduce Samantha to everyone. What do you think, Yale?"

He shifted, obviously ill-at-ease. "Whatever you wish."

"Good, then we shall do that," Marion said, and opened the door.

Inside was a bedroom decorated in peacock blue and peach. Candles were already lit, and a fire burned in the hearth. Samantha walked across the carpet. It was so deep and rich, she wanted to take off her shoes and stockings and feel her bare feet against it. The bed with its silk curtains was large enough for four people. "This room is gorgeous."

She glanced up at the ceiling. To her relief, the painting was of ancient goddesses lounging in the setting sun.

"More temperate, is it not?" Marion said, guessing Samantha's thoughts.

"I prefer it to the others I've seen."

"I thought you would," Marion agreed with a smile. "The room has a private bath over there." She nodded to a door between a heavy carved wardrobe and the bed. "And there is a sitting room that connects this room with Yale's."

She opened the sitting room door to reveal a

connecting room with a high-backed settee, a table in front of it, and two upholstered chairs. They all looked quite comfortable.

Marion pointed to the window. "The window overlooks the garden. It's not a large room and there is no fire, but it is very cozy and quite private. Let me show you your room, Yale."

On the other side of the sitting room, she opened a door that was directly opposite Samantha's.

Samantha couldn't resist following. Yale's room was much the same as hers—the heavy four-postered bed and curtains, the wardrobe and a desk and chair—only blue silk was the predominant color. Across his ceiling, fat, lazy satyrs lounged beneath branching trees.

"How appropriate," Samantha murmured under her breath, but he'd heard her.

His eyes sparkled. "I shall accept that as a compliment."

Before she could rally an answer, Wayland tapped on the hallway door and entered without waiting for admittance. "Is everything fine?"

"Yes, very good," Yale said.

Wayland went directly to his wife's side. They didn't touch, but Samantha sensed they didn't need to. There was something about the way their gazes met. Something special and exciting. Something that made her feel as if she intruded.

She glanced at Yale, wondering if he had noticed the same thing.

He wasn't paying attention but yawned.

A yawn she immediately echoed.

"Did you see Charles?" Marion asked.

"Yes," Wayland said pleased. "When he heard the sound of my voice, he woke up and gave his papa a big smile. I didn't find him fussy at all."

"Wayland, you promised not to wake him."

"I didn't. He woke on his own."

"I don't believe you," she answered, but there was no heat in her words. She reached up and brushed a strand of her husband's hair back in place. "Did you put him back down?"

"Poor tyke," Wayland said. "It wasn't his teeth at all. One touch from me and he went right to sleep."

"Wayland, he's a baby," Yale said, interrupting their private conversation. "He doesn't know anything."

"He knows me."

Yale snorted his opinion of that. "Babies don't have the brains to know one adult from another."

Even as Marion exclaimed that it wasn't true, Wayland said proudly, "All my sons knew me from the beginning."

Yale shook his head. "You're going daft, brother. Babies are babies. I daresay I could pick up your Charlie, coo at him a bit, and he'd call me Papa as well as you."

Marion bristled at the thought but Wayland silenced her with a hand on her arm. "Don't argue with him, my love. We will leave it to Samantha to show him the error of his ways. Mark my word, he'll be as giddy and proud over the birth of his first child as I was."

He nudged his wife toward the door. "But we should go and give these two their peace." He paused in front of Samantha and placed his hands on her shoulders.

"Welcome to Penhurst...sister," he whispered for her ears alone. He gave her a brotherly kiss on the cheek.

Sister.

She hungered for what he offered. The children, the companionship of a family. A husband.

"The maid and valet will be here shortly," Marion called out from the hall. "They've probably gone to fetch water. The kitchen is a bit of distance from the bedrooms. If you need anything, you have only to ring or come to our rooms. They are the last ones down this hall on the right. The nursery is across from it."

"Thank you," Samantha managed to say, just before Wayland decisively closed the door and she and Yale were alone.

Alone in his bedroom.

For a second, they stared at each other.

Then Yale said, "What did my brother say to you?"

His question startled her. Her mind went blank. She sensed he would not appreciate Wayland's meddling.

"He wished us welcome to Penhurst." Her face flushed with heat. She knew what Wayland had really meant. He'd been reminding of her duty to the family. Of her responsibility to persuade Yale to stay in England.

He hummed his doubts.

"You do not believe me?" She edged her way to the sitting room door.

"You have a tendency to blush when you feel guilty."

Samantha covered her cheeks with her hands. "It's the fire. This room is unusually warm."

The corners of his mouth curved into a smile that let her know he thought she was stalling.

"Well, I think I'll go to bed." She moved into the sitting room.

He followed.

"Good night," she said.

He didn't answer, but picked up a green glass paperweight from the table in front of the settee. "I'd forgotten about this."

"What is it?"

"It belonged to my Uncle Roscoe. When I was about John's age, he told me there were pixies trapped inside it and it was very special. He always used pixies as the excuse for anything untoward that happened. And he'd make me blow on it and rub it for luck whenever I was intimidated or needed a boost of courage." He ran his finger over the smooth green glass. "I believed his pixie stories." He grinned up at her. "I blamed them a time or two myself. Once when I'd broken Mother's favorite vase and another when I let the hunting dogs into the sitting room at Braehall because I feared they were too wet and cold to leave outside. Both times, Mother was furious, but once I told her about the pixies, she let me by without a well-deserved punishment."

He looked around the room. "This is all so strange. I feel like I'm in the same house, and yet it isn't. I expect everything to be the way it was eleven years ago, and it is . . . but then again, it's not quite."

"Eleven years is a long time to be gone."

"Yes. But I don't feel as if I've changed. Everyone else has. I had assumed they wouldn't, that I could return and Roscoe would be here with Louise." He shook his head. "And who would have thought my brother would be so silly about his children?"

"Silly? I think it is a delight to see a man take so much pride in his sons."

He set the paperweight back down on the table. "Sam, I'd like to be with you tonight."

For a heart-splitting second, she wasn't sure she understood him correctly. "Why?" It was the only word her voice could croak out.

He gave her a crooked, self-conscious smile. "Because."

Her knees felt suddenly shaky. She gripped the door handle to her bedroom for balance. "I don't believe you are talking about sleeping on the floor, are you?" Thank God, her voice didn't tremble.

He crossed to where she stood. "No, I wasn't."

Samantha leaned back.

He rested one arm above her head against the door. "Returning here has brought back so many memories." She could feel his breath on the skin of her neck. "I feel the need to be with someone tonight. Is that wrong of me?"

No.

"I don't know." Her voice had gone breathless. She couldn't think clearly when he was this close to her. Her reflection was mirrored in his dark eyes. He wet his lips and she realized he was going to kiss her. It was so tempting, and yet—

She ducked under his arm, slipped into her room, and closed the door before he could so much as move.

Leaning her back against the door, she held her breath. Her heart pounded in her chest. What would he do next?

She listened . . . and after several minutes, heard the door to his bedroom close.

He'd done nothing.

She felt equally disappointed and reprieved.

The knock on her bedroom door sounded like gunshot. Samantha jumped and then chastised herself for being so foolish. It was her maid, Emily, a gentle, matronly woman carrying a pitcher of warm water.

Samantha used the water to wash her face. She wished she could bathe away her troubles as easily.

"You look tense, my lady," Emily said. "Come sit on this bench and let me brush your hair."

Her ministrations were exactly what Samantha needed. Slowly the tension ebbed from her shoulders.

"That was wonderful, Emily. Thank you."

"Yes, my lady." The maid helped her dress in her faded flannel nightdress and Samantha crawled into bed. She'd hoped to fall asleep the moment her head touched the pillow, but she didn't.

Instead, she lay wide awake long after Emily left, staring at the peach silk canopy over the bed. She wondered if Yale slept. Probably. He never seemed bothered by an overstrong conscience.

The lonely minutes ticked by, dragging like hours.

Why hadn't she let Yale into her bed? It was what Wayland wanted. It was her duty as Yale's wife.

It hadn't bothered her to keep him out their nights at the inns, so what was different now? Why did she feel so guilty?

Because it was what she wanted . . . but for all the wrong reasons.

She wanted a family. Seeing Wayland and his sons made her ache for children. It came on her in that moment. Before, she'd envied those whose babies she had helped bring into the world. But now she wanted one of her own. Now, it was a possibility. She could even be with child . . . although she didn't feel any different than she had before her marriage.

She recognized her yearning as the emptiness that had been inside her for so long. The emptiness she hadn't known how to describe.

She wanted love.

But Yale did not love her. He would leave her.

But once he left, she would have his baby to love. Furthermore, Wayland and his family could not turn their backs on her if she was the mother of Yale's child.

Still, her conscience bothered her. It seemed cold-blooded. Wicked, even . . . especially when a part of her body grew hot and anxious at the thought of his touch.

His kisses.

The feeling of him inside of her.

She rose from the bed and padded to the door on silent feet. She opened it and slipped into the sitting room. The curtains were back, and moonlight spread across the settee and shone on the green paperweight.

Pixies. Perhaps they were responsible for the sudden madness she felt.

This was wrong, terribly wrong—and yet she could not turn away.

She approached his door.

For a second, she debated knocking, and then discarded the idea. What if he was asleep?

She would not wake him. Not for this. If he was awake, fine . . . if he slept, she would return to her room.

Gingerly, as if it was a hot iron, she placed her hand on the door handle and slowly turned it.

The door didn't make a sound as it swung open.

Here too the drapes were hung back. This room was darker than hers because of the blue walls and curtains, yet the edge of the bed could be seen plainly in the moonlight.

The fire in his hearth was almost out. A whiff of cold air skipped across the floor and tickled her ankles.

She listened, expecting to hear his steady, even breathing.

"Sam?"

His voice came from the shadows of the bed. He sat up, the moonlight catching on the hard planes of his chest, his face still hidden by darkness.

"Sam, what are you doing here?"

She opened her mouth to speak, but the words froze in her throat.

"Is something the matter?" he asked. His leg moved as he prepared to get out of bed.

Samantha didn't know what to do. And because she'd gone too far to turn back now, because she'd gambled on fate and fate had made its choice, she reached down, lifted the hem of her nightdress, and pulled it over her head. She tossed it aside and stood naked before him. Her body tensed in the cool night air and she shivered, vulnerable . . . and fearful of her own audacity.

There was a heartbeat of silence.

Then his deep voice said, "Come here."

Chapter 13

The first step was the hardest. Samantha's feet seemed to have turned into anvils, heavy, clumsy, numb.

Yale's face was hidden in shadow, except for the gleam of anticipation in his eyes.

Her knees bumped into the edge of the bed before she realized she'd reached it. She almost lost her balance but caught herself in time from pitching forward onto the bed.

There she stood, in indecision.

Yale's hand moved. He flipped the bedcovers, indicating a space beside him. He was naked. She could see the length of his bare thigh and her mind fantasized the rest. Her mouth went dry.

When she didn't move, Yale moved over to her side of the bed and into the moonlight. The covers slipped away, revealing that he was already hard and ready for her.

The intent expression on his face held her spellbound as he reached out and placed his

269

hand against the side of her breast. His thumb touched her nipple. It puckered and hardened in response.

She lowered her gaze to where he touched her, his tan skin dark compared to the whiteness of her breast. The room seemed to turn hot and close around her. She stopped breathing, waiting for what he would do next.

He surprised her with a question.

"What are you doing here?"

She blinked and lifted her gaze up to his face. He watched her.

Her mind scrambled for an answer. *Why was she here?*

"I don't want to be alone anymore."

Her words astonished her with their honesty. She felt she stood before him, completely defenseless.

His answer was a low, deep groan. He came up out of the bed and embraced her. The length of him pressed against her stomach and he raised her up, his hands cupping her buttocks, to let her feel his need for her. His lips came down on hers, the kiss fierce, hungry, as if he'd held himself at bay for too long and could no longer.

He lay Samantha on the bed, her head on the pillow.

His lips left hers and came down to cover one taut nipple. She gasped, burying her fingers in his hair and feeling the pull and tug of his mouth deep inside her.

Her legs opened in invitation. She was ready for him. She ached for his touch. When his hand swept up her thigh and stroked her, she closed her legs around him, wanting him there.

He kissed her neck and whispered in her ear, "I have waited so long for this." His fingers entered her, testing.

At his intimate touch, Samantha wanted to cry out, but didn't.

Something was wrong. Something wasn't right. In spite of the aching need she felt for him, she flinched, shying away.

His hand stopped moving. "Sam, what is it? Did I hurt you?"

She didn't answer. What could she say? She didn't understand herself.

She looked up at him with puzzled eyes and then understood . . . *Dear God*—

The realization struck like a flash of blinding light, brighter than any sun, exposing her.

She truly was in love with him.

That was the reason she had crossed the distance between the two bedrooms. Somewhere in their journey from Sproule to London, maybe even before, she'd fallen in love. It was so obvious, she was surprised she hadn't recognized it sooner.

But he did not love her.

The thought filled her with an indescribable sadness.

"Sam?" His voice sounded angry. He sat up,

moving away from her. "You don't want this, do you?"

She shook her head no, tears starting to fill her eyes. He caught a tear on the tip of his finger.

"Then why are you here?" he asked again.

Samantha wasn't sure of those reasons herself. The arguments that had seemed so sane and rational when she was in her bed were suddenly confusing, crazy, insane. Terrifying.

Without his love in return, she felt as if she prostituted herself. But she also felt another emotion, a stronger one: *fear*.

No other man had ever made her knees so weak or had so completely captured her imagination or had kept her grounded by listening to her talk about her doubts.

Yale could do that, all of it.

And when he kissed her, it was like stars shooting into the heavens.

He'd warned her once against falling in love with him . . . but she hadn't heeded his warning.

Now, she would be doubly hurt when the time came for him to cast her aside. Why had she not protected her heart? Lying here naked beside him, she felt common, cheap. She could be any woman to him.

Her breath caught in her throat in a small sound of despair.

"Damn!" Yale swore viciously, and rolled out of the bed on the other side. He came to his feet. "Why are you here?" he demanded. He was still proudly erect. He looked down at himself, swore again, this time colorfully, and pulled the sheet off the bed, wrapping it around his waist.

Samantha reached for the satin bedspread to hide her own nakedness. Her body still throbbed from the heat of his touch; her cheeks burned with embarrassment.

Yale raked his hair back with his hand. He stood in the moonlight and she could see every line on his face. "What are you doing to me, Samantha? And why?"

"Doing to you? I don't understand—"

"Oh, you certainly do," he said, ruthlessly cutting her off. "You know *exactly* what you are doing, and that's playing me for a fool! I've just spent a good portion of the last week burning for you, and now tonight you walk in here, take off your clothes, and practically beg me to take you. But you don't want to be here, do you? You started, but you changed your mind."

This was worse than she had imagined. She felt dishonorable, a fraud. "I will finish. Come back to bed. I'll do it."

"Damn you, Sam, damn you, damn you, damn you." He stormed across the room, having to kick the tail of the sheet out of his way and then realizing how ridiculous he looked, he sat down in an armchair by the window.

She came up on her knees. "I don't understand why you are so angry," she said around the lump forming in her throat.

He looked up at her, his hard, glittering gaze

boring straight into her. "Did Wayland put you up to this?"

His accurate guess caught her unawares. Too late did she realize her face gave her away whether she spoke or not.

He gave a half laugh and sat back in the chair. "Why am I not surprised? My brother. He started with little digs at first. Belittling words about Rogue Shipping and my present status in the world. Nothing serious, only letting me know that perhaps I'm not as well off as I wish to be. But then this morning, he let me have it full bore."

"Is that when you were arguing?"

"Oh yes. He announced that it was time I lived up to my responsibilities and stopped pretending to be a businessman. God, he sounded just like Father."

He stared at Samantha a second. "And I'm not surprised he'd try and use you. That *is* why you are here, isn't it? Because Wayland encouraged you to come to me."

"Yes." It was hard to say the word.

Yale nodded. "I've been in England less than two weeks, and already I'm surrounded by the hypocrisy." He sat forward. "But I didn't expect it from you, Sam. I thought we understood each other. I had faith in your honesty."

His words inspired guilt. She felt a need to defend herself. "You question *my* honesty? You married me under an assumed name!"

"And you'll never forgive me for it, will you?

Tell me, Sam, what did Wayland use to convince you to throw yourself at me? Money? A better house than I could afford? What? I would have given you all those things and more any one of the last several nights instead of sleeping on the floor, playing the monk."

"He told me it was my duty."

"Your duty?" Yale repeated. He stood up. "I don't want you in my bed out of *duty*. I don't want some guilt-ridden vicar's daughter weeping as I labor over her like a peasant. I'm not without honor, Sam. No matter what my brother and family believe."

A wave of shame rolled through her. "Yale, please, it's not what you think. I just wanted—" She broke off before confessing her innermost desire. She wanted a baby. He'd accuse her of worse mistreatment if he knew the truth. And then he'd never believe what lay in her heart.

And she could never tell him.

When she didn't speak, the set of his face hardened. Without another word, he turned to his wardrobe and began getting dressed.

"What are you doing?" she asked.

"That should be obvious."

"But why? Where are you going?"

"Does it bloody matter?" He angrily stomped his foot in his boot, putting on first one and then the other.

"Yale . . ." She searched for words. "I'm sorry. I don't understand—"

"Leave it, Samantha. Not another word. Just

leave it." On that, he opened the door and marched out into the hall.

His booted feet made no sound on the hallway carpet, but she could sense his movement. She waited, hardly daring to breathe. In her mind's eye, she could see him going down the stairs and across the foyer, and then opening the door. She could almost hear it slam behind him.

He was gone.

Just as she'd feared.

He'd left her.

Samantha rolled herself up in his bedspread, buried her face in his pillow, and cried.

Yale didn't care where he went. He strode out of his brother's house and took the first left until he came to the end of that street and turned again, this time to the right. And turned at another block, and then walked and walked and walked. He'd forgotten his hat and overcoat but didn't even feel the cold winter air.

The most errant part of his body was still stiff and erect and it only made him angrier that he'd wanted her so much.

Sam! He could curse the day he'd met her. She was driving him to madness. One minute she was all moral righteousness, and the next she was doing his family's bidding, offering herself like some harem slave.

But then, he realized with a snort, she couldn't be anything other than what she was. He wasn't surprised her conscience had gotten the better of her. She could no more play the whore than he could the beggar—and it was time Wayland and all the other dukes of Ayleborough understood that fact!

The worst of it was, he wanted Sam. Memories of the hours they had spent in bed together that first night were burned into his mind. Her passion rivaled his own—when she wasn't feeling guilty!

After a good half hour of walking, he finally started to calm down and came face-to-face with one hard fact: he wanted Samantha as he'd never wanted another woman before.

He ached from wanting her.

He'd rather be drawn and quartered than feel the way he did now. Oh, there were a good many things he admired about her . . . one minute she exasperated, another she challenged, and in the next she worked her way into his heart—

Yale almost stumbled over his own feet. He came to halt.

What the bloody hell was he thinking?

His heart remained free, unfettered. He was a self-made man, completely independent of the society, country, and family that had bred him.

And yet . . . he *wanted* to be around Sam.

He actually treasured those nights he'd spent on the floor of her room feeling a bit like some sort of chivalrous knight—

Dear God, it was happening! A few more days with Samantha and he'd be daffy in love!

Yale wanted to roar with frustration.

He began walking again, his pace brisk.

He *couldn't* be in love. Love was like thunder-bolts and lightning—he hadn't felt any thunder-bolts with Sam, not even a sizzle . . . well, maybe a sizzle, he amended, remembering the scene in his bedroom. Actually, *more* than a sizzle—but not a thunderbolt.

Love was the sort of thing where men and women mooned about over each other. He and Sam argued. Of course, he found her spirit invigorating. Intriguing, even.

But love never lasted, no matter what the poets said. Yale couldn't imagine himself shackled to one woman. There! At last a statement his conscience couldn't challenge.

Of course, he really didn't want *other* women right now. The only one he longed for was Samantha.

"Blasted woman," he said under his breath.

Wayland had seen it. In some mysterious manner, his older brother had divined that Samantha was the one person Yale wanted to please.

He'd have to hide his feelings better. Ignore her. Better yet, set sail for his spice plantation in Ceylon. Whatever he did, he couldn't let her know how deeply his affections ran for her. Ever.

In fact, he was just starting to realize how deep they were himself.

Only the oceans knew such depth!

Yale stopped his furious walking. Where had such a poetic notion come from? He avoided poems. Avoided poets! And yet here he was, thinking in poetry.

His hands hung loosely at his side and he felt suddenly tired and strangely defeated, both alien notions.

He was in danger of falling in love with Sam . . . and she did not return it. She saw him as duty, a responsibility.

He didn't want to be a duty; he wanted to be a lover. Maybe that was it. Perhaps if they were lovers he would tire of her and return to his normal self. It was a possibility.

Slowly he became aware of his surroundings. He didn't know how far he'd walked or what time it was.

The streets here were dark. Too dark. Little light spilled out from what few grimy windows were lit. The air smelled of rubbish and human waste. In the distance a dog barked and a woman laughed, the sounds eerily alike.

This wasn't the London he remembered. It was more like the bowels of Calcutta.

He walked on at slower place, the hair on the back of his neck warning him of impending danger.

A hard shove against his back sent him stumbling into the ink-black shadows. Struggling for his balance, he felt a small hand reach for his purse.

Pickpockets!

Landing heavily on the ground, he heard one pair of footsteps running off. The thief's accomplice jumped over Yale's body and went running in the same direction down a narrow alley.

Yale cursed. He'd been in hellholes from Bombay to Macao and kept his purse. He had not come to London to be filched.

He was on his feet in a blink of an eye and running after the thieves. He tripped over small crates stacked in the alley but easily caught himself and pursued. The alley came out on a narrow street.

He feared he'd lost them.

"The cove's chasing us!" a voice cried out. "Split up!"

Yale heard one set of running footsteps go in one direction and another in the opposite. He guessed which one was the bastard with his purse and followed him.

The hard exercise and the thrill of pursuit were exactly what he needed to clear his mind. His legs ate up the ground between him and his quarry.

Then he had a break. The boy ran across a broad street toward a park. Moonlight flashed like a beacon on the pickpocket's shirt.

Yale was right behind him. As the pickpocket ran toward the dark shadows of trees, Yale launched himself up into the air and tackled the boy. The two of them grunted as they hit the ground with a thud.

Yale grabbed hold of the lad's collar and gave him a shake as he brought both of them to their feet.

He whirled the thief around to face him and found himself staring into the wide, frightened eyes of a child.

A thieving child, he remembered, recovering from his surprise. "I want my purse. Give it back."

"I d-don't know anything about a purse."

Yale gave him a rough shake. *"I want my purse."*

The boy's teeth were chattering. Yale didn't know if it was from the cold or from fear. The lad wore little more than a thin shirt, breeches and a ragged coat.

He pulled the boy into the moonlight and pinched his ribs. "I haven't seen such a scrawny lad even in India."

"Please, s-sir. L-let me g-go."

"My purse." He held out his hand.

"Arnie took it," the lad blurted out. "He got it from me while we were running. Back there, when you ran into those wooden crates."

"And where is Arnie?"

"I don't know."

Yale bent down to look him in the face. "Yes, you do."

"I don't! I don't! I swear, sir."

"Well, then perhaps the magistrate can get it out of you."

"No!" the boy cried, truly terrified now. "You can't take me to the magistrate. If you do, he'll throw me in prison or deport me."

"Which is not a bad idea," Yale agreed ruthlessly.

"But me sister," the lad said, huge tears welling in his eyes. "She'll starve. I'm the only one that takes care of her. Mum said I had to."

"And where is your mother now?" He didn't believe a word the little bugger had to say and gave him another shake for effect.

"She's dead, sir. Took ill with the influenza and died."

Now he had Yale's attention. "Recently?"

"No, sir. She died a year ago. I've been taking care of us."

"By picking pockets?"

"It beats sweeping chimneys."

"I can't agree with you."

"I tried it, sir. I hired on as a chimney boy. But the sweeps are mean, and once I got stuck in the chimney and the sweep was going to go off and leave me while the man we did the job for started a fire. The sweep had his money. He didn't care if I got burned or not."

Yale frowned. He'd heard of boys burning before. "How old is your sister?"

"She's eight, sir."

"You speak well. Did your mother teach you?"

"She was a seamstress. Me pa was a clerk for G. G. Dobbins and Son until he climbed a ladder and fell and hit his head."

"Did it kill him?"

"He never was quite right and died soon after.

Mum said it was freak thing that happened. I don't remember because I was too young."

"How old are you now?" Yale asked, thinking the boy looked barely ten.

"I'm twelve. Old enough to be a man."

"And old enough to steal from another man's pocket and cry about it," Yale shot back.

His words reminded the boy of his peril. "*Please* don't take me to the magistrate, sir."

"Can you get my purse back?" The boy's cheeks were gaunt. In the Orient, he had seen hunger before. He had not expected it on the streets of London.

The boy shook his head. "Arnie and the others would kill me for trying to take it back from 'em, even if I knew where they were. I'd be dead before morning."

For a moment, Yale suspected the boy of high drama until he looked into his eyes. His fears were real.

"What is your name?" Yale asked.

The boy wasn't going to tell him until Yale gave him another shake. "Terrance."

"Terrance." Yale tested the name. "Not exactly the name for a thief."

"I am not a thief, sir," Terrance said, two large tears rolling down his cheeks. "I just started it because of me sister. If she doesn't get good food and someplace warm, she'll die."

The tears running down his dirty face reminded Yale of the tears that had welled in

Samantha's eyes . . . and made him feel culpable in the lad's bad luck.

A part of Yale warned him he shouldn't believe a word the lad said. But another part, this new part touched by Samantha, wondered if the story was true—and he couldn't turn his back on the boy if it was.

He tipped the lad's chin up to look him in the eye. "Well, Terrance, I'm out my purse and in a foul mood for it. Let's go and find that sister of yours."

Terrance immediately started to struggle, attempting to break Yale's hold. "No, sir! You can't. She didn't do anything. She's a wee thing who's never done anything bad. Take me to the magistrate, but leave her alone, I beg you."

Yale jerked Terrance's arm. "I'm not going to harm your sister. But I believe a man should do anything but be a thief."

"I've tried, sir. It's either that or starve."

Yale knelt down to his level. "And if I found you something to do where you wouldn't starve, would you continue to steal?"

"No, sir, I wouldn't."

Yale studied him a moment before saying, "All right. I believe you." And he did. "Now come, let us go fetch your sister."

Terrance dug in his heels. "And what are you going to do with us?"

"You'll find out when you get there. But I promise you this, it will be better than how you are living now."

Terrance considered his words, eyeing Yale carefully. Then he squared his painfully thin shoulders. "Alice and I will go with you, but if I find out you are playing tricks, sir, on my mother's grave, I will not forgive it!"

Yale almost smiled at the oath, but realized that this young boy had more bottom than most men he knew. "Aye, I will answer to you," Yale assured him.

Terrance began walking and Yale followed. They moved back the way they had come and Yale shuddered to think of a girl of eight alone in this filth and poverty.

Samantha woke the next morning, heavy-lidded and tired. The day was overcast with high lead-gray clouds. It looked as if it might rain. She wondered what time it was.

Sitting up in Yale's bed, she groggily half-expected to see him sleeping on the floor or sprawled in the chair. But he was neither. And she was naked.

Her nakedness sparked shameful memories of the night before. He had walked out. He'd left her.

She hated the knot forming in her stomach. Hated caring when he didn't. Hated the thought of having to answer to Wayland for his brother's leaving.

She climbed out of the bed and hurried over to where her nightdress lay in a heap on the floor. She pulled it over her head as quickly as she could.

Then she heard it . . . snoring. It was a light sound and came from beyond the bedroom. Cautiously she opened the door to the sitting room.

Everything in there was just as it had been the night before—except that the door of her bedroom was slightly open. She couldn't remember if she had closed it or not.

Skittish, she rang for the maid. Something was not right . . . but she couldn't quite put her finger on it.

Now knowing that help would be on the way, she bravely tiptoed over to the door of her room and pushed it open. A heartbeat later she wanted to laugh at herself in relief.

Yale slept flat on his back, sprawled in the middle of her bed on top of the sheets. The bedspread was in a pile on the floor at the foot of the bed. He'd taken off his coat, but still wore his shirt and breeches. His feet were bare.

Funny, he had appealing bare feet. Almost as appealing as the growth of beard that covered his lean jaw, and the tousled look of his hair. In spite of his broad shoulders, he appeared almost boyish.

He snored with the pleasure of uncomplicated sleep.

As if drawn to him by a magnet, she tiptoed over to the side of the bed and pushed his hair back from his forehead. It felt good to touch him.

For a second, she toyed with the idea of waking him and then changed her mind. She liked watching him this way.

And all too soon, he would wake and they would have to discuss issues and problems Samantha would rather not address.

At that moment, there was a light rap on the hallway door. Emily was here.

Samantha hurried to open the door, raising her finger to her lips to warn Emily to be quiet. The maid took one look at Samantha's husband stretched out on the bed and covered her mouth to stifle a giggle.

Samantha motioned with her head for Emily to go into the sitting room. She felt nervous. Servants were notorious gossips, and it made her uncomfortable that they would know such intimate details as in which bed her husband had spent the night.

Emily nodded that she understood, but signaled that she needed to get Samantha's dress. She silently crossed over to the wardrobe and looked in askance for which dress Samantha wanted her to bring.

Samantha nodded toward her wedding dress. Wearing it would give her confidence to face whatever happened this day.

Samantha picked up her hairbrush and started to leave the room first. Emily hurried to follow, almost tripping over the bedspread on the floor. She looked down and startled Samantha by screaming.

"What is the matter?" Samantha asked.

Emily dropped the dress. "There's somebody under that bedspread, my lady." She shied away toward the door even as Yale opened an eye.

"What was that confounded racket?" he asked, with very little humor.

"There is someone under there!" Emily declared. The "someone" sat up under the bedspread and she screamed again before running out into the hall, shouting for help.

"Why is she going on that way?" Yale asked, coming up on his elbows.

Samantha still didn't think he was entirely awake. She gripped her hairbrush and pulled the bedspread off the "someone."

Or "someones."

Two grubby children huddled together, wide-eyed and frightened, at the foot of the bed.

Samantha relaxed her militant stance. She looked at Yale, who was scratching his beard. "I found them," he said, as if that explained everything.

At that moment, Wayland, Marion, a footman, and the frightened Emily charged back into the room. Everyone but she and Yale were dressed and ready for the day.

"What is going on here?" Wayland commanded.

"There!" Emily said, pointing at the footboard. "Next to that bedspread. I saw something move."

Wayland came around the bed and looked at her in confusion. "They're children." He turned to Samantha and then to his brother. "What are children doing here?"

"They are my guests," Yale announced. He got off the bed and stretched. "In fact, Sam, I brought the girl to you but didn't have the heart to wake you up last night. She's ill. Can you have a look at her and heal her?"

"Sick?" Wayland echoed. "Sick with what?"

"Well, yes, of course I can try," Samantha said, slightly disconcerted by the swift change of events.

Wayland stepped forward. "Absolutely not! You can't mean to let those filthy children stay here in this house—especially *sick* children. Have you gone mad? They are a danger to my sons."

"I could not leave them on the street," Yale said.

"Oh, but Yale—" Marion started, and then broke off. She motioned to Emily. "Go and make sure Nurse doesn't let the boys out of the nursery. Hurry, now!"

The maid ran to do her bidding while Wayland exploded in anger.

"I can't believe you did this, Yale. Have you *no* common sense? And just when I believed you had changed, you pull a trick like this! Where in the name of all that is holy did you find them?"

Yale leaned against the bedpost, the set of his chin stubborn. "I caught the lad picking my pocket."

"Pickpockets!" Wayland's face flushed with outrage. His mouth opened and closed as if words had failed him. He whirled on the footman. "Bates, throw this riffraff out!"

The younger child, the girl, gave a soft cry of distress. The boy put his arms around her.

But as the footman moved forward, Yale stepped protectively in front of the children. "You will not touch them."

Chapter 14

Bates stopped and glanced with uncertainty at the duke. Samantha held her breath.

"They are my guests," Yale said to his brother. "If they can't stay, then I will leave with them."

"Oh, God," Wayland swore. He motioned Bates out of the room. The moment the door closed, he exploded. "I thought you'd changed! I was beginning to believe you had more sense than all this. Worse, you are putting me in an untenable position. I cannot have—" he waved his hands at the two grubby children as if words failed him, *"people like them* under my roof. It's unheard of."

"Wayland, stop being so dramatic," Yale snapped. "They're children. Nothing more, nothing less. They have no parents or home. You'd be grubby, too, if you'd been forced to live the life they have."

"*You* are the one who doesn't understand. Don't you remember anything that happened years ago? Society has all but forgotten who you are and the details of your disgrace—but not for long, once they catch wind of this. What you are doing is unheard of."

"What rot," Yale said. "I'm my own man. I'll do what I wish. If I choose to nursemaid a multitude of children, I will. "

"Yes? Well, what of Samantha? No one does this sort of thing. You will draw attention to yourself. It will remind people of the scandal."

"Oh, yes, what a frightening black sheep I must be. Taking in sick children. What will I do next?" Yale mocked his brother.

"Damn you, Yale, you understand exactly what I mean."

"I do, brother. You mean that I'm welcome as long as I obey your rules. You are the twin of our father."

"Yes? Well, now I'm beginning to understand a little of his side of the story!"

Samantha stepped between the two men. "Please, both of you. If you wish to argue, take it to another room. These children are innocents and you are frightening them."

At her words, the men looked down at the children. The girl sobbed in earnest. Samantha dropped to her knees and placed a hand on the girl's head. She had a slight fever and her chest was congested, but that was all. Still, Yale had been right to bring the child in from the cold. A small fever could rapidly develop into something life threatening.

Marion squeezed her husband's arm. "Wayland, perhaps you *are* overreacting a small bit."

He frowned his answer at his wife, then turned abruptly and stomped to the door. "Keep your brats away from me and my children. As soon as they are well enough, I want them out of this house." He placed a hand on the door handle. "Oh, yes, Marion and I have decided the best way to reintroduce the two of you into society is to start with a small dinner for only the members of the family this evening. She is having the invitations sent out. Next week we'll stage a ball in your honor."

"Killing the fatted calf?" Yale murmured.

Wayland's eyes narrowed. "I advise you to pay a visit to your tailor."

Yale bowed, the gesture polite—and mocking. "I do not want a ball. As for this evening, you may introduce Samantha. My family and Society turned their backs on me years ago and I'll be damned if I perform in front of any of them like a trained bear."

Wayland jerked open the handle of the door. "Defiant to the end, aren't you? Come, Marion." Without another word, he left the room.

However, Marion lingered behind.

"I will order beds made available for the children in the servants' quarters. Samantha, tell Fenley what you need in the way of effecting a cure for this girl and he will see your wishes are carried out. Oh, yes," she said, pausing in the doorway. "I have asked the dressmaker to visit this afternoon. If she doesn't have anything suitable for this evening, then perhaps we can find something from my closet that you may wear."

"Thank you, Your Grace," Samantha said, the sentiment heartfelt.

Marion smiled and then glanced up at Yale. "He really is glad to have you home." She left the room.

Yale and Samantha were left alone with two very frightened children. The girl was shivering.

"Come now," Samantha said in a soothing voice. "Everything will be fine. What is your name?"

"Her name is Alice," the boy answered.

"And this is her brother, Terrance," Yale said, sitting on the edge of the bed. He seemed remarkably unconcerned after having had such a serious argument with his brother.

"Well, Alice," Samantha said, "there is no reason to be afraid. The duke and duchess are going to see that you have plenty of food and a warm bed." She looked at Terrance. "Did you really attempt to pick my lord's pocket?" He seemed so young for a criminal act.

"It was the only way he could feed his sister," Yale said, defending the boy.

But someone had taught Terrance pride. He answered Samantha honestly. "Yes, my lady, I did."

"And you know what you did was wrong?" She ignored Yale's muttered "Jesus." She'd talk to him about using the Lord's name in vain later.

"Yes, my lady, I did, and I won't do it again. Unless . . ."

"Unless what?" Samantha asked.

"Unless I have to feed my sister."

Samantha placed a hand against the boy's cheek. "I understand. Now, let us see what we can do to make her well." She came to her feet and crossed to where her medicinal basket set next to the heavy wardrobe. Digging into it, she pulled out the cloth bag of feverfew and the makings of a poultice for the girl's chest.

She rang for Fenley, who arrived promptly. "Fenley, this is Terrance and his sister Alice. Children, this is Mr. Fenley. He will take the two of you to good, clean beds and see that a tea is made of this herb. Alice must drink all of it. After I have dressed, I will prepare a poultice for her chest. Terrance, it will be your responsibility to see that Alice does as I ask."

"I will, my lady," he vowed earnestly.

Samantha smiled in approval before saying, "Fenley, these children are both frightfully dirty. I'm a firm believer in cleanliness. Please bathe them."

The children gasped in surprise.

"I am not going to bathe," Terrance said stoutly.

"You will if you stay here," Yale answered.

"Then I do not have a choice," the boy said morosely. "I can't leave without my sister." He looked so miserable, Samantha couldn't help but laugh.

"Go with Fenley," she told him.

"I'll take the little one," Yale volunteered gallantly, and lifted Alice up into his arms.

As Samantha watched them leave, she realized Terrance and his sister trusted Yale implicitly—and he had not let them down. He would have left the house rather than bend to his brother's suggestion of throwing the children back into the street.

Her wedding gown still hung on a peg. She started to dress.

She was brushing her hair when Yale pushed open the door of her room leading to the sitting room. He leaned against the door frame.

He crossed his arms. "So, do you agree with my brother that I'm mad to have brought these children here?"

Samantha paused, the brush poised in the air. She lowered it before asking, "Does it matter what I think?"

He made an irritated sound. "Yes, of course."

She answered honestly. "The girl truly is sick. She needed shelter. However, it is Wayland's home, and he is thinking of his own children. He doesn't know what disease Alice suffered from, and all diseases spread so quickly. I lost the Ryman baby to what I'd thought was a simple cold in less time than it took to bring him into this world. You may have jeopardized your nephews' lives. Furthermore, telling Wayland that the lad was a pickpocket was not the way to make him feel charitable toward the child." She drew a deep breath for courage and said, "But I think you knew that when you said it."

Yale's eyes blazed with anger. "I didn't give him one thought." He shoved away from the door. "I should have known better. You're like my family. All of them put the worst interpretation on anything I do." He left the room.

Samantha stared after him. Where had such a hot-headed outburst come from?

It dawned on her that since they'd left Sproule, he'd been playing little games with her, and suddenly she'd had enough. She wasn't one to hold back her opinion when asked—and if he didn't like it, he shouldn't bother asking. She marched out into the sitting room and walked straight to his bedroom door.

She didn't bother to knock because he probably wouldn't answer if she did. No, she just barged right in and caught him half-naked, his shirt in his hands. The valet was busy pouring water into a basin. Samantha's arrival so startled him, he overflowed the basin.

He hurried to wipe up the mess, but Samantha had no patience. "Out," she ordered.

The man scurried out of the room.

Yale blinked in surprise. "Samantha?"

"Yes, it is I," she answered tightly. "And I have a few things I want to say to you."

He started to open his mouth, but she held up her hand to stave him off.

"I have just spent the morning entertaining everyone in the house in my nightdress. I have found myself placed in the unenviable position of being between two brothers who can't seem to sit and talk civilly for five minutes and iron out their differences—"

"It's more than that. We have years of differences!"

"I do not care," she responded, effectively shutting him up. "But the next time you ask my opinion, you will stay and listen to what I have to say, or don't bother to ask it at all. Am I clear?"

"Sam—"

"Next!" It felt good to argue with him, to push aside her uneasy emotions. "I think your brother is a bit overbearing, but I also I believe you bait him. Why did you bring those children here?"

"Because they were sick."

"And perhaps because you knew it was something your brother wouldn't like?" she questioned him suspiciously.

"I didn't even think of him."

"But you should have, Yale. It is his house, and whereas I don't want those poor souls out in the freezing cold, you knew it would upset him. Just as you've known what would upset me."

"That's not true!"

"It isn't?

He spread his hands. "What have I done wrong?"

"Oh, let's start at the beginning, shall we?"

She ticked off on her fingers her counts against him. "You've lied to me—"

"I explained that!"

"You married me under a false name—"

"That's the same as lying to you. They were both the same incident, Sam, you can't count them twice."

"You *bedded* me," she said, as if he'd triggered her memory. "And then told me you were going to *leave* me."

He threw his shirt down on the chair. "Unfair, Sam. I always intended to take care of you."

She ignored his protests. "Then you dragged me to London and your family, and you won't even be here for dinner this evening when I have to meet them all."

"What?" He made a face. "What are you talking about? Are you saying you are in this pet because I'm not going to be there for dinner this evening?"

"Pet? Is that what you think I am in?"

"Yes."

"Well, you're wrong! I'm angry!"

"Samantha, I don't understand you. When I want to be by your side in bed, you toss me onto the floor—"

"What does our argument have to do with bed?" she ground out.

"—Then, my brother snaps his fingers and you are naked in my room—"

"Yale, that was a mistake." Samantha immediately regretted pressing her complaints. "I shouldn't have—"

"*You're right* you shouldn't have. Then you side with my brother over Terrance and Alice."

"I'm *not* siding with him."

"You aren't?" he said in patent disbelief. He placed his hands on his waist. "Then why am I receiving this lecture? One of many I've had to bear over the past few days."

She made an exasperated sound. "I said you were right."

"Yes, and then accused me of doing it to annoy my brother."

"What I was saying is that you did the right thing, Yale, but for the wrong reasons."

"The wrong reasons! God in heaven, woman, you could drive a saint to madness."

"I wish you would not take the Lord's name in vain," she said self-righteously.

"Jesus, Mary, and Joseph," he answered. "It's not enough that I perform a charitable act, I must do it for the right reason! Is that not truly insane? No 'Thank you, Yale,' or, 'That was well done,' " he mimicked in a falsetto voice. "Instead, my motives are suspect. My brother is ready to throw those children out into the street, and you think I should be more understanding!"

"You don't understand what I'm trying to say—"

"Yes, I do!" He walked up to Samantha and bent down until he looked her straight in the eye. "But do you know what really makes me furious?"

"No, what?"

"The fact that I could kiss you right now! You'd probably hiss and spit at me like an angry kitten, but it might be worth the trouble."

Samantha could scarcely believe her ears. "Isn't that like you? I'm trying to have a meaningful discussion, and you want to kiss me! Well, I have no desire to kiss you."

"You lie."

"I do not."

"Don't dare me."

"I'm not!" she said firmly.

"Samantha, that was the wrong thing to say."

One look at the fire in his eyes, and she agreed with him. She turned and started to run, but his hands took hold of her arms. He turned her toward him and his lips came down over hers.

His kiss was brutal, full of anger. And she allowed her own ire to show, matching him stroke for stroke. These weren't the soft, yearning kisses of before; this was a test of wills.

He broke the kiss off first. "You won't give quarter, will you?"

Her lips felt bruised and sore, and the beat of her heart pounded in her ears. "Will you?" she challenged.

His eyes softened. "What do you think?" And he bent to kiss her again . . . except suddenly Samantha knew that she could not withstand another onslaught, especially one that wasn't edged with anger.

She pushed away and ran.

Yale followed her to the door. "*Sam!*"

She ignored him, dashing into her room, and pushed the door shut. A second later, he slammed his door.

She picked up a pillow and threw it. And then another, and another. He was arrogant. Stubborn. Selfish!

She heard him stomping around the sitting room.

If he thought she would open this door, he was wrong. Let him be the first one to apologize. She was the injured party.

At one point, she thought she heard his booted steps come to the door. She sat up in bed, her heart in her throat. For a second she could almost picture him on the other side, his hand poised to knock.

But then she heard him walk away. His bedroom door opened and closed. She waited as one frozen, listening. A few minutes later, she heard him pass on his way down the hall.

Samantha caught a glimpse of herself in the mirror and barely recognized the white-faced woman with large, sad eyes who stared back at her. At no other time in her life had she felt so confused about her own mind.

Less than a week ago, her world had been simple. Everything had been either wrong or right. Now, she didn't know what she thought or how she felt—except for the fact that she loved him.

Hopelessly loved him.

The anger inside her evaporated.

She wished she were made like other women. They could laugh and flirt and hide their feelings. Some of them had had many lovers—but she'd had only the one and knew instinctively there would be no other man for her but Yale.

"Dear Lord," she prayed, "how does one live with a broken heart?"

Yale clumped out of the house, thoroughly disgusted with everyone inside it.

It had felt good to kiss Samantha. Too good. A man couldn't think clearly when a woman tasted like that. Of course, this was the first time he'd ever had a woman turn his world upside-down before.

He'd almost begged her forgiveness. For one heart-rending moment, he'd stood in front of her bedroom door prepared to go down on his knees to her.

But then he'd come to his senses. Samantha didn't love him. She'd told him as much.

Well, he didn't love her. She was too complicated. There wasn't a man alive who could understand her. He was tired of trying.

The silly thing was, she'd cared for him more when she'd thought him penniless than she did now that she knew he was a rich man with powerful family connections. Any other woman would be happy as a cat with fresh cream. But not Sam.

No one had ever dared to question his motives before.

She not only dared—worse, she had been right! He hadn't thought of the danger of bringing a sick child around his brother's children.

The woman irritated him beyond reason!

Hailing a hack, he went down to the docks. The *Wind Eagle* sat at her moorings, just as he'd left her before he'd made his ill-fated trip to the North Country. He went into the office of the warehouse owned by his shipping company. The clerks in the office jumped up from their chairs at his appearance. At last he was in a place where people respected him.

He took off his jacket and went to work. His desk was piled with correspondence and his banker was begging an audience. Work always kept his life in perspective.

Women never did.

Samantha couldn't spend the day moping. She had promised to make a poultice for Alice's chest and she would do so—even if what she really wanted to do was pack her bag and take the earliest mail coach back to Sproule.

She prepared the poultice and then Emily led her up to the servants' quarters on the third floor where Alice and Terrance were staying. Since the servants were all occupied with their chores elsewhere in the house, this floor was very quiet.

Samantha excused Emily at the staircase and followed the sound of someone reading. In a small dormer room, close to the back stairs leading down to the kitchen, she found Alice in bed sleeping. Terrance sat quietly on the floor beside her bed, listening to Fenley read a book.

Samantha paused in the doorway, surprised to see the manservant here.

Fenley finished the last words of the story before rising from his chair. "Good morning, my lady. I was entertaining our guests."

"I see that. Did you enjoy the story?" she asked Terrance.

"Aye, my lady."

"Terrance knows his letters and is good with numbers," Fenley said with approval. "I believe that once His Grace hears that, he will think better of the young man. Perhaps we will find a position for him in the duke's household."

"Why, that is wonderful," Samantha said, while Terrance beamed proudly.

"Me mum said she would watch over us from heaven, and it seems as if she has," Terrance said. "Just when things got so bad I was afraid we'd starve, Lord Yale saved us. He'll never regret it, my lady. I promise he won't."

"I am sure he will not," Samantha assured him. She sat on the edge of the bed and gently woke Alice to place the poultice on the girl's chest. Alice rolled right back to sleep.

Samantha felt her forehead.

"Is she going to be fine, my lady?" Terrance asked anxiously.

"Yes," Samantha said with complete confidence. "Sleep is the best healer, although you are most fortunate Mr. Carderock found you when he did."

"I know that," Terrance agreed readily. He paused a moment and then said, "I am sorry we caused so much trouble for his lordship this morning."

Samantha tucked the covers around Alice's painfully thin shoulders before saying, "His lordship and the duke are brothers. They argued as brothers do argue."

Fenley chuckled his agreement.

"Now, take care of your sister and watch her closely," Samantha told Terrance. "I will have some clear broth sent up and you must make sure Alice drinks all of it."

"I will," the boy promised.

"I'll come back and check on her in an hour or so."

"Yes, my lady." Terrance made a clumsy bow, and Samantha smiled at him.

She left the room. Fenley followed her out into the hall.

"I'll personally see that the broth is sent up from the kitchen, my lady."

"Thank you, Fenley." She lightly touched his arm. "It's nice of you to take an interest in those children."

"It is no chore at all. I've always enjoyed the strays Master Yale brought home."

Master Yale. She had not heard Fenley refer to Yale that way. She liked the paternal sound of it.

He started for the back stairs, but Samantha's voice stopped him.

"What do you mean about Yale bringing home strays?"

The servant turned to her. "Master Yale always came home from school with some poor boy or other who didn't have anywhere to go . . . or didn't want to go where he should. Master Yale had a soft heart when he was a child. It was a characteristic of his I've admired. For a while, when he was a young man on the town, I thought he'd lost it. It is good to see that in spite of his being a successful man of business, he has returned to his youthful compassion. I believe a gentleman needs compassion."

His words struck uncomfortably close to the heart of her worries . . .

"His Grace said you know all the family secrets."

Fenley gave a small bow. "I have been privileged to be with the House of Ayleborough for a good many years."

"Then you probably are aware of the differences my husband had with his father?"

His watery blue eyes watched her carefully now. "They argued often," he said bluntly. "Master Yale never was one to bow to authority, whether from his father or the headmaster of whatever school he was attending at the time. The old duke was much like His Grace. Their immediate thoughts and fears are for their own loved ones and the good of the family. Master Yale was always a bit irreverent toward those topics."

Samantha polished the smooth wood of the stair banister with the palm of her hand, debating a moment before drawing a deep breath and asking, "Why was Yale disinherited?"

Fenley frowned.

"I know it isn't proper of me to ask. But everyone seems to know except me, and there is no one else to whom I can turn except you." She placed her hand on his arm. "Yale would only say something flippant, and if I asked the duke, he would huff for me not to worry about it. But I *do* worry. You see, I've heard stories, and yet in many ways he doesn't fit the image of the man in the stories."

Samantha felt heat rush to her cheeks as she added, "In some ways he does."

Fenley's eyes sparkled with silent laughter. "Oh, he always was a rogue with the ladies."

"I'd heard that Yale was disinherited because of women, but His Grace mentioned that wasn't true. He said it was because Yale squandered money."

"Young Master Yale did spend rather freely, but not any more than any other idle son of a rich father."

"Then what happened?"

Fenley shook his head. "I don't know if I should tell you. It's not important anymore."

"Please. I must know." She pleaded with him with her eyes. "I want to know."

"Well, someone should tell you," he relented. He looked to either side in the hall to ensure they were alone. "You understand, don't you, my lady, that in families what seems as nothing to an outsider can be very serious to the persons involved?"

Samantha thought of the numerous family disputes her father had been called upon to resolve as vicar. Some of them had been quite petty. "I know what you are saying."

"Good." He drew a breath and then said, "In my opinion, the argument between Lord Yale and his father had to do with control. Whether my lord wishes to admit it or not, he is very much like his sire."

"Is he?" Samantha had not noticed. "My memory of the old duke was of a kind, gentle man."

"Yes, well, in his younger days, the old duke loved a challenge. He was opinionated and headstrong. No one told him what to do."

"Much like Yale is now?"

Fenley smiled. "Exactly. Wayland was always more biddable. As the oldest son, he had had it drummed into him what was expected. He was a good student and took his responsibilities seriously, just as his father wished him to. Meanwhile, Master Yale had a difficult time in school—I do not mean that he is not intelligent; he is. He's quicker than a cat on most matters. But he is not studious."

Samantha shook her head. "I cannot imagine his energy confined to a schoolroom."

"It was difficult. And once his mother died, he turned into quite a handful. I've always believed he felt left out of the family. His brother and sister had the same mother, who was undoubtedly the old duke's favorite wife. Poor Master Yale was years younger and didn't even look like the rest of them."

"I see the family resemblance."

"But he didn't," Fenley reminded her gently. "He was a lonely child even though he was popular and had friends. He was always very handsome, and women had a tendency to mother and make over him. Men gave him the benefit of the doubt. Of course, he was spoiled rotten and became a wild little prankster. You should ask about some of his more outrageous stunts at school. He was sent down from Eton three times before they finally said they didn't want him back."

"And the old duke was not happy hearing that."

"Absolutely not. Although he managed to get Yale into St. John's College. He lasted less than six months there. Of course, his father didn't know about it because Master Yale didn't come home. He hied himself to London, used his father's good credit, and set himself up in grand style."

Samantha laughed at the thought. It sounded like Yale.

"It was funny," Fenley agreed. "Here he was, a lad of nineteen with his own residence, flank of servants, and memberships to the best clubs. The first bills arrived on the old duke's desk about the same time as the letter from the chancellor of the college. The duke had me accompany him when he made the trip from Northumberland to London to confront his son. Master Yale had hosted a party the night before. We literally had to kick the empty wine bottles out of our way to walk across the floor. Master Yale was in a drunken stupor."

"His father was angry?"

"Not at first, but he grew angry when Master Yale showed no remorse. The lad was in with a bad crowd and had been fleeced shamelessly at the gaming tables. I believe Master Yale was embarrassed, but as is so often the case with youth, he'd hoped to extricate himself from these embarrassing debts with false bravado."

"So they argued."

"Bitterly. The son was not about to admit he was wrong; the father grew more angry that his son was not more obedient. So the duke decided to teach Master Yale a lesson."

"One that didn't work out the way he'd planned."

Fenley shrugged. "I could have told him that.

The lad had his father's pride. He would not come begging back."

Samantha thought on everything he'd said. She hugged her arms against her waist. "He refuses to stay in England. He wants to leave."

"Of course he does," Fenley said. "His brother doesn't understand that it was easy for him to follow his father's orders because someday *he* would be the duke. But Master Yale had no such opportunity before him. He is ambitious. Nor is he the kind of man who can easily do another's bidding. He would not be happy to stay here and do nothing more than carry out his brother's orders."

"Have you told His Grace this?"

"He has not asked me."

Samantha studied the old servant. She liked him. She trusted him. And because she had need of someone to confide in, she whispered, "He wants to leave me."

Fenley considered her words a moment, then said sadly, "I am sorry."

"I love him." She raised her eyes to meet his.

The manservant touched her shoulder. It was a fatherly gesture.

"Have you been in love?" she asked.

"I spent thirty-two years with my sainted wife. She was the light of my world. She died five years ago. I think of her every day."

"I fear I will feel the same way about Yale. He's exasperating and stubborn and independent, but I don't think I will ever love another as I love him. Oh, Fenley, what shall I do?"

"Love isn't something you cage, my lady, and keep to yourself. It's given from one person to another. If that person does not wish to be with you, you can't force him."

Samantha drew a deep, shuddering breath. "Another woman might manage to make him stay. A woman who is more beautiful and sophisticated than I am."

Fenley laughed. "Master Yale is made of sterner stuff than that. The only way you can keep him is if he wishes to stay with you."

"And if he doesn't?"

A sad look stole into Fenley's eyes. "Then you will build a life without him. Your heart will hurt, but you will mend. You are a strong woman, my lady. You will go on."

Samantha shook her head, denying his words. "I wish I'd never fallen in love. Death would be preferable to the pain I'm feeling now."

"No," Fenley answered, clasping her hands between both of his. "Love enriches the spirit. It gives meaning and depth to our life. When my wife died, I prayed that my life might be taken, too. I wanted to crawl into the grave with her. But now I think back on our years together and all the pain I felt at her loss is balanced by memories of unequaled joy and happiness."

"But your love was returned," Samantha reminded him sadly. "Will I feel as you say, even if my love is never returned?"

He smiled at her, his expression that of a gentle grandfather. "Would you be happier never to have loved at all?"

Samantha thought on his question. She erased the fears and doubts and instead just considered her love for Yale and what those words really meant.

It appeared in her mind's eye almost as something set apart from the rest of her, a bright, shining thing, pure and unwavering . . . filling her with the beauty of its presence. Her heart soared with the gift of it.

She loved Yale Carderock just the way he was. She saw his flaws, the differences between her character and his . . . and none of it mattered. What did matter is that he'd changed her in ways she hadn't even noticed until this moment. Before, she had been adrift, a shadow of a woman, incomplete and half-formed.

Now, in spite of the fact that he did not return her love, she felt stronger. Yes, that was it. In this moment of realization, she almost felt powerful. Yale had done more than take her out of Sproule; he'd taken her out of herself.

His presence in her life was a gift.

And she would never regret having fallen in love with him.

"I love him," she said, and then repeated it, her conviction stronger than before. "I will always love him, but you are right. Love is not a reason for despair but a cause for celebration."

"I hope someday he returns your love."

Samantha kissed Fenley's aged cheek. "I hope

so, too. But even if he doesn't, you have helped me to understand. Thank you."

With those words, she left to see the duchess, her heart much lighter.

Chapter 15

The butler's jaw dropped open when Yale sailed through the door of Penhurst in his new finery. The man's reaction was everything Yale could have wished.

The tailor Yale had patronized before he'd left on his journey to Northumberland—and from whom Yale had heard of his father's death—had finished the new wardrobe and delivered it to the ship.

Yale took off his greatcoat to reveal a marine blue jacket cut in the latest fashion. He knew he looked the very model of a wealthy man. His buff breeches hugged his thighs, while the gleaming black leather of his boots reflected the light from the room's candles. He even had a new hat.

His fine attire excited an even better reaction from Fenley, who almost missed his step and walked into a marble column at the sight of Yale. His recovery was quicker than that of the butler. "Lord Yale, I must say you look splendid."

"Mr. Carderock," Yale corrected, as he handed his hat to the butler. "And thank you for the compliment, Fenley. It is not often I've had a chance to dumbfound you."

"Not that you didn't try years ago," Fenley answered complacently.

Yale smiled at the memory. "Ah, but you were always more than equal to my youthful transgressions."

"You tested me, my lord, you tested me."

Yale laughed and then asked the question uppermost in his mind: "Tell me, where is my wife?"

"She is in the nursery with the duchess," Fenley answered.

Yale dusted a piece of imaginary lint from the sleeve of his jacket. "I believe I will go see her." He started for the stairs.

"You will be joining the family this evening, won't you, my lord?" Fenley asked.

"No, I won't be able to. I've been asked to dine with the Prime Minister." It gave him great pleasure to say those words. "Timothy, please see that Beast is brought round to me at half past seven."

"Yes, my lord," the butler said with a bow.

Yale climbed the stairs, eager for Samantha to see him in his new finery and to tell her the good news about his dinner with the prime minister.

He was disappointed to find only his sister-in-law in the nursery. She carried the baby on one shoulder.

"Oh my, Yale, you appear quite the Corinthian," Marion greeted him. "You've even cut your hair."

He self-consciously flicked his fingers through the short curls cut in the latest style. "Thank you," he said and then paused. "Actually, I should say th*ah*nk you." He drawled the words out with the practiced boredom of a well-established dandy.

Marion laughed at his clowning and turned the baby to look at him. "There he is, Charlie, your Uncle Yale. Isn't he fine? All he needs now is a snuff box."

The baby blew a bubble from his mouth and it was Yale's turn to stare. He'd never seen such an ugly baby. Charlie had a big, bald head, protruding ears, and a nose that looked uncomfortably like Yale's own.

"Isn't he *adorable*?" Marion asked proudly.

Yale grasped for words. "My thoughts exactly."

"Here, hold him." She didn't wait for a response but shoved the baby into Yale's arms.

For a long second, uncle and nephew stared at each other with uncertainty.

"I must run to my room for a moment," Marion said. "Nurse is taking a much deserved rest. You don't mind watching Charlie for a few minutes, do you?"

"Well . . . no, I guess not."

Marion smiled. She was already on her way to

the door. "I knew you wouldn't. I'll be right back."

"Wait," Yale said, following her to the door and still awkwardly holding the baby. "Where is Samantha?"

"Getting ready for this evening," Marion said over her shoulder. "You are going to join us, aren't you? Twyla and her husband will be here, as well as Uncle Norris and the rest of the family."

"I can't," Yale said and then told her, with no small amount of pride, his momentous news. "I dine with the Prime Minister tonight."

Marion paused in the door, her eyes widening in surprise. "Lord Grenville?"

"The same. I met him while having a late lunch with some bankers today. He wants to hear my thoughts on the Indies trade."

"Why, Yale, that is wonderful." Marion's expression turned wistful. "We will miss you, of course. By the way, Samantha and I had a lovely afternoon. She is a very special person."

"Yes, she is," he answered perfunctorily.

Marion shook her head. "It is all right, Yale. She told me the two of you weren't a love match. I must have sounded silly, babbling on the way I did last night."

"You didn't," he murmured, because he felt she expected an answer.

"Anyway, Samantha explained to me that the two of you have agreed to live apart."

"She did?" The news surprised him. When

had she changed her mind about their arrangement?

"Yes. She also told me that Wayland had wanted you to stay, but she's made it very clear to both of us how important your other life is to you."

Yale didn't know how to digest this piece of information. "Really?"

Marion nodded. "She is an eloquent spokesperson on your behalf. Wayland is not completely satisfied, but he is growing accustomed to the idea of your leaving again. Besides, you are giving us Samantha. She is such a joy. Please have no fears. We shall love her like a sister."

"I . . ." Yale paused. He didn't really know what he was going to say. He hadn't expected that his plans to leave would meet with such blessing. "I appreciate that."

Marion smiled. "I'll be right back." She left the nursery, closing the door behind her.

Yale stared after her, not even thinking about the baby in his arms—so he was completely unprepared for the child to let out a peacock-shrill wail.

He looked down at Charlie. The babe's forehead was puckered with worry. "She'll be right back," Yale assured him. "There's no sense in getting worked up."

His words didn't seem to reassure Charlie, who scrunched up his face in preparation for a good cry. Yale panicked.

He started walking and talking to the baby—

foolish stuff, nonsensical. He told him about meeting the prime minister and being invited to dine. It was silly to talk this way to a baby, but Charlie actually seemed interested. He grabbed Yale's lapel with one hand. His short little legs kicked beneath the long skirts of his baby dress. He kicked the dress high enough for a sock-covered foot to stick out. Shifting the baby's weight to balance on one arm, Yale couldn't resist touching that small foot. He could feel the tiny toes inside the sock.

Charles watched him intently while chewing on his free fist.

"That's what your problem is. You're hungry, aren't you?" Yale told him. He held up his finger.

Charlie reached over and started gumming his uncle's finger just like a trained bird. Yale watched in amazement. The wee lad drooled something terrible.

"You will be the bane of your tailors," Yale warned him. He studied the baby's profile. "Actually, your nose isn't that bad. Rather distinguished, I think."

Charlie raised his gaze to meet his uncle's but did not offer comment or stop his chewing. Yale thought he could feel the beginnings of teeth against his finger. He wondered what they looked like and might have opened his nephew's mouth to peek except for the sudden rush of warmth he felt on his arm . . . directly on the spot where Charlie's little bum sat.

A man didn't have to be intimately familiar with babies to know what had happened. Charlie had soiled his nappy.

With both hands, he held Charlie out and away from him. "What have you done?"

Charles had the audacity to smile, kicking his feet in excitement.

Yale raced over to the door, still holding the baby in out in front of him. However, when he got to the door, he found he couldn't open it unless he changed his hold on Charlie.

Yale wasn't about to run further risk of staining his new clothes. He yelled. "Marion? Marion! Someone! Come help me."

He listened for footsteps. He heard nothing.

"A house full of servants," he muttered to the baby, "and when you need one, not one can be found."

Charlie blew bubbles at him. He was quite good at bubble blowing.

Then, Yale heard footsteps coming toward the nursery. He stepped back from the door expectantly. It opened . . .

. . . And in walked Samantha—but she looked completely different than when he'd last seen her.

Her glossy brown hair had been gathered up high on her head. A gold ribbon threaded through it tamed the riot of curls. He had the impression that he could pull on that ribbon and her hair would tumble down around her shoulders to where breasts swelled daringly above the low-cut neckline of a rose muslin dress.

The rose color gave her skin a healthy glow and a sparkle to her brown eyes. A sash of the same gold hair ribbon around the high waist of the dress emphasized the fullness of her breasts. In fact, Yale found it very difficult to take his eyes off them. He could almost swear he could see the pink of her nipples.

As she moved toward him, the material clung and outlined her legs, including an entrancing V at the top of them.

"Dear God, Sam. Are you wearing anything beneath that dress?"

She stopped dead in her tracks, her eyes widening. "I beg your pardon?"

Too late, Yale realized he'd said the wrong thing. "I don't mean that you don't look fetching and all that." She looked more than fetching— she looked delicious.

"But," he continued, stumbling for words, "is that really the sort of dress a vicar's daughter should be wearing?"

Her cheeks turned bright red. "It is the height of fashion. Marion picked it out for me."

"Marion?"

"Yes, it's hers. The dressmaker cut it down for me."

Yale stared. His conservative sister-in-law would wear such a thing? And then he realized he never would have noticed. Whereas with Sam—

Charlie's cry interrupted his thoughts. He still

held his nephew straight-armed in front of him.

"What is wrong with Charles?" Samantha said. She moved forward and took the baby from Yale. She held him with a practiced hand.

Grateful for her intervention, Yale confessed, "He has messed in his nappy and I can't find anyone to change it. Watch out for your dress, now."

"Oh, pooh," Samantha said to Yale, but with her gaze on Charlie. "I can change a baby's diaper and not worry about my dress."

Charlie smiled up at her.

She carried him over to the dressing table and laid him on it. Yale trailed behind them.

"If he's all dimples and kisses now, it's because he saved the odious part for his Uncle Yale."

Samantha laughed, lifting Charlie's baby dress and working to unfasten the knots of his diapers. She removed it and wiped his bottom with a damp cloth.

Yale stood at the edge of the table, feeling a bit out of place. "Do you like my new clothes?" She hadn't said anything about them yet.

Samantha stared at him as if just now noticing his finery. She gave a rueful smile. "You look very handsome. And you've cut your hair." She reached for a clean diaper from a pile on the table for that purpose. "I like it."

But his earlier wish to impress her seemed flat and false. Instead, he studied her carefully. "Actually, you are the one who has changed."

She laughed silently. "Do you mean my new hairstyle?"

"No, I mean, yes." He shook his head at his verbal fumbling. "I like it. I also think your dress is very attractive, too."

She blushed prettily and said, "I am wearing a petticoat."

Now it was his turn to be embarrassed. He should have reacted with more sophistication. "I was being silly. You caught me by surprise."

"Oh, you will be taken by surprise when you receive the bill from the dressmaker. Marion kept ordering one dress after another. I don't know when I shall wear them all."

"Marion was quite right to see you outfitted properly. Don't even think about the bills. I would not mind even if you ordered a hundred dresses."

"I'm not so sure Marion didn't."

He laughed, but then added softly, "Still, there is something different about you. Something that has nothing to do with the dress or the hairstyle." He reached over and tipped her chin up to look at him. He drank in every detail of her face before he said slowly, "You almost seem more relaxed. More at peace."

"I am." She lifted Charlie up in her arms, taking his fisted hand in hers. "I've finally accepted my fate." She kissed the baby's tiny fingers.

"Your fate?"

"I do not want to force you to stay. What is the word men often use to describe marriage?

Shackled. I do not want you to be *shackled* to me.''

Yale wasn't sure of her meaning. She was saying she was cutting him loose? Without recriminations? Or at least a few tears?

For a second he felt as if the floor had disappeared beneath his feet. He placed a hand on the changing table for balance, not certain how he should react, how he wanted to react.

She smiled. ''I do admire your new clothes too, Yale. You look just as a man should when he is ready to take his place in the world.''

Yale remembered his news. ''I dine with the Prime Minister tonight.'' The words sounded hollow.

''Yes, I heard. I met Fenley on my way up the stairs. We shall miss you this evening, but I'm sure yours will be a very important dinner.''

''He wants to know what I think of the Indies trade.''

She stood rocking back and forth with the baby in her arms. Charlie cooed to her. ''Your brother will be very proud of you.''

Yale ran the fingers of one hand back and forth along the wooden rail around the changing table. ''What of you? Are you proud of me?''

She gave him a smile that was like a ray of sunshine shooting through the gloom. ''Yes, I'm proud of you. And even though the circumstances of our marriage were a bit unorthodox, I'm glad you married me.''

Time seemed to suspend itself. ''Why?'' he

asked, staring into the open honesty of her golden brown eyes.

"Because . . ." She started and then stopped, looking away a moment. He wondered what she was thinking.

"Because why?" he pressed.

She faced him. "Because now I have a home."

"Oh." He rocked back on his heels, strangely deflated. He didn't know what he'd expected her to say—or what he'd *hoped* she would say—but whatever it was, it wasn't what she'd said.

He leaned one hip against the table. "That is it?"

Her smile turned bittersweet. "Is there anything else?"

Yes, me.

Yale hedged away from the thought. He felt like a man making his way across a thin sheet of ice. If he wasn't careful, he might admit to something he'd regret later. "No, nothing."

She nodded as if his answer had been what she had expected. "I explained to Marion that we are not a love match."

"She told me that."

"Yes. I told her you wanted to swim in waterfalls."

"Waterfalls?"

Her smile was shyly self-conscious. "Don't you remember telling me about swimming in the pool fed by waterfalls? I thought I'd never heard of anything so lovely. Marion said she hadn't, either."

He didn't answer. He couldn't. He watched Charlie try to chew on his own foot and felt just about as silly and awkward.

At that moment the door opened and Marion breezed into the room. "I'm so sorry it took me longer than I expected. I hope you don't mind, Yale. Oh, has my Charlie been good?" She took the baby from Samantha and hugged him close.

Charlie ignored his mother's kisses. Instead, he stared at Yale, his expression awake and curious—as if to say, "There is my uncle Yale the buffoon."

Because that was how Yale felt.

"Doesn't Samantha look lovely?" Marion said, calling Yale back to attention.

"Yes," he agreed readily. "Most lovely—"

He was struck by a new realization, a disturbing one. Samantha looked like a stranger. He had the unusual sensation that she was drifting away from him.

"She is going to be the Toast of London," Marion predicted.

"I'll be labeled a bumpkin from the north, once they hear my accent," Samantha said.

"Your accent is lovely," Marion disclaimed. "Such a lilting sound, and not so harsh as a Scots accent. She shouldn't worry, should she, Yale?"

"No," he murmured, now picturing Samantha as the rage of the London Season. It wasn't an image he liked. Men would flock to her, drawn by her accent. They would know immediately that she was fresh from the country and think her slightly naïve.

And she was. She had no idea of the evils that lurked in Society under the guise of polished manners. Men who wouldn't hesitate to take advantage of her.

Or did she know? Was that why she was so willing to cut him free?

But he couldn't stay. He had to go. He had no choice. Nor could he let his jealousy show. He didn't want to appear a complete fool.

"Don't forget, the dinner bell will ring in one hour, Samantha," Marion said. "And Yale, I told Wayland that you have been honored with an invitation to dine with Lord Grenville. He doesn't like the man's politics, but he hopes you put in a good word for the family."

"Of course I will."

"I know that," she said indulgently. She reached up and kissed his cheek. "You are a good brother and I am happy that you returned to us, even for this short a time."

"Thank you, Marion." He meant the words.

"Now come, Samantha. We must make one last check of everything downstairs to ensure all is ready."

"I am certain *something* needs to be done," Samantha said. "I can't imagine entertaining this many guests on such short notice."

"Oh, but I have help! And I know many's is the time you entertained the whole village of

Sproule and didn't have one extra pair of hands to help you," Marion said, and the two women left with Charlie bouncing on his mother's shoulder.

Yale found himself alone. The only one of the trio who had given him a backward glance had been bubble blowing Charlie.

He walked to his room, disconcerted by these contradictory feelings. He'd always known his own mind. He was a man. Men knew what they wanted.

But the only thing he knew right now was that he wished Samantha had not been so anxious to hurry off with Marion.

His valet waited impatiently for him. He'd already been informed by the butler that Yale dined with the Prime Minister and wished his master to make the best impression possible. He heartily approved of the new wardrobe that Yale had sent over earlier from the ship.

Yale had to suffer the valet's ministrations while the little man prattled on about shoe polish and finished seams, a conversation that didn't interest Yale at all. Instead, he listened to the sound of coaches arriving outside his bedroom window, facing the street.

The Carderock family, when second and third cousins were included, was actually quite large. From the greetings he could hear, it sounded as if everyone had turned out to be introduced to Samantha.

Yale waved the valet away and undertook to

tie his own neckcloth. He was tired of the man's fussiness.

He was just getting the knot right when he heard a sound in the sitting room. He opened the door and caught Samantha reaching for the green glass paperweight.

She looked up in surprise. "Oh, I'd thought you'd gone." She wore a shawl of cream shot through with gold threads. Kid leather gloves covered her arms to the elbow.

"I'll be leaving shortly."

"I'm sorry you won't be with us tonight. I'm just a little nervous, but I'll be fine," she hurried to add. "I just thought it might be a good thing to rub my palm over the pixie paperweight. I felt I needed some magic."

"You don't need magic, Sam. You're beautiful."

Her eyes sparkled from his compliment. "Thank you," she whispered.

They stood staring at each other.

She moved first. "Well, I must go downstairs." She turned and started for her bedroom.

Yale was tempted to call her back, and yet something stopped him. Probably his own good common sense. He didn't need a woman in his life.

He didn't need anyone.

So why did he feel left out?

He watched her until she shut her bedroom door and then returned to his fuming valet. It didn't take long for him to finish dressing after that.

He wore formal evening dress, white knee breeches, a dark wine velvet coat, and a white swansdown waistcoat. He took his silk hat from his valet, told him not to wait up, and started down the stairs. As he entered the foyer, the sound of laughter carried from the receiving room and echoed off the marble. Most of the guests had arrived and there was only him, Fenley, and a few footmen waiting for stragglers.

"Beast is waiting for you, my lord," Fenley said. One of the footmen held out Yale's greatcoat.

"Yes, thank you," Yale said absently. He didn't move to put his arms in his coat. Instead, he was drawn to the murmur of conversation. He wandered closer to the receiving room.

The doors were open; the room was full. He spied Wayland and Marion and was surprised that they had included the older boys in this family gathering. After six in the evening, he and his siblings had never been allowed out of the nursery. For their part, both Matthew and John acted well behaved.

Twyla was there. She was still blond and blue-eyed, with a miniature version of the Carderock nose . . . but she'd aged. She had wrinkles, and her waist was thicker. She appeared happy and healthy, not completely like the sharp-tongued sister he'd left eleven years before.

By her side stood a man whom Yale hadn't

met. His manner was so supercilious toward her, Yale knew instantly this must be Twyla's husband, the one Wayland had labeled the "twit."

Then he saw Samantha. The crowd shifted and there she was. She stood not far from the twit. Graceful and composed, she talked to two young women of around her same age. The women must be cousins that Yale had long ago forgotten. Certainly he didn't recognize either one now.

But there was no doubt in his mind that Samantha outshone everyone in the room. He knew how nervous she was, and his chest swelled with pride at her courage.

She listened intently to something one of the women said and then shook her head ruefully. He wondered if they had asked about him . . . and if she wished he were there.

If she wanted him to be there.

And then Sam laughed.

He could hear the sound not just with his ears, but with every fiber of his being.

At that moment, in that very instant, he was hit by the fabled bolt of lightning. The one prudent men avoided. The one he had never believed existed.

He was stuck by Love.

Yale staggered back a step, humbled by the magnitude of his love for Samantha. Why, it had always been there, he realized with a sense of wonder, maybe even from the first moment they'd met—except that today what he felt for

her was larger and grander and more encom-
passing than anything he'd ever imagined.

And tomorrow his love for her would be
greater still. He knew it in the depths of his soul.

Walking the streets of London, he'd thought
that he might be falling in love with her—in fact,
he'd feared it. But now, watching her laughing
eyes reflect the candlelight . . . his fears seemed
silly. Groundless. Vain, even.

"My lord, your coat." The footman's voice
sounded as if it came from a great distance.

Almost in a daze, Yale turned and looked at
him.

While his whole being had been profoundly
changed, everything else had stayed the same.
No one was different save him.

And maybe that was one of the beauties of
Love. That no one else could feel what he felt. It
was special and unique . . . and all his.

He looked back at Samantha. A man had appeared at her side to offer her a glass of wine.
Yale didn't recognize him. A ripple of irritation
went through him. "Fenley, who is that man
talking to my wife?"

Fenley peered at the man a moment. "That is
your cousin Richard. He is twice removed on
your father's first wife's side of the family."

Yale didn't remember Richard. But he knew
he didn't like him. The man was a fop. The
points of his collar were too high, and the green
and yellow stripped waistcoat was vulgar.

Then Samantha laughed at something Richard said. Yale almost growled.

"Is there a problem, my lord?" Fenley asked blandly.

"No problem," Yale said, his eye still on Richard. "However, send Beast back to the stable and please see that a message is sent to Lord Grenville. Convey to him my sincere regrets, but I will not be able to dine with him this evening."

"Shall I include a reason?" Fenley asked.

"Tell him I must dine with my wife," Yale said, already walking toward the receiving room.

Chapter 16

Samantha listened politely as the man introduced to her as Cousin Richard droned on about his wine collection. Her head hurt from trying to keep all the names straight with the proper faces. The person who had made the strongest impression had been Uncle Norris because he used a tin ear horn and shouted as if everyone else was deaf.

She was just taking a sip of the wine Richard had brought to her when a prickling sensation raced along her neck.

He was here.

Her heart seemed to stop beating. She turned. Even the air in the room took on a new and vital energy.

The crowd shifted. Conversation died out. Everyone moved toward the door—and she knew without looking that her husband was there.

The wall of guests parted forming a corridor between her and the man she loved. He was a

336

handsome sight in his wine velvet evening jacket and white satin breeches. But what riveted her attention was the expression on his face.

He was looking at her with such love, she knew that her dearest dream had been answered.

Love! Bright, shining, *wonderful* love. It was there for everyone to see.

She didn't know whether to laugh or cry from the joy in the moment. Tension, fear, hope—all had lain coiled tight and deep within her, and now they sprang free, leaving her to bask in the glory of love.

She held out her glass in Richard's direction—fortunately, he took it, because she would have let it drop if he hadn't—and began walking toward her husband. The noise and quiet murmurs of the guests faded to be replaced by the beating of her own heart.

He held out his hand to her.

Samantha stopped, almost afraid to go forward.

He took the last steps to bring them together, his stride sure. His warm fingers closed over hers.

"Yale." She released his name on a sigh and only then realized she'd been holding her breath.

He raised her hand to his lips and pressed his kiss against it. "Forgive me, Samantha. I have been so blind."

His deep, husky voice was no louder than a

whisper, and yet if he had shouted the words, she could not have been more glad.

"Yale, I love you."

His gaze met hers. "I love you. With all my heart."

Samantha laughed and threw her arms around his neck, completely forgetting they had an audience. Her feet left the floor as Yale picked her up and held her close. Here, in his arms, was where she belonged. Here was her home.

Wayland's voice brought them back to reality. "Yale, aren't you late for your engagement with the Prime Minister?" he asked slyly.

Yale set her down on the ground, his arm resting possessively around her waist. "Actually, I've changed my plans," he said easily. "I wouldn't want to disappoint my family."

A huge smile split Wayland's face. "Then let me be the first to raise a glass and welcome you back, brother." He nodded to the others. "To my brother."

"To Yale," several voices echoed, and they all drank his health. Marion signaled for the servants to refill glasses.

Yale turned to Samantha and started to say something, but he was interrupted by Twyla's crisp voice, "Well, the prodigal has returned home at last."

"It is good to see you, too, dear sister."

"I suppose you believe we all welcome you with open arms?"

"I know that would be too much to expect

from you," Yale answered smoothly. "May I say, you haven't changed over the years?"

Twyla snorted. "Neither have you. I hope you don't believe we will all sing your praises. Wayland is far more forgiving than he should be."

Wayland, whose expression had turned wary the moment Twyla had come up to their younger brother, stepped between them. "We are *all* glad to have Yale back, just as we value the contributions of *your* husband, my dear sister."

His conciliatory words did not set her mind at ease. "I pray you don't forget that," she said. "While Yale has been off wandering the world, Harold has worked very hard. It hasn't always been easy for him. You've often asked him to do things that were beneath his dignity. I would not want to see him lose what is rightfully his because of Yale's return."

"There's enough work for every member of this family," Wayland said firmly.

"Besides," Yale said, "there is a difference between my life and that of the prodigal son."

"Really?" Twyla said with polite disinterest.

"Yes, the prodigal son was poor in spirit and in pocket. Whereas right now, I am the richest man on earth. I have my wife and my shipping company. I can ask for no more."

Marion placed her arm around her brother-in-law's shoulder. "I am so happy for you both," she said. "And, Twyla, put aside your doubts. We are a family again. Let us celebrate."

Wayland took his wife's hand. "Yes, Twyla,

listen to reason and put your fears to rest. I love both my siblings equally and I will never give you cause to worry."

"Oh please, I'm glad he's not *dead*," Twyla admitted. "I just don't want to see Harold left out."

"Twyla, don't be ridiculous," Yale said with impatience. "If you wish for me to sign a paper relinquishing all claims to the House of Ayleborough, I will do it. I don't need the money. I have everything I want. I have Samantha."

Suddenly, everyone in the room clapped. Yale and his brother and sister turned to see that they were the center of interest. Even Uncle Norris had heard Yale's declaration.

Samantha's cheeks burned with pleasure and embarrassment. "I can't believe you said that in front of everyone."

"I'll say it again," Yale offered stoutly. "I love my wife." And he kissed her!

This time, his relatives did more than clap; several shouted with good-natured ribbing.

Marion motioned for the butler to announce dinner. As cousins and aunts and uncles passed Yale and Samantha on their way into the dining room, they offered congratulations to their couple.

Uncle Norris stopped in front of them and said in his gruff, overloud voice, "Always did like you, nephew. Said you had spirit! Good to show some spirit now and then!"

After he'd passed, Yale whispered, "I always felt he hated me when I was a child. He was forever advising my father not to spare the rod. Fortunately, Father didn't listen to him."

"People have a tendency to be overbearing with the very young," Samantha observed.

"We must endeavor not to do that ourselves," he said sternly.

"Yes, my lord," she said with mock humility, and Yale laughed.

As the last person went in to dinner and they were alone in the receiving room, Yale turned to Samantha. "Now I know why I had to return to England." He rubbed the back of her hand he held. "It wasn't just my father I needed to see. I needed to stand in the middle of all of them and feel the way I do now."

"Which is?"

"Completely accepted. I used to hear them whisper about my mother. She didn't ingratiate herself with any of them. But now I realize they aren't bad people. For the first time in my life, I feel whole and completely accepted." He looked down at her. "Not for the reasons that I had anticipated, but because of you."

Samantha blinked back tears of happiness. "I don't think you will ever say anything that will mean as much to me as those words."

"Then I will say them every day."

She would have thrown her arms around him, but Fenley's voice interrupted them. "His Grace bids you come join the family at the table."

"I don't want to have dinner with them," Yale said, for her ears alone. "I want to be alone with you. We have several nights of our honeymoon to make up for."

His words sparked an answering need inside Samantha—and a blush that must have gone all the way to the tips of her ears.

"Master Yale," Fenley reminded him.

"Yes, Fenley, I'm coming," Yale said, taking Samantha's arm. "I know better than to ignore him when he calls me 'Master Yale.'"

Samantha laughed. As she walked by Fenley, he winked, the movement so quick, she could have imagined it.

Of course, Yale saw it. "Why did Fenley wink at you?"

"Perhaps he's part pixie," Samantha said, then laughed with joy.

Dinner was almost interminable. The conversation was lively enough, but Samantha heard very little and could eat even less. Her complete concentration was on the man across the table from her, her husband.

She understood what Yale meant about feeling whole. That's how she felt, knowing he loved her. No more doubts; no more fears.

At last, after the tenth and final course had been served, Marion signaled for the ladies to leave the men to their port. Samantha couldn't help a lingering gaze at Yale. He didn't appear too happy, either.

Earlier that afternoon, Marion had said that sometimes the gentlemen of the family could take as long as an hour over their port, depending on how interesting the gossip was. She'd also engaged an Italian singer to entertain the family after dinner.

Samantha didn't know if she could wait that long to be alone with Yale.

The women adjourned to the receiving room, where pots of tea and coffee were set up for their enjoyment.

"Come sit next to me," Marion's mother, Lady Orcutt, ordered. She wore her hair powdered and piled on top of her head. She was Marion's only living relation. "I want to hear the rest of this story about you and that young rake Carderock."

"I don't think he's a *rake*," Samantha said, defending her husband. She had at one time, but her opinion had completely changed.

Lady Orcutt laughed. "Don't you know, girl, rakes make the best husbands." She leaned close to Samantha's ear. "Wayland is fine enough for a duke, but he's so reliable. I wonder how Marion has lived with him this long without growing bored."

"Mother," Marion warned, as she handed Samantha a cup of tea.

Samantha smiled. Marion had warned her that her mother was "as pointed as a brass tack."

However, at that moment Bates, bearing a note on a silver salver, approached them.

He offered it to Samantha. She looked in confusion at Marion as she broke the seal. The note read, *The two orphans need your attention immediately* in a bold handwriting.

There was no signature.

"What is it, Samantha?" Marion asked.

"A note saying Terrance and Alice need me." She looked to Lady Orcutt and Marion. "You will excuse me, won't you, Your Grace?"

"Of course," Marion said. "I hope she hasn't taken a turn for the worse."

"What is this about orphans?" Twyla asked, but Samantha had already risen and was moving toward the door.

Behind her, she heard Marion sigh audibly and launch into a tale of Yale's orphans.

She had just climbed the stairs to the first floor and was preparing to climb another flight when she heard someone whisper her name.

She turned. Two strong arms reached out from the shadows. Before she could think, Yale's lips came down on hers.

Samantha gasped in surprised and then relaxed into the kiss. Her arms went up around his neck.

This was where she'd longed to be.

He lifted her up into his arms and started carrying her down the hall to their room. His lips did not leave hers.

She was the one who broke off the kiss.

"The children—?"

"The children are fine. I used them as an excuse to get you up here. I couldn't wait any longer—especially through an Italian singer!"

Samantha tilted her head back and laughed. One of her kid slippers slid off her heel. It hung on her toe for just a second and then dropped to the carpet. "My shoe."

"Leave it," he said, and shoved open his bedroom door with his shoulder.

The room was dark except for the fire in the hearth.

Yale walked over to the bed and stood Samantha on it. The cotton mattress was cushy under her feet. "What are you doing?" she asked.

"I'm going to undress you," he said, pulling her shawl through her arms and tossing it aside. "And then I'm going to make sweet, mindless love to you." He began pulling at the lacing at the back of her dress.

Samantha captured his hands and brought them forward. "And *then?*"

His dark eyes met hers. "And then *what?*"

She kneeled, holding his hands in front of her. "Are you still going to leave me?"

Yale shook his head. "Sam, I must return to Ceylon, but I will come back to you. I will *always* come back to you. My business is very well developed. Perhaps I can spend a few months there and the rest of the time with you. But I can't make promises. It's not an easy trip."

"Something could happen to you." Now she had a fresh worry.

Yale shushed her. "Or a hundred different accidents could befall me in London. There are no guarantees in life, my beloved. I've become a man of the sea. I built my business with my own sweat and by my own wits. It is like a child to me. But please know there is one constant."

"And what is that?"

"My love for you."

Samantha reached up and placed her cheek against his. She could feel the scrape of his whiskers, the warmth of his body. He smelled as warm and inviting as those spices his ships carried. Her fingers rested against his neck and she felt the beat of his pulse.

"Sam, I know it is a lot to ask of you. You didn't even want to leave Sproule. I will understand if you cannot accept me the way I am."

In answer, she kissed him.

She would take each day as it came, and when they were parted, she would pray and wait until they could be together again.

"I love you," he said.

"I will never tire of hearing those words."

He laughed, his teeth flashing white in the shadowy light. "Then I will say them often."

His finger moved, hooking inside her bodice, pulling it down below one nipple. He brushed the light corset she wore over her breasts. The nipple puckered and he placed his lips over it.

How wonderful it felt to have him touch her again! She buried her fingers in his hair and held him close. He moved to her other breast and she leaned so far back she lost her balance and they fell on the bed together, his leg over hers, his arm under her head.

They both laughed. "We're clumsy," she said.

"We just need practice," he answered, nibbling the hollow of her collarbone while his fingers finished unlacing her dress.

"Yes, practice," she agreed dreamily, and began untying his neckcloth.

He paused and rose just long enough to remove the wine velvet jacket and toss it off the side of the bed.

Samantha ran her hands up and down his sides. "You are so handsome. When I saw you in the doorway this evening, my heart almost stopped."

"You're beautiful," he whispered.

"No, I'm not," she quickly denied. "I'm rather plain."

"Oh, Sam, nothing could be further from the truth. I love your eyes and the way they flash when they are angry. When you are concerned or upset, they are like small mirrors into your soul." He kissed each lid reverently.

It tickled and she couldn't help a little giggle.

"And your eyebrows!" he said.

"My *eyebrows?*"

"Yes." He ran the pad of his thumb first over one brow and then the other. "They are so straight. When you are angry, they come together in a little V. When you are happy, they almost dance."

"Dance?" She laughed in earnest now. "I thought you were telling me my *good* points."

"I am. I love your eyebrows." He placed a kiss

on each one, before rubbing his cheek against hers. Her skin burned from his whisker stubble.

"I like your cheeks, too. Your skin is smoother than the petals of a rose, and your nose . . ." He paused.

"What about my nose?" she dared him.

"It goes very well with your eyebrows."

"You cad," she said, smiling. "My nose is half the size of yours."

"But mine is distinctive," he said proudly. "My father, my brother, and even young Charlie have my nose. You know what they say about men with strong noses."

She shook her head.

Taking her hand, he lowered it to his breeches. She could feel his desire for her. "They are stronger in other ways, too," he said, his voice turning husky at her touch.

Samantha ran her hand down and up the length of him. During their estrangement, she'd dreamed of touching him this way. She knew how to pleasure him.

The time for being playful was past. They began to undress each other in earnest and were soon naked. Their clothes had been thrown every which way on the floor around the bed.

Yale's hand ran up her thigh and she sighed with pleasure as he found his way to her core.

"You've got beautiful breasts," he whispered, tracing the curve of her nipple with his tongue.

Samantha whimpered from the feel of it.

He growled, "I can't wait any longer, Sam."

Without warning, he rolled on his back, picked her up, and sat her on top of him.

Samantha gasped as he slid into her. She pressed her knees against either side of his body, taking in all of him.

"This feels good," he whispered.

"Yes." The pins had long fallen out of her hair. The gold ribbon held a portion of it in place, but the rest flowed down her back.

"Ride me, Sam. Make me come inside you."

He leaned her forward so that her palms rested on his chest. Slowly she began moving.

His hands rested on her hips. They watched each other, their gazes locked. She loved having him this deep inside her. She loved being in control.

They moved in harmony, each knowing what the other liked. They had learned that already and now sought to please.

Their pace quickened.

Yale's head went back, his eyes closing as he raised his hips, the better to thrust into her. His powerful arms held her close. His skin glowed in the firelight.

Samantha didn't know if she could stand much more. She felt as if she rode him beyond anyplace she had ever been before. It felt so good it almost hurt.

And then she reached it: the pinnacle. He was deep inside her. She pressed her knees against him, her hands on his shoulders, holding onto him. Pleasure, joy, rapture ran though her, over and over again.

He shouted her name. She felt his seed release within her and then, pulling her down, he kissed her over and over and over again.

Later, they lay naked in each other's arms, the silk bedcover over them for warmth. Samantha reached up and ran her finger down the length of his nose. "I think it is a very noble nose," she said, breaking the silence.

He grinned, knowing she wasn't talking about noses. "It has its purpose."

"It is a noble purpose."

He fitted her to him. "I would not wish it on daughters. I would want them to have a loving nose like their mother."

"But our sons would be proud to be like their father."

He laughed. "Oh, Samantha, you are the jewel of my life."

"It was an incredible nose this time," she answered drolly.

"It was, wasn't it?"

She nodded, and then, to her surprise, felt him stir. She sat up, her hair over one shoulder. "You can do it again? So soon?"

His smile was cocksure. "With you, I can do anything."

They didn't bother coming out of their room the next day. Their desire for each other had been denied for too long.

Nor did they just make love. They talked.

Samantha had never felt this close to another human being. She didn't care if they ever came out of the bedroom.

On the morning of the second day, she woke, cuddled up next to him. "I love you," she whispered.

He smiled, his eyes closed. "You keep saying that and I shall believe it is true."

"It is true," she insisted, and gave his nipple a little bite.

His eyes opened. "You love me enough to eat?" he asked in surprise.

"I could," she answered.

"Really?" he demanded, and began tickling her.

She tickled back. They were both laughing and rolling over the bed when a knock at the door interrupted them.

"What is it?" Yale shouted, rising naked from the bed.

"It's the footman, Bates, my lord," came the answer from the other side of the door. "I have a letter for you. It was just delivered. The messenger said it was of some urgency."

"Slip it under the door and I shall look at it later," Yale said.

He turned to Samantha. "Now, where were we?" he said, and then with a mighty leap, jumped back into bed.

Samantha shrieked with laughter. Holding her, he kissed her forehead, her ears, her chin, her nose. "I don't know when I've ever been so happy," he said.

She put her arms around his chest and listened to his heart beat. "It almost doesn't seem right, does it? Like something terrible will come and take it away from us."

Yale raised his head to look down at her with exasperation. "Nothing terrible will happen. And if it does, I will protect you. I'm your knight—" He grinned before adding, "Without any armor."

She giggled, but then added seriously, "You are my rock."

"And you are the brightest light in my life."

Samantha felt the threat of tears.

"Sam, why are you crying?" He brushed her lashes with the tip of one finger.

"Because I'm happy. Because I have you."

"We have each other. Come now, let us bathe and see what the rest of the world has been doing while we've played."

He rang for bathwater for the two of them. Samantha didn't rise immediately. She wasn't really ready to give up this haven. The sheets smelled of him. She rolled herself up into them and lay there listening to him move around the room.

Yale picked up the vellum envelope the footman had slipped under the door. He broke the seal and read the message.

"What is it?" Samantha asked.

"It's from my banker. He asks for an audience

today. Says it is a matter of some importance."

"Can't it wait until tomorrow? Then we could spend another day in bed."

Yale laughed. "Business never waits. But I will make it short, knowing you are here waiting for me. Perhaps you shouldn't dress but just stay right there the way you are."

"Will it make you return home faster?"

"It might make me never leave," he said, putting a knee on the bed. He kissed her hair, her ear, and her neck, and they were soon in each other's arms. And neither of them rose to get dressed until much, much later.

Samantha found Marion in the nursery. She had Charles and John with her. Matthew was in with his tutor. John drew a picture for his mother while she and Charles practiced his standing.

"Good morning, Samantha. I didn't know if we would see you today or not."

Marion was smiling, but Samantha felt her cheeks heat with color. "I'm so sorry that we didn't stay for the Italian singer the other night."

Marion shook her head. "She was a disappointment. Uncle Norris fell asleep. He snores as loud as he shouts. Then Twyla and my mother got into an argument over some opera. Family gatherings can be so annoying. So. I take it everything is good between you and Yale?"

"Oh, Marion, he is the most wonderful man. I don't know how I could ever have doubted him."

"He gave you plenty of reason, but Wayland and I are happy he has atoned for his sins. And of course, Wayland is still hoping that now that you and Yale are truly man and wife, Yale will stay in London and help him. It would be so nice to have you here. And if you don't want to live here, you can get a house of your own. You and I can go out looking. Someday our children will play together."

Samantha placed her hands on her stomach. She could already be carrying Yale's child. The thought pleased her.

Still . . . "I don't know what Yale's plans are, Marion. I know he is thinking that he may spend most of the year in London, but he'll have to visit Ceylon to look after his business interests."

Marion waved a dismissive hand. "Yes, in the beginning. But when you and the children are here, he will change his mind and not want to go to wherever that place is so often."

"Perhaps," Samantha said doubtfully. She changed the subject. "Terrance and Alice are getting along well. I was just up to see them."

"Yes, Fenley is very pleased. He'd thought at first of training Terrance for the household staff but changed his mind and has talked to His Grace about letting the boy apprentice as a clerk."

"That is very generous of His Grace."

Marion smiled. "He is a good man."

Almost as if their words had conjured him, Wayland appeared at the nursery door. John jumped up to greet his father. Even little Charlie bounced up and down excitedly.

But for the first time since Samantha had known him, Wayland did not have an answering smile for his children.

"My love, is something the matter?" Marion asked. "You don't look as if you feel well."

"Do you know where Yale is?" he asked Samantha. "Fenley and the butler say they haven't seen him."

"He had an appointment with his banker this morning," she answered. She felt the first stirrings of alarm. "Has something happened to him?" She was halfway to the door before Wayland reached out and took her arm.

"No, Samantha, nothing has happened to him. At least, not physically."

"What do you mean?"

"I dropped by my club for lunch. I heard word that Yale is done up."

"Done up?" The expression didn't make any sense to her.

"A typhoon hit Ceylon. The man I spoke to is involved with the East India Company. He said Rogue Shipping was completely destroyed by the storm. It hit Trincomalee Bay. Eleven ships were sunk. They were mostly my brother's. The man told me Yale is ruined."

Chapter 17

The three of them, Samantha, Marion, and Wayland, waited in the downstairs sitting room for Yale to return home. The servants were given instructions to notify them immediately upon his return.

Fenley suggested a footman be dispatched to Yale's ship in the London harbor, and Bates was sent. He sent a message back that no one had seen Yale on the ship or at a warehouse he owned. Bates would wait until Lord Yale appeared or he was sent orders to return to Penhurst.

"What of his banker?" Samantha asked. "Could he still be there?"

Wayland didn't know, and because he was not one to cool his heels, he went himself to call on the banker who had sent the early morning message. He returned two hours later. "The banker said Yale received word of the typhoon without comment, other than to thank the man for the information, and he left. Yale did not mention where he was going." He paused. "I sent out a fleet of footmen to search the pubs and ale-houses."

"Yes, that might be where he is," Marion agreed.

But Samantha had her doubts. Since his influenza and the brandy bottle, Yale had shown a singular lack of enthusiasm for strong spirits of any sort.

Marion insisted on lunch trays being brought to them, since she and Samantha had not yet eaten. But Samantha was too worried to attempt even one bite.

Standing by the window overlooking the winter garden, she racked her brain, trying to think of where Yale could be . . . and came up with nothing. The only thing left for her was prayer. She said the same prayer over and over, "Dear God, please send him home to me."

In late afternoon, Twyla joined them. "I came as soon as I heard. Harold said rumors are flying. They say Yale is bankrupt. Is it true?"

Wayland nodded.

She approached Samantha. "Last night, I was a bit churlish. I shouldn't have said what I said. Certainly I did not wish something like this to happen. Will you forgive me?"

Samantha didn't know what to say and then realized that Twyla was apologizing to her because Yale wasn't there. "He will be back. You can say this to him when he returns."

Twyla and Wayland exchanged glances. Samantha turned to her brother-in-law. "What is the matter? Why do you look at each other that way?"

"It's nothing, Samantha," Wayland assured her. "We just worry because this is so much how it was years ago."

"We even waited in this same room, didn't we?" Twyla said.

"No, the library."

"Yes, I remember now," Twyla said.

"Waited for what?" Samantha demanded.

Wayland didn't answer. Twyla suddenly studied the pattern of the carpet.

It was Marion who had the courage to say, "They are talking about the first time Yale disappeared. The old duke had been certain that Yale would come home with his 'tail between his legs,' as he put it. But he didn't; he vanished. My father-in-law set up a vigil in the library. He did wait in this room at one time, Twyla. You were right about that." She said to Samantha, "One of us was always with him. On the third day, he sent out runners. That's when we learned he had boarded some ship as nothing more than a crew member and left England."

"But he wouldn't leave like that now," Samantha said firmly. "Not without saying something to me first."

Marion was by her side in an instant. "You are right, he wouldn't. He'll be home. We must just wait a little longer."

But Samantha couldn't wait. The seeds of

doubt had been planted. Her trust in Yale was too new. She asked Wayland to take her down to the docks: "I want to see his ship."

He reluctantly agreed.

The twilight gloom was cold and wet and suited Samantha's mood perfectly. The hours of the morning when she had lingered in Yale's arms seemed almost a lifetime ago.

"The *Wind Eagle*," Samantha said, reading the name in gilded letters across the bow.

Wayland knocked for the coachman to stop, and they went aboard. The captain was a young man with a gruff bearing. He was honored to meet Mr. Carderock's new wife.

"I have a wife and three children of my own," he said.

"Are they here in London?" Samantha asked, more out of politeness than genuine interest. She studied the piles of rope and the orderly confusion of the deck. A ship seemed much larger from a distance than it did when one stood on board.

"No, they were in Trincomalee."

"Trincomalee? Isn't that where the typhoon hit?" she asked.

"Aye. I pray they are alive."

His words brought the force of the tragedy home to her. Samantha reached out for his hand. "I am so sorry." The man's eyes misted and then he looked off from her.

"No need to be sorry. It's God's will," the captain said. He took a moment to gather himself.

"It's hard, not having word. Mr. Carderock was by here as soon as he heard. From what he says, a good number of lives have been lost on land. I can only pray until I return home."

"I shall pray with you," Samantha promised. "Tell me about your children."

"Oh, I'm not the only one," the captain said. "A quarter of our crew has family back there. It's a good place to live if you don't mind giving up the English winter."

"I know my brother will do everything he can for you," Wayland said somberly.

"Thank you, Your Grace," the captain answered. "But we all know that. He's a rum one, he is. Best man to work for in the Orient."

Samantha and Wayland returned to Penhurst after that. Both were silent, lost in their own thoughts.

Yale had not returned home in their absence. It was already dark. Marion and Twyla still waited up in the sitting room.

Samantha didn't go with Wayland to join them. Instead, she went to her room. A fire had been laid in the hearth, but it hadn't been lit. She set the candle she'd carried with her on the chest of drawers.

"Dear God, where can he be? Please bring him home to me."

At that moment, a small draft eased open the door leading to the sitting room. Samantha went to close it and stopped.

He was here.

Pushing open the sitting room door with the palm of her hand, she looked into the darkness of the room.

Yale sat on the settee, his long legs stretched out in front of him, his boot heels resting on the table. He twisted the green glass paperweight in his hands. She could see the flash of glass as he turned it over and over. If he knew she was there, he gave no indication.

And then he looked up. "You've heard." It was a statement, not a question.

"I've been worried about you. We've all been waiting for you."

"I needed to be alone," he answered.

"How long have you been here?"

"Since after I called on the banker."

"The servants—"

"I came in the back way, Sam. No one saw me. I needed time to think."

She entered the room and crossed to him, kneeling on the floor beside where he sat. "What did you need to think about?"

He surprised her with a smile, "About what an unlucky bastard I am." He kept flipping the paperweight, first in one hand, then the other. "Not even pixies could save me, Sam. Everything I worked for is gone."

She placed her hand over his, halting its movement. "Not everything, Yale. I'm still here."

Their gazes locked.

"You shouldn't be," he said. "I'm no good, Sam. My father was right. I am a wastrel."

"Your father never thought any such thing." She came to her feet. "He loved you. He didn't always do what was best for you and maybe he didn't understand you, but he did love you. And *I* love you. I will not let you push me away, Yale Carderock."

He set the paperweight aside and came up to take her in his arms. "Sam, I love you. I want nothing more than to be with you."

"But?" she asked, holding her breath for the answer.

"I must leave," he said dully. "The bankers think I'm finished, but that isn't true. I have a warehouse and one ship. Plus a plantation in Ceylon. I will rebuild my company."

"Then why are you sitting here alone in the dark?"

He placed his hand against the side of her cheek. "Because I don't want to leave, Sam. By rights, I should be gone on the morning tide . . . but I can't. I want to be here with you."

"Would you stay and work with Wayland?"

He laughed. "No. I could never do that . . . and yet I can't leave you either, but I must. The worst part is that I don't know when I will return. It depends on the island and how bad things are. I could be gone for well over a year or more, Sam."

"A year or more," she repeated, a sick feeling in the pit of her stomach.

His arms pulled her close and she rested her head against his chest, her arms around his waist. Closing her eyes, she drew a deep breath.

He was so warm, so real, so secure. "A year," she repeated again.

His arms tightened. He rested his chin against her head. They stood this way in the dark, holding each other as if they would never let go, and then Samantha heard a small, distinct voice inside herself.

It spoke clearly. It was not her voice. She knew it . . . and she heard it as plainly as if someone was in the room with her. The voice said, "Go with him."

Go with him.

Of course she could go with him. "I'm going with you."

"What?"

It was so simple! "I am going with you," she said, and turned toward her bedroom. "I must pack if we are going to leave in the morning. My packing will be easy. I don't own much."

He caught her hand before she'd taken two steps. "Sam, you can't go. I won't take you with me."

"Why not?"

"Because it is dangerous." He took ahold of her by both arms and bent to look in her eyes. "You don't know what a storm of that magnitude is like. Trincomalee is a safe natural harbor. For it to be destroyed, the typhoon could have leveled the whole island. Until you experience a typhoon, you can't imagine how much destruction Nature can wreak. Food, and even water, may be scarce. Disease will run rampant."

"All the more reason for me to go," she said calmly. "Yale, I am a healer. From what you have described, my skills will be needed."

"It's too dangerous. If something happened to you, my whole life would be meaningless. I have to believe that you are safe here in England."

She almost laughed. "This sounds like what we were talking about this morning—only then *I* was the fearful one. What is it you said? A hundred accidents could befall one right here in London?" She pulled back from him and he released his hold. "Yale, I want to be by your side. Together we will rebuild Rogue Shipping."

"Sam, it isn't an easy life. The tropics claim many lives."

"Oh, pooh, I'm a bonny North Country lass. I'm strong, Yale. Furthermore, you might as well resign yourself to the fact that I won't let you leave without me. Ever. Do you understand? I want to swim in a pool at the base of a waterfall. I want to see everything you described to me, including those giant stone gates shaped like a lion's paws."

He studied her a moment and then, to her relief, he smiled and she knew she'd won. "I'll take you with me," he agreed. "But I will never forgive myself if anything happens to you."

"It won't, Yale. This is how it was meant to be. I know it in my soul. Now come, let's tell Wayland and Marion our plans."

She held out her hand and he took it. But instead of leaving immediately, he brought her hand to his lips and kissed it. "With you, I can do anything." They left the room then, arm in arm.

Samantha had no regrets over her decision. She told Yale that she felt as if it was meant for her to go to Ceylon with him. Maybe it had been preordained from the beginning, she told Yale, when they'd first met in the Ayleborough vault.

Yale's family did not want them to leave, but they understood, and supported, Samantha's decision to go with her husband. "He needs someone," Marion assured her. "You will help him build a good life there. But please do not forget us."

"I could not," Samantha said. "You are my family."

Once word was out that the *Wind Eagle* would sail immediately for Ceylon, those with friends and relatives on the island petitioned Yale to take messages, clothing, and presents to their loved ones. He promised to deliver each and every one.

The morning papers wrote about Yale's confidence in making the return trip. To his surprise, bankers were not as reluctant to extend credit as they had been immediately upon hearing the news. There was a very good possibility that Rogue Shipping would survive with little trouble.

Samantha laughed and claimed the pixies living in the green glass paperweight must be working magic. Marion agreed and insisted they take it with them.

Three days later, Samantha and Yale stood side-by-side on the dock, prepared to board the *Wind Eagle*. Wayland and Marion and the boys had come to wish them a safe voyage. Even Twyla had come to see them off, although she said she had never in her life risen before dawn for anyone.

"Thank you, sister," Yale said.

For a second Twyla's lower lip pushed out, and then she answered, "You're welcome, brother." She reached up and gave him a hug.

Yale looked over to Wayland. His brother stood a little apart from the others, his arms crossed against his chest. Yale walked over to him.

"Thank you for all you've done for me and Samantha."

"You are family," Wayland said curtly. He looked away a moment and then said, "I wish you would stay. Who knows when we shall see each other again?"

Yale placed his hands on his brother's shoulders. "I will return. The last time I left, I did so in anger. I left with nothing, and to my surprise, I returned with nothing. Now I leave with everything that is important to me—my wife and the goodwill of my family. You are my brother, Wayland. You're a good man, a fine father, and the most worthy one to head up the family and be the duke. I respect you. I love you."

Marion took Samantha's arm and both of them held their breath, waiting for Wayland's response.

"Brother," was all he said, before he reached out and hugged Yale.

Samantha's eyes filled with tears. She glanced at Marion, who was similarly affected. They hugged each other.

Wayland stepped back and cleared his throat. Samantha thought she could see his eyes water a bit, but he held true to himself. "Don't forget us," he told Yale.

"Never. Samantha and I will return for a visit." Yale clapped a hand on Matthew's back. "Perhaps someday you can send one of your sons to me and I can show him a bit of the world."

"I will do that. And perhaps you will be sending one of *your* sons to *me* someday," Wayland said.

Yale laughed. "I pray that happens." The two brothers stared at each other a moment and then Yale added softly, "Take care of Beast for me."

"Come back and ride him from time to time."

"I shall." Yale turned to Samantha. "It is time to go."

There was flurry of last-minute promises and kisses, and then Samantha found herself walking up the ship's gangway. Her stomach was nervous, but not from fear. She was excited.

Once they were on board, the captain gave the order for the ship to be prepared for voyage. Yale and Samantha stood side-by-side and watched as the *Wind Eagle* pulled away from the dock.

Matthew and Joseph charged along the dock, racing the ship and shouting to their uncle Yale, who'd become a great favorite in a short time. Marion held Charles's hand and made his tiny arm wave good-bye. Even Wayland waved.

"I still think he is an ugly baby," Yale whispered to Samantha, as he gave one last farewell salute to his family.

"Aye, but he has character," she assured him. "You can see it in his nose."

The two of them laughed before Yale turned serious. "Any regrets?" he asked her softly.

"None," she replied.

He kissed her hand and led her to the bow of the ship and their future together.

Epilogue

~~~~~~~~~~~~~~~~~~~~~~~~~~~~~~~~~~~~~

Ceylon
1808

Yale paced the covered walkway between the main house and the lush garden. His plantation was located in the hills, where it was a touch cooler than the tropical heat of the coast. A soft, steady rain pattered against the red tiled roof and ran in a stream off the ends of the gutters.

The rain was left over from the thunderstorm the night before.

The change in the barometric pressure had started Sam's labor. Her pains had been coming at regular intervals since one in the morning. Now, almost ten hours later, Yale was growing concerned. Certainly it couldn't take this long to have a baby.

The walkway passed the shuttered windows of their bedroom. He could hear Samantha's heavy breathing and her soft whimpers. A Tamil midwife calmed her in a low voice.

369

Yale wished he'd been able to send for the British doctor in Trincomalee instead of relying on the local midwife, but the heavy rain had prevented it. Not only that, but Sam had assured him everything would be fine. And he'd listened because she was so often right.

Over the past year and a half, they had built a good life for themselves. His fortune still wasn't completely restored to its former glory, but in Ceylon, he was a wealthy man. Besides, money didn't matter as long as he had Sam by his side.

Contrary to his fears, she'd blossomed in the wild beauty of the tropics. His vicar's daughter who had grown up knowing only the boundaries of Sproule had developed an insatiable curiosity about everything. She'd attended a Hindu marriage ceremony, climbed Adam's Peak and seen the indentation in the shape of a giant foot that the Buddhists believed had been created by Buddha, and had explored the sacred city of Anuradhapura.

But Yale's favorite memory was of taking her to the waterfalls hidden deep in the jungle. They'd camped out under the stars. When the moon was high, they had swum in the pools' cool depths and felt the spray of the waterfalls.

That was the night the baby had been conceived. They both knew it. It had been a magical moment between them.

Now, Yale wished he'd never touched her. For

the hundredth time, he turned on his heel and paced the length of the walkway.

Just as he came even with the shuttered windows, Samantha cried out his name.

Enough with waiting!

Yale dodged into the house and hurried to their bedroom. He burst in unannounced.

Samantha's face was so sweaty and pale, he feared she had to be sick. She cried again, her knees bending. Two household servants were holding her in a seated position.

He rushed to her side. "What is it? What can I do?"

The midwife answered him in Tamil. "This is the way it is," she said. "Missy wife is doing well."

Yale didn't think Sam was doing well at all.

"Yale." Sam's voice was weaker than he'd ever heard it.

He knelt by the bed and took her hand. "What is it, darling?"

"Just hold me," she whispered. "Just be here."

Yale was scared. He put his arms around her and held her close. "Give me the pain. Let me do it for you."

Sam forced a smile. "If I could have, I would have called you hours ago." She was even able to laugh at her joke.

What spirit his wife had! What would he do if he lost her?

The midwife ordered Sam to push. Yale whispered the command in her ear.

"I'm so tired," Sam said.

"I know, darling, but just one push more. It'll soon be over. You'll see." He hid his own fear behind false bravado.

"Yes . . . it . . . will . . . be . . . fine," Sam muttered, building her strength for another push.

"Everything you have, Samantha," Yale said. "Give it all that is in you."

She looked at him as if to say she had nothing left, but then he felt her body tense as she pressed down hard, holding her breath at the same time.

"It's coming! It's coming!" the midwife shouted.

"It's coming," Yale translated. Samantha had been learning Tamil, but it was still a difficult language for her.

She laughed, the sound almost giddy. "One more push, right?"

At the same moment, the midwife ordered, "One more push!"

"Right," Yale agreed.

Her gaze on him, Samantha summoned a reserve of strength and made one last push.

The midwife gave a shout.

Yale turned just in time to watch the baby's head emerge. "It's coming, Sam. It's coming!"

A small body slid out of his wife. It was amazing. He came to his feet to look closer. The midwife was talking excitedly in Tamil. She was exclaiming over how big the baby was.

Then, to his surprise, she thrust Yale's son into

his hands, the cord still attached, and began rubbing the baby down with soft cloths.

The baby gasped with a startled jerk and then its mouth opened and out came a loud, healthy wail. Samantha began laughing and crying.

"We did it, Yale! We did it!"

He couldn't answer. He was witnessing a miracle. As he tilted the babe, his eyes opened. They were large, blue, and a bit unfocused—and then the baby blinked and looked directly at him.

Father and son took the measure of each other.

Yale couldn't speak. As he looked into his son's eyes, he had the impression he could see his own father in them. And his father's father, and so on and so forth until the beginning of time . . . and he knew then, in that moment, that his own father had forgiven him for all his failings as a son.

Because now Yale understood a father's love.

The midwife cut the cord and tied it off. She was still speaking and working on Samantha, but Yale didn't pay attention to her words.

He sat down on the edge of the bed, holding his precious son with both hands. "He recognizes me, Sam. Right off from the first breath, he *knows* me."

She placed her hand on his arm. "Of course he does. You are his father."

Suddenly, the world was a better place. For this child in his hands, he would slay dragons. He'd protect him, and love him, and cherish him. He would teach him to be a man . . .

Yale leaned over and kissed his wife. "Thank you."

She laughed tiredly. "You had something to do with it."

"Ah, Sam, my life was nothing before you."

She blushed and it pleased him that he had touched her. "Wrap the baby up in the quilt the women sent from Sproule, will you?" she asked.

He did as she'd requested. When the colorful quilt had arrived several weeks ago, along with a note from Squire Biggers and Vicar Newell and the village ladies congratulating them on the impending baby, Yale had laughed. Who needed a quilt in the tropics?

And yet right now, it seemed the perfect thing to wrap his son in.

Samantha reached for the baby and placed him to her breast. Their son latched on and suckled immediately. She gave a soft, happy sigh.

Yale stretched out on the bed beside her. He slipped his arm beneath his wife's head and watched, fascinated by this moment between mother and child. Reaching out with one finger, he traced his son's long fingers curled up in a fist. Nothing had ever felt as soft as this newborn skin.

"He's perfect," Samantha whispered.

"Aye, he is," Yale answered. "After all, he has my nose."

The two of them laughed.

"What shall we name him?" Samantha asked.

"How about after our fathers?"

"Barrett Leland?"

"It's a good name."

"Yes, a good name to go with Carderock." She smiled up at him and he caught his breath.

"You've never been more beautiful to me than at this moment," he said.

"Oh, Yale." She rested her head in the crook of his arm.

For the first time in his life, Yale felt content, complete. There would probably be more struggles in his future, but wherever he was, whatever he did, he knew he would be the victor. Life held meaning. Life was good.

"Because of you," he whispered to Samantha. "All because of you."